Captive's Deception

Lori Laidlaw

Published by Lynda French, 2024.

This is a work of fiction. Similarities to real people, places, or events are entirely coincidental.

CAPTIVE'S DECEPTION

First edition. July 9, 2024.

Copyright © 2024 Lori Laidlaw.

ISBN: 978-1998074327

Written by Lori Laidlaw.

Table of Contents

To all those who yearn for freedom and find it in the arms of a lover.

About Captive's Deception

Dora

Saturday night's dinner party turned into a massacre, Sunday morning I witnessed a murder, and by Monday I'm a hostage in an Outlaw Biker clubhouse.

I'm a pampered, privileged, home-schooled, bride-to-be who has been taught since birth to never, ever tell anyone my name. I really wish I was a better liar...

Viper

I've got to call her something so I chose Poison: harmful, insidious, and sneaky. Sometimes there's an antidote but usually it's fatal. Often looks beautiful, can be addictive.

She's my captive but am I being deceived by the killer body and great big brown eyes of this Mafia Princess? How much danger am I putting my MC in by having her here? Why the hell didn't I kill her when I had the chance? How can I ever let her go?

Content Advisory: Adults Only!!! This DARK romance takes place in the gritty, violent world of an outlaw MC.

Note from the author: I guarantee NO cliffhanger and HEAs for all the couples.

Playlist

Great Songs for the Road

"Born To Be Wild" by Steppenwolf

"Bourbon In Your Eyes" by Devil Doll

"Changes Are Coming" by Daughtry

"Face The Face" by Pete Townshend

"Frankenstein" by The Edgar Winter Band

"How You Remind Me" by Nickleback

"Hush" by Deep Purple

"I Love Rock 'n Roll" by Joan Jett and The Blackhearts

"In The Mood For You" by The Record Company

"Keep On Truckin'" by Eddie Kendricks

"Life Is A Highway" by Tom Cochrane and Red Rider

"Little Red Corvette" by Prince

"Lust For Life" by Iggy Pop

"My Sharona" by The Knack

"Poison Ivy" by The Coasters

"Pour Some Sugar On Me" by Def Leppard

"Radar Love" by Golden Earring

"Rock The Casbah" by The Clash

"Truckin'" by Grateful Dead

"Tube Snake Boogie" by ZZ Top

Kidnapped

Dora

1st Rule: *Carjack the Mercedes of a man called Viper and you'll be killed.*

2nd Rule: *When you're dead the girl you left behind now belongs to the Satan's Tears MC.*

Steve is so excited when he spots the unattended white Mercedes saying *I can boost that no problem* as he wheels us into the rest stop of the conservation area. I feel too beat down to share his enthusiasm but I nod and hope my smile isn't just me baring my teeth.

I know it's ridiculous to be riding on the back of a ten-speed while I'm on the run but what choice do I have? Steve scared me half to death when he glided up beside me without a sound because of this bicycle. I think I've used up my fear quota because I didn't scream.

Up until then I was running into the forest to hide behind a tree whenever I heard a car. No way would I be hitchhiking – especially around here – but my sore feet convinced me to accept a lift from this boy on his bike. Even though we're not going much faster than I was walking.

At least it isn't raining anymore. In last night's wet I felt the dampness deep in my bones, and stumbling around in the dark didn't help. Today the sun isn't shining but the temperature is comfortable and I can see where I'm going. Too bad I don't know where that is. I don't even know where I am now. Well, I know I'm on a highway that runs alongside a state park but I don't know what either are called.

The moment I climbed on the bicycle Steve promised he'd ditch it as soon as we found a car he could steal and then we'd *ride in style*. The Merc parked here is a wagon so not exactly stylish but it will be comfortable and roomy. I know because that's the model our housekeeper uses for grocery shopping.

Of course I don't say anything about that to Steve. I met him for the first time about thirty minutes ago and while he's a nice kid I already know he's not my knight-in-shining-armor. Even though it's still technically summer I've been chilled since I woke up so it will be nice to get out of the wind and into the shelter of a car.

I get off the bike first and then Steve dismounts. We can't see any other people and the Merc is the only car here. The deserted rest stop feels kind of creepy in the gloom of this overcast day.

"The driver must be in the can so go stand outside the restroom and distract him by crying or something. Or maybe it's a woman driving this car? same deal, just start crying while I get to work here," Steve instructs.

I know I can cry. I've been holding back my tears for about twelve hours by now. That's been tough to do but I'm afraid that if I let loose I might never stop.

I head over to the restrooms, limping a little on my blistered feet. I start wringing my hands because that's something I've read about although I've never seen anyone do it before. Actually I could cry just from the relief of using a real bathroom with running water.

I plan to hop up on the counter and soak my poor feet in the sink. I've got streaks of blood and dirt on my arms and legs, my hands are a terrible mess, and God knows what my face looks like.

I'll get a good wash with hot water and– I'm startled out of my thoughts by a yell, a scuffle, and a scream. Swinging around I see Steve on the ground with his head bent at a funny angle and his eyes staring at, but no longer seeing, a dark-haired stranger.

I try to release a high-pitched scream of my own but no sound comes out although my mouth is wide open. I can't pull in a deep enough breath, not even a shallow one. This attack happened so fast, so unbelievably fast! I didn't even get the restroom door open.

The huge man in a suit and tie looming over Steve catches my gaze and his blue eyes pin me in place. With just a few long strides he's on me grabbing my arm and dragging me back to the car. The Merc is his car. He beeps his key-fob to open the driver's door and part of my brain realizes Steve didn't even get that far.

The big man flings me inside and shoves me down on the floor. Although he's pushed the car-seat as far back as it will go it's still a cramped space. Once he gets in I'm trapped between his legs. I cringe away from him trying to make my size, I'm a couple of inches over five feet, even smaller if possible. I'm so scared of this guy and I don't want to do anything to make it worse.

"Stay still. Don't touch the pedals. Don't say anything. Don't touch me. Do what you're told and you'll live." He rumbles at me in a gravelly voice accompanied by a look that warns against arguing or whining.

A line my English tutor taught me comes to mind now: *What fresh hell is this?*

I'm squashed in this cramped space but since I'm still breathing I'm not complaining. I'm too scared anyhow. I finally do manage to breathe in a huge gulp of air but I don't dare scream now so I swallow it down and that's given me hiccups. Probably because it's so smoky in here.

The nasty man is staring at my neck as if he'd like to snap it too. From the unnatural way Steve lay that must be how this guy killed him.

I keep repeating the same litany over and over in my mind: *don't tell him your name, don't say anything.*

I hunch my head down into my shoulders and when my widely stretched eyes meet his which are narrowed in meanness my mind just gives up. There's no room to fall so my body just sags in a faint.

Viper

Of all the fucked-up stupid flukes... who would figure on some punk trying to rip off the car? Now I've left behind some guy's body and I've kidnapped his girlfriend. Fuck-fuck-fuck!

I'm really struggling to hold my temper in check because I've gotta get under control. Dammit I didn't mean to kill that kid, killing just brings trouble, but I totally lost my shit. When I realized that this punk was trying to steal the car... fuck me.

Now I'm stuck with this teenage bitch who I'll kill if I have to but hell, I'm supposed to be keeping a low profile.

I've been so careful, sticking to the speed limit and staying in the middle lane, putting my cigarettes out in the ashtray instead of tossing them from the window, doing nothing to get noticed and now this.

First of all it's complete and utter bullshit that I'm even behind the wheel of this cage but when shit came down then fuck, as VP of the club I had to step up and help my Prez out.

I shift my legs around, they're too long for this car, and tip the girl closer to the door. That gives her a bit more space but you'd never think so from the looks she's giving me. Seeing her frightened white face staring up makes me grind my teeth in frustration. What the hell am I going to do about her?

When her and the kid showed up at the rest area of course I noticed her, she has a hot body, really long hair, and a pretty face although it's kinda dirty. It's as if she'd had a rough night although he looked okay.

I'm minding my own business taking a whizz behind a tree because no way am I going to let the Mercedes out of my sight. It's packed to the brim with cash and it should be the Prez's Old Lady driving the damn thing, not me. Then this fucking kid has the fucking balls to try to steal my wheels! Fucking death wish.

If I'd meant to kill him I'd have popped her too but him dying like that was such a shocker I didn't think, I just knew she was a witness so I grabbed her. Big mistake.

I huff out a pent-up breath and give the girl a menacing look, satisfied when her impossibly big brown eyes widen even further with fear except then she passes out! But maybe that's for the best because I've got another hour's driving before I'm home.

The gates of our compound swing open as I approach. I'm glad to be back, relieved that both me and the money are safe.

The girl wasn't out for too long and I have to give her credit for sticking to my *no talking* order because she hasn't uttered a sound. The quiet gave me a chance to think about how I'm going to explain things to Banger. I don't want to add to the problems our Prez is currently shouldering but he has to know what went down so I figure I better tell him right away.

"We're here," I inform the girl, opening the car door and pushing her out onto the ground. She doesn't say anything but I see her wince as she straightens up. I guess she got stiff and cramped crouched under the dash. Too bad, I'd have stuffed her in the trunk but this car doesn't have one.

Getting out I stretch too. Even with the seat pushed back at 6'2 my legs feel constricted. I hate driving a cage, I'd much rather be riding my bike. Naturally our club only rides American-made Harley's and there's a long line of them parked outside our garage.

I can see one of the prospects, looks like Kyle from here, is polishing my Low Rider till it gleams. I'm glad to see Banger's Fat Boy here and Dog's Sportster as well as his Classic. Good, we all need to talk.

Pushing the girl ahead of me I notice how crumpled, dirty, and wrinkled her dress is. I'm finally getting a good look at what she's wearing and it looks like... party clothes? Who puts on a silky dress to ride on the back of a bicycle through the state park? and wearing strappy high-heels?

Reaching out I grab her shoulder forcing her to look up at me. Even in those shoes she's really short, I figure about a foot less than me. She wobbles a bit and I see that her eyes aren't focused until she blinks. They're a pretty shade of light brown and go good with her dark blonde-brownish hair.

I realize I don't want to take her into the clubhouse not knowing a thing about her so I bark out: "How old are you? Who are you? What's your name?"

Her eyes flit back and forth on my face but she doesn't answer so I try again, speaking a bit more softly this time since I know I scare her. I mean, she just saw me off her boyfriend with my bare hands. "C'mon little girl, tell me your name."

But again I just get a slow blink in response. Abruptly I knock her to the ground and nimbly stepping behind her shout: "Hands on your head!" and she quickly obeys.

Moving around to face her I observe: "You weren't reading my lips then so you sure as shit can hear, and you understand English. My name's Viper, what's yours?" Still nothing from her although she's closely following every word. "Can you talk?" Her eyes are still huge as she gives a very slight shake to her head.

"Hmm. Can't talk or won't?" Of course she doesn't answer me. I almost reach out to give her a hand up but stop myself in time. I don't know yet what role she's going to play.

By now everyone who is outside is watching so I jerk my head towards the clubhouse and walk away certain that she's following me but not bothering to check. After a few steps I hear her scrambling to get to her feet.

The indoors is dim compared to the bright sunshine outside and I realize it's still early in the day. With everything that's happened it feels much later. As my eyes adjust I can make out a dozen or so men and women at the bar and from the sounds of pool balls clacking there are at least a couple more playing the tables.

The girl steps through the doorway behind me and immediately I sense people taking notice of her. Of course it's Fiona who strides right over demanding information. As clubhouse manager I suppose she has that right but that doesn't mean I have to like it.

"Who's this?"

I quirk up an eyebrow at her abrupt tone and pause before replying: "I'm not sure. Possibly a hostage, definitely a witness – either way she's become an unavoidable, accidental guest. Can you get her something to drink? water, food, whatever."

Fiona's upper lip curls slightly as her gaze sweeps up and down the younger girl. Fiona's almost my height so she has to step back to look down. Her eyes narrow slightly as she takes a closer look, beyond the obvious dishevelment, before replying: "Maybe a hostage... that's an expensive dress and those are very expensive shoes. What's her story?"

"Fucked if I know," I answer with a smirk. "She doesn't talk."

"Well that just about makes her a perfect woman, eh sweetheart?" Dog has approached quickly and now crowds the girl looking her over with his trademark wolfish grin. He should have been called Wolf since he's a sexual predator but instead he got Dog for being a hardcore hound. "I bet I can get her to talk, or at least scream my name while I fuck her like she's never been fucked before," he declares.

"If she's just a witness I'll have to kill her so yeah, in that case you can fuck her first, but she might be a valuable hostage so you're gonna have to keep it in your pants for now. Hardware can check her out."

Dog's as big as I am but a couple of years younger. He's by far the best-looking guy in our MC. His big hands are reaching out to follow the path his eyes have taken but I push the girl away from his grasp. I feel her trembling from fear or shock as I shove her towards Fiona to take care of.

Before they leave Fiona turns back and giving me in my suit the once-over says "Viper you look good dressed up like a businessman."

I don't return her smile when I reply: "I always look good."

She's about to say more but just then a couple of arms snake around my waist and a sultry voice purrs: "Viper always looks soooo HOT!" Glancing over my shoulder I see that I'm being groped by Bebe. With her big fake tits and big fake lips she's a club favorite.

Personally, I never fuck the club whores but I let her suck me off one time and found out those lips can't grip very tight. I briefly stroke Bebe's cheek, smiling at her compliment, but I don't have time for any bullshit right now.

Turning back to Dog I gesture for him to come with me.

"Aww Viper," he whines, "I love a girl with long sandy hair that I can wrap around my fist while I move her head where I want it. And when her hair is that long I can wrap it round and round my dick."

"Jesus, Dog do you ever quit? C'mon, we've got to have a meeting with Prez." I say, shouldering him to go in the opposite direction.

Dora

The woman with the angry blue eyes latches on to my wrist with strong fingers. She's really tall – about 6-foot? – and I have to tilt my head way back to look up at her. Which hurts. I'm stiff and aching after that never-ending car-ride. She's dressed all in black from her skinny jeans to a fitted vest with a lacy camisole underneath and she looks really tough, no way am I fighting with her. It won't take much for me to just lose it and I can't, I've got to keep my wits about me because these aren't safe or friendly people.

That man Viper called Dog is just as big as he is and very handsome. I mean, he's terrifying and he said horrible things as he leered at me but I still noticed his good looks. Both he and Viper wear their hair long but Dog is a curly blond while Viper's is straight and a very dark brown.

The place seems dark which I guess makes sense for a bar. I can smell tobacco smoke, weed, and beer but it's not a bad odor so I figure they must keep it clean. There are a lot of other people in the room but I don't look around in case I draw attention to myself. The less I see or know the better.

I'm still fuming at Viper's *little girl* comment. I'm twenty-one now! I was so indignant I almost spoke up but caught myself in time. I must keep silent. No one can find out my name. That's always been drilled into me, an unbreakable rule, because terrible things will happen if our enemies find me.

I'm pretty sure the big man isn't the foe my family warned me about but he might still recognize the name. I can't say anything.

Pulling, the tall woman leads me towards the bar but goes past it into a room behind. A kitchen. Opening the fridge door she gestures to an impressive array of sodas and juices and I grab a bottle of water that I chug right down. That makes her smirk as she says: "Go ahead and have another if you want." So I do, but this one I sip on. She's really thin so I'm not surprised when she doesn't take anything.

"My name's Fiona," she says, pulling a chair out from a large table. It has banquette seating curving around one end and lots of chairs. She walks around and takes a seat on the other side. I sit down in the chair she indicated and do my best to look meek and respectful. I recognize this type of woman and know that her angry eyes prove she's got an angry, dissatisfied nature.

She leans in a bit and lowering her voice says: "It's okay now, it's just us girls, so tell me kid what's your name?" I blink a lot, as if I'm fighting back tears, and put on a frightened look as I just sit there staring back at her.

With utmost conviction I know she'll never like me and we'll never be friends and I don't feel the slightest regret over that. Keeping up the pretense of polite interest is really hard, I just want to put my head down the table and either sleep or bawl my eyes out. I'd really like to pee, too.

A few other women enter the kitchen, lining themselves up around Fiona. They're all older than me and rough-looking but sexy with it. Their clothes are... unusual. Super-short skirts that are skin-tight even when that's not a good look for the wearer.

Not one of them is smiling, and there's palpable animosity surrounding them. I'm definitely not welcome here. Considering what I've gone through and what I've seen both yesterday and today I really don't care if they want me or not. I'm barely holding on as it is.

Suck it up bitches, I tell them silently, *because I sure as shit don't want to be here*. My cousins would be teasing me over my language but what the heck, I learned those words from them! I don't let my thoughts show on my face although I don't care if my weariness comes through.

"So what's the deal with her," asks a blonde whose roots are in dire need of a touch-up, jerking her chin towards me.

"Don't know, Bunny," answers Fiona. "She doesn't talk."

That's caught their attention and they draw in to look more closely at me, some puzzled and some frowning, guess they're all ableists here.

"So she's... a dummy?"

Fiona just shrugs and Bunny responds by making a *hmmph* sound.

Looking over Fiona's shoulder I see a calendar on the wall and have a sudden inspiration. Hurrying over to it I stab my finger on today's date and grab at my crotch. The women give me confused looks wondering if I'm mental.

Then the one who was hugging Viper, I think her name is Bebe, cries out: "I got it! she has her monthlies. Calendar means time of the month. That's what she's tryin' to say!"

Fiona gives me an appraising look and a frown. "She might just be faking it, trying to make the guys keep their distance." But a comment like that makes no sense to these women. Even I can tell that they do their very best to get the exact opposite reaction from the men.

Jerking her chin at me Fiona says: "Let's see."

It takes me a moment to realize what she means and I give her a frown of my own when I do understand but I comply.

Reaching under my dress and hooking a finger into my thong I pull it down far enough to show a bloodstained mess. Every woman in the room has dealt with this since puberty but they all pull back in disgust like it's something brand-new to them. What drama queens.

I'm not on my period but my ploy has worked and the one I'm sure now is Bebe takes me to a good-sized restroom. Fetching a packet of tampons from under the counter she hands it to me with exaggerated gestures – maybe she thinks her pantomime will help me hear? before thankfully leaving me alone.

The relief at letting my guard down, even for just a moment, brings tears to my eyes. I won't cry, not around these women, but I'd sure like to let go. It's a blessing to actually sit down on a toilet.

My thong is bloody because I used it to clean up as much gore off my body as I could. I sneaked my jewelry into my panties when I was on the bike behind Steve but, luckily, I'd moved the diamonds to my mouth when I came to huddled on the floor of the car and Viper was busy muttering his thoughts.

I take out one tampon to insert because Fiona's accusation sounds like a good idea to me. I stuff my engagement ring and matching earrings in with the rest. I'm not worried about any of these bikers looking in here.

I am sorry about losing the solitaire pendant. The full set was a wedding tribute, a family tradition, from the Vendetti's and worth a fortune.

I'm pretty sure the platinum chain broke when I fought to get away from that last FBI agent. I wonder if he kept the necklace? I'm sure he'd realize something of that quality would substantially increase his government pension but he'd be much safer turning it in for the reward. If he survived the shoot-out, that is.

I can't think about any of that right now, though. I have to pay attention to what's going on and be alert for any chance to escape.

Finishing up at the toilet I give my hands a good wash and look at my reflection. My hair is a tangled mess with leaves and bits of twig stuck in it. My face is ghostly pale with shadows under my eyes. Trying to run through the forest in the dark was dangerous and I don't know how many times I fell. I mean, twice for sure but it looks like it happened way more than that. I'm lucky I didn't break something. Lucky... yeah, right.

The fact that I only managed a couple of hours' fitful sleep shows. But surprisingly the deep horror at what I witnessed doesn't, and after I wash up I just look like a regular girl.

Banger

I look at my best friend and VP in total disbelief. "Are you shitting me, Viper? You kill some guy and bring his girlfriend back to the clubhouse? For what, a party? Why the fuck didn't you end her?"

"I don't know Prez. She's just a kid. I'm sorry this shit happened but that guy? he must have had a pencil neck or somethin' because I only wanted to pull him away from the car, give him a few taps, and scare the living shit out of him."

"Aw fuck me, Viper, I don't need any more shit right now." I've got the temper promised by my red hair but I bite back the words that hover before I insult my best friend.

"Shit I know and I'm sorry Prez. And..."

"What? Spit it out, man."

"The girl's connected to money. I thought so from her clothes and Fiona confirmed–"

"Wait a sec," interrupts Dog. "You said you saw her wheeling into the rest area sharing the guy's 10-speed so if she's rich then she's got to be a runaway, right?" Our Sergeant-At-Arms has a quick mind when he isn't clowning around for pussy.

The three of us are standing in the meeting room we use for *church* and now I march over to the kitchen nook and grabbing a bottle of Jack pour myself a shot. I'm too pissed off to offer it around.

Viper comments: "Good point. Unless she was somebody's hostage who managed to escape?"

"Well why are you guessing? Just ask and if she won't tell you then make her."

"That's the other thing..." Viper begins and I can feel my anger ready to blow. He must see it because he hurries to explain that the girl's a mute. "She can hear but she can't, or won't, talk."

"Can't or *won't*," I repeat staring him down.

"I'll work on her. Maybe she's just been too scared of me after what she saw..."

"I gotta get the fuck outta here, jeez." I throw back my drink and leave the room only to be confronted by my sister waiting outside the door for her turn to bring trouble.

"Banger that girl can't be here, the other women don't want–"

I cut my twin off saying: "Fee I don't, and never will, give a shit about what those bitches want."

Fiona's so thin I easily push her out of my way and head back to my room and my own problems. Now I've gotta add this new bullshit to the list. My fucking wife should be here with me, helping me. Aw fuck I can't think about Kimmy now, I miss her too much.

Dora

After I finish in the restroom Bebe leads me back to the kitchen but Fiona immediately gets up saying *come with me.* I have no choice but to follow. We only get as far as the hallway and then have to wait outside a room marked *Private.*

We can hear loud male voices raised in anger but not the actual words. "Go wait over there," Fiona instructs pointing to the doorway of the main room where I first came in. I hover, uncertain where exactly I'm supposed to stand and really I'm too tired to care. I prop myself against the wall and will my legs to keep me upright.

The closed door is flung open and yet another big man, this one a redhead comes storming out only to tangle up with Fiona. I want to hear what they're saying but once Dog spots me he hurries over and I back away.

"Fuck, if you're not gonna have the bitch then I will," he declares. Roughly grabbing my wrist he pulls me along till he finds a chair and yanks me down into his lap. He's huge and well-built, like the rest of the men I've seen here, and again I note that he's by far the most handsome, and shockingly so. I mean, this guy is drop-dead gorgeous with his wavy curls and bright blue eyes. I'm mesmerized by the tattoo on his face. *On his face!*

The red-haired man has stomped off down the hall in the opposite direction so Fiona joins us. She says nothing but the way her eyes jump from one to the other shows she's very interested in what's going on.

Viper comes up behind her and his lips thin slightly as he snaps: "Dog, don't touch her." The words *she's mine* are unspoken but everyone feels them hovering in the air. The pause enables me to scramble to my feet and step away from Dog.

Is Viper my protector? or is he planning on using me himself? No, he's a killer and I'm in danger of being murdered after he or any of them - or even all of them - rape me.

"Hey, you found her so sure you get to have her first but bro, fuck her already so the rest of us can get a taste."

"Christ no, I don't want her at all. Touch her? Fuck no, it'd be like touching poison ivy. Keep your hands off."

Like a hunter stalking his prey Dog looms over me close enough that I can feel his hot breath against my face. He's been chewing cinnamon-flavored gum. Or maybe eating those hot little candy hearts? at the thought I almost bark out a nervous laugh. I'm definitely at my wit's end.

I draw back but he just leans closer. "Are you sure? 'cause I've lived with the itch of crabs so I sure as shit could live with her kinda itch," smirks Dog.

"You're really pretty, aren't you Poison Ivy?" His eyes actually sparkle but I don't know if that's due to his enthusiasm or my reluctance.

"Dog, we've had a lot of shit going on lately and we don't need to invite more trouble."

Fiona speaks with a veiled barb in her tone as she questions: "Trouble? Why? because she's just a witness, right? isn't that what you said?"

When Viper turns his cold gaze her way she lowers her eyes but not before a challenging look flares across her face. It looks to me like Fiona is trying to push his buttons in a weird way of showing she's attracted to him. Doesn't seem like the feeling is mutual. "What's your point, Fiona?"

Dog suddenly exclaims: "Hey, with all the bad luck and shit maybe she's like that typhoon Mary chick!

"That was *Typhoid Mary* and she spread disease. This one is just... bad news. So keep clear of her."

"I get it, VP. Dummy is off-limits."

"*Poison Ivy* can be her name now," says Fiona, "Like the old song."

"Poison works," says Viper with finality, turning a dark look on me. I shiver not out of fear but exhaustion and that makes me cold. I'm fighting to stay awake because I don't feel safe with these men in front of me nor the rest of them gathered behind.

Jerking his head Viper signals for me to follow. If I was speaking I'd have let loose a small *woof* since he's treating me like a dog.

Viper

I give her one of my meanest looks and all she does is yawn in my face. I almost smile, she's kind of fucking cute.

Letting her know she should follow I take her to my room so she can sleep, even though it's still afternoon. I hear Fiona ask where we're going but I ignore her 'cause I'll be back in a minute.

I've lived in this room for ten years now. Back when I was a prospect I shared the loft space above the garage with the other club hopefuls but once I got patched-in I got my own room, with a toilet and shower, in the clubhouse. I've never lived so well. Sure, when Banger's family practically adopted me I stayed at their place lots but this is my own place and I've always felt secure here.

Banger's almost four years older than me so he got his patch and his room way before I did. We spent a lot of time hanging out there. He didn't move out until he got married, and I'm still here in mine.

There's no marrying in my future, not with my history. Sure, his parents set a good example of family life but that lesson arrived too late. I'd already learned way more than I wanted to about the devious viciousness of wives and mothers.

There's not much stuff here, just my bed, dresser, chair, and a big screen TV. I never bothered with a stereo because there's always loud music playing in the clubhouse. I keep my work stuff in my desk in our meeting room and everything there is always locked up. So there's nothing this girl can poke her nose into if I leave her here for a couple of hours.

I change out of my suit hoping I don't have to put it on again for a long time. I need to talk to Hardware to see what he can find out about this girl but fuck it, I really need a ride to clear my head because today has been a royally fucked-up day.

As soon as we got in the room Poison made a bee-line for the bed and flopped face-down on it. She went out like a light and watching her sleep now makes me realize she really is very young.

Melva Flaherty crocheted an afghan for *both of her boys* many years ago, although I'm only her unofficially adopted son. Mine lives at the foot of my bed so now I shake it out and lay it over Poison. She squeaks out a contented little sigh in her sleep and that makes me smile. If she farted I'd laugh out loud.

Locking the door I head back to face the battle I'm sure is brewing up in the main room. Tough, I'm going for a ride first.

Tracing

Viper

Arriving back in the main room of our clubhouse I see that a fight or a bet or something has caught hold of everyone's attention. Perfect. Moving purposefully I skirt the crowd and am out the door in moments. I love my club but sometimes it's just a relief to get away from everybody.

The days are still long as we near the end of August so I can easily ride for hours if I want before it gets dark. Night riding is great when I'm out with my brothers but it can be hazardous for a lone biker.

Right now all I need is to open the throttle and let the wind challenge me. I'm hoping it will clear all this shit outta my head so I can deal with the trouble I brought to us. The Satan's Tears MC is my life and I will do everything and anything to protect it.

I experience my own special kind of peace after burning up some miles. Turning around I head back to the clubhouse, 100 times better able to deal with the shitstorm that'll be going on there.

As soon as I get inside I catch sight of Hardware and forget all about the arguments over the girl. He's a huge man, easily 300 pounds of bulky muscle standing 6'6", and one of our enforcers.

He's also incredibly gifted with any kind of digital device so he spends most of his time hunched over a keyboard. Right now he's sitting at the bar doing something between a phone and an iPad.

"Hardware!" I call, "Perfect timing, my man. Let me buy you a beer."

I slide onto the stool beside him and our prospect Jimmy serves us right away. Other than me killing that boy nothing that happened earlier is private so I tell him about everything else. The death –

murder – will be mentioned in our next church but I'm not going to compromise myself by talking in front of prospects or club whores.

"Lemme re-cap," he says when I finish and take a long swig after so much talking. "Young girl... is she of legal age?"

"Oh yeah, she's definitely full-grown," I assert.

He snorts and I think he's laughing at me but what did I say that's so funny? before I can ask he continues:, "Probably rich, dressed for a party, at the rest area of the forest looking messy like she slept rough, and not speaking, that it?"

He summed it up accurately and in far less time that I took to explain. I nod and watch as his big fingers fly across the iPad as he sets a search in motion. Moving onto his phone he brings up a Google map of that part of the forest and zooms in on something. I try to see what he's looking at but there's too much glare on the screen for me to get anything from my angle. After a minute or so he turns back to the iPad and swipes through some news items.

"Okay, there's a real ritzy restaurant, Portofino's, that's rented out for private functions set right in the forest here," he points to the area of the map he's enlarged.

"How did anyone buy land and get permission for a commercial property there?" I ask.

"Maybe they owned the land before the state took over? I dunno, anyway it's there. Oh this is interesting... uh-huh, hah!"

"What?" Impatiently I interrupt his mumbling.

"Hmm? Oh, I just found somebody covering their tracks and it's always fun to chase down stuff people are trying to erase. Something did happen and it's been removed but nothing is ever totally deleted from cyberspace. I'm gonna need some time but I will find out what these fuckers are trying to hide and I'll let you know."

"Okay. Shit, how much time do you need?"

"The more you keep talking to me the longer I need."

I punch him in the arm and laugh, saying "Asshole."

Just then Dog distracts us all by climbing up on the stage and whistling loudly for attention. It's only a small stage with a dancer's pole but we get in strippers to perform on Friday and Saturday nights and it's good entertainment.

One of the club's most lucrative gigs is running a crew of exotic dancers through the outlying strip clubs in this region. We bought a used Class C Coach for $100 K to house and transport the girls. It sleeps eight, has a kitchen, and there's even a mini-laundry. The brothers take turns providing protection and security but Dog runs the operation. We send six dancers on each trip which will last up to two months. The girls take turns driving and there are two bikers flanking the camper. The dancers earn enough to take a few months off after each tour.

The strip clubs pay us plus we get a percentage of the door. We give the girls a base fee and they keep any extra money they earn from the customers. In between shows the girls do lap dances and probably more but we don't care and we don't ask for a share of their earnings because we're not pimps.

Some clubs request matinee sex shows featuring girl-on-girl action and our ladies love it. Most of them are in relationships with each other and since the strip-clubs pay big for those shows they're always huge money-makers for the strippers. If the girls are happy everyone's happy.

Since plenty of brothers are willing to take a turn none of us has to go out on an escort tour if we don't want to. The girls can be fun and getting out on the highway for a good run is always fucking A but hanging out at the clubs can be a headache.

The club owners and managers range from criminal to hardcore sleaze but Dog gets on with them okay. Actually he gets along with everyone – even women, despite the way he talks and acts around them. It's like he's got a permanent hard-on or something.

At a recent church meeting Dog's report included problems with a girl who goes by *Sadie Corvette*. A couple of brothers hmmphed in recognition of the troublemaker. I had to think for a minute before recalling who she is. Sadie Corvette isn't pretty exactly but she's a great dancer and damn sexy.

The audience loves her but her fellow dancers sure don't and neither do we. She's always trying to run the show, wanting this and that for herself, and trying to take slots away from the others. We've had complaints that she doesn't play nice during the lesbian performances even going so far as to physically hurt her partner. No one wants to pair up with her.

Banger instructs Dog to tell her *next trip she's on probation and if she makes any trouble then cut the cunt loose*. We're not going to put up with *prima donna* bullshit even from a very popular act.

We also provide bouncers for the local strip clubs but they hire their own girls. We've got a good working relationship with the organizations that own these places and everybody makes money.

The room's quieted down now for Dog who hollers: "It might be Sunday night but the weekend ain't over yet. Who wants to see a live action sex show starring yours truly? and who's gonna be my co-stars?"

Rubbing his hands together he looks over to where the club whores are congregating. "I need some big tits – oh is that you yelling *pick me, pick me* Bebe?"

She wasn't, but now she just shrugs good-naturedly and sashays up onto the stage.

Bunny calls out "Well mine aren't big but they're real and they're perky. They'll bounce in your face when I'm climbing your pole."

"Tell you what, I'll take Bebe's tits as a pillow behind my -head while you ride me reverse cowgirl so I can squeeze your luscious ass."

The audience greets this with a cheer and Dog is quick to demand they show their appreciation by keeping the three of them well-lubricated with drinks. "Okay bitches, let's get naked!

Somebody loads up seventies disco tunes on the sound system and the women on stage are soon jiggling their tits and twerking their asses while Dog is waving his dick at them. The three form into a series of poses groping and kissing before fucking each other just as Dog suggested. Bebe's resting his head between her pillowy tits while he's smacking Bunny's plump butt as she rides him reverse cowgirl. Holding her hips firmly in place Dog strokes deep into her pussy until he hits her A-spot. Bunny's legs shake in a frenzied orgasm and the men shout their approval.

After Dog cums Bunny straddles his face for some tonguing while Bebe captures his cock in her boobs and rubs and licks his crown until he's ready to fuck again. They shift positions and now Dog pulls Bebe forward far enough that her big tits are squashed against his chest while they kiss. Bunny's moved down to suck his balls and she's fingering Bebe's butt-hole. The crowd loves it. The rest of the club whores are circulating among the bikers ready to start some action of their own.

The girls are determined to use Dog's cock one more time and take turns passing him from one hot mouth to the other until he explodes. Both of them then smear his cum over their tits and while Dog gives directions they play with each other, fingers slipping into holes while thumbs rub clits.

They roll on the floor even though it's messy and sticky. Their bodies are filthy with fluids and the dirtier they get the more the audience likes it. I'm reminded of the mud wrestling entertainment from way back when and wonder if we could revive some of those contests outside before summer ends.

Dog shouts that he'll *handle the color commentary for all the guys who are too vain to wear their glasses.* That gets a big laugh and he follows through, too. Grabbing the microphone so he doesn't have to yell he scoots right down and starts giving a play-by-play description in the low-pitched voice of a golf commentator:

"Bebe's got Bunny pinned with her legs bent in some crazy yoga position that forces her pretty pussy wide open. Bunny's getting her ass cheeks rubbed by Bebe's big tits. I'm looking down and all I can see is masses of glorious pink skin. Poor Bunny is getting the licking of her life!

Bebe's holding back the... what's it called? foreskin? the hood? of Bunny's clitoris and that poor little bundle of nerves is sizzling in Bebe's hot mouth. It's completely exposed and all shiny and red and swollen and I want to have a little taste myself but it doesn't look like Bebe's in the mood to share. She just keeps edging this poor girl and not showing her one iota of mercy. I'd ask her to explain but her tongue is waaaaayyyy too busy and Bunny's talking gibberish so..."

The brothers are hushed and leaning in to enjoy the performance Bunny's orgasm is a prolonged howl of pleasure with her hips bucking and her heels drumming while Bebe keeps sucking her clit trying to take her over the top for a third time tonight. The men raucously cheer the girls on.

Dog says: "I hope you were all paying close attention brothers because Bebe sure has set the bar high." That elicits clapping and whistles. "Bebe I need you to tell me a couple of things, one: whose dick has Bunny been pining for lately?"

"Ranger!" declares Bebe, looking out into the audience. The bikers part to let a tall man come forward. He doesn't need any pushing as he hurries up on stage to claim his prize.

Scooping Bunny into his arms he carries her off like a bridegroom calling over his shoulder "I gotta fuck her in the shower 'cause she dripping wet!" The guys all roar their approval at his crude comment.

Dog turns back to Bebe who's kneeling on the stage showing off her generous curves. "Okay Bebe you obviously came up with the right answer to that question. I said there were two things I wanted to know and the second one is: now that you're feeling all proud about dominating Bunny how do we put you back in your place, hmm? I think you need a big strong man with a firm hand to show you who the boss is, am I right brothers?" He yells the last question and everyone starts hollering advice from *spank that sweet ass* to *choke her with a big dick.*

"Hmm, why not both? What do you think, Bebe? do you need a *good girl spanking?*"

She plays up to him beautifully by twiddling with her hair and swiping her top lip with the tip of her tongue. "Maybe Dog, but only if I can get a *bad girl fucking* to go with it!" She sure knows how to play to the room!

Dog starts up a chant of *Tiny! Tiny!* and our biggest brother, a giant of a man, lets himself get shoved forward. It only takes him one step of his long legs to get up on the stage and his big muscular body towers over the well-built blonde.

Tiny is a quiet man, always bashful around the club whores, but he doesn't hesitate to lift Bebe up over his shoulder. When he lands a smack on her upturned bum Bebe wriggles and squeals *oooh, that stings!* The audience voices its disappointment at missing the show when Tiny carries Bebe away but it's a good-natured grumble because no one begrudges the shy man his fun.

Dog pulls his jeans back on, he always goes commando, and heads over to the bar for a drink. There's plenty of backslapping going on as the brothers argue over who gets to buy him a bourbon.

He looks at me with his shit-eating grin and I have to smile back even as I shake my head at him. I would never get naked and perform like that in front of everybody but I can enjoy it when he does. Dog's a showman, and a hound, and he can always be counted on to bring us a party.

Hardware was busy with his computer but still managed to catch most of the show. His eyes glittered with interest which is a surprise. He's always had his share of pass-arounds swarming him but he never seemed to care one way or the other.

It must have been the live sex show that caught his interest. I'll mention to Dog that maybe he should ask Hardware to go out on the next strip-club tour. Away from the clubhouse he might enjoy indulging in some menage action.

Now he signals to me and we head to a quiet corner of the bar.

"You got something?" I'm eager to hear what he's learned.

"Yeah, there was an incident involving shooting early yesterday evening. All the articles have been removed but I found them in my archives of deleted news items. They're interesting ones, because the incident involved at least two Mafia families, possibly three, and the FBI. Lots of shooting, lots of death, and nobody came out a winner so everyone wants it hushed up."

"That must have cost them big time."

"Big bucks for sure, but some real Mafia Royalty was involved. It says here that the Spagnolos and the Vendettis were *celebrating the betrothal of Loretta and Gualtiero*, two of their kids who are now as good as married. If they're still alive, that is. These engagements only last days because once an agreement is reached everyone wants it signed, sealed and delivered. Maybe your girl is Loretta Spagnolo?"

"Jesus, what a name!" I chuckle and he joins in. Hardware's laugh is booming and everyone nearby looks our way smiling at the sound before returning to their conversations. Good, they don't need to know our business.

"If that's who she is..." I begin then stop to think.

He picks up my thought finishing: "Then she's either our biggest payday or our death warrant. She could be her and important, or just a guest like a distant relative who no one will look for. See on the map here? If she got away from the venue and entered the forest anywhere along here it's not too far to the highway. She'd have to walk a fair ways to the restrooms here, though, but it could be done."

"Fuck, I gotta get hold of Prez 'cause he's gonna want to hold church to discuss this with the club. I mean... damn, we've got to figure out our options." *How much trouble is this putting me in now?* I wonder .

Hardware nods, all serious now. "I'll keep looking online, see if I can come up with more info and maybe some photos."

"Photos yeah, that would be real good, thanks man."

I know Banger is busy with his family stuff so I send him a text instead of calling. Less than five minutes later I get a group text telling everyone to meet first thing tomorrow for an emergency church.

I finish my drink but say no to another. It's been a long day, too much driving in a cage and too much stress with the punk and the girl... a mafia princess? I need to sleep.

Ignoring Fiona's voice calling out to me I head upstairs to my room before remembering the girl's inside. Fuck.

I stomp down the hall making enough noise to wake her and rattle the handle when I unlock the door. It doesn't make any difference. She's completely flaked out. Poison is still in her wrinkled dress and hasn't moved an inch from the same position she flopped into, right in the middle of the bed.

Well, she's little and doesn't take up much room, I think planning to just undress and climb onto my side of the bed when I change my mind. I don't know where it's come from but a wave of anger washes over me. I'm well fucking aware that I'm being unreasonable but an overwhelming urge to disturb Poison takes hold and I roughly shake her awake.

She pulls herself mostly upright blinking and groggily mumbling an unintelligible complaint. Sleeping made her seem very young but it's nothing compared to being woken suddenly. She looks like a 10-year-old the way she's rubbing her eyes.

"Get up and take my boots off, Poison. Make yourself useful."

I flop down in the armchair and manspread. She screws up her face into an angry pout and seethes at me for a long minute. I don't know what thoughts are going though her head but I'm pretty sure they revolve around my death. *Good!* I tell myself, *I want to piss her off. I want both of us pissed off.*

Reluctantly she comes forward and bends down but soon realizes she'll have to kneel to grab hold of the heel of my leather boot. It's not wet or muddy but it's not clean and she frowns over the task. She tugs but motorcycle boots are reinforced for safety which means they're heavy and she needs all her strength to yank hard. Her small hands look soft, unused to doing any kind of manual work. Well that's about to change.

"Get on with it, little girl," I order and her eyes shoot daggers at me. I give her a closed-mouth smile that I know makes me look like a sarcastic asshole. That's accurate. When she finally gets my boots off I tell her she doesn't have to clean them until the morning – this time – so she gets up to go back to bed but I stop her by loudly calling: "Hey! Socks and a foot rub. Chop-chop."

I don't even bother to hide my chuckle when a look of pure hatred comes my way. She drops heavily to her knees again and with a look of deep distaste hauls off first one sock then the other. I showered this morning but that was many hours ago so I'm sure both socks and feet have a sweaty smell.

She balls up the socks and puts them beside my boots. With a huge sigh she lifts my foot onto her thigh and using both hands starts massaging from the toes down to my heel. It feels like heaven.

Watching her on her knees concentrating with her eyes downcast makes me imagine holding her in that position while I deep-throat that pretty mouth. I wonder if I'll ever get the opportunity? Well of course I can get it, the question is *will I take it?*

She's not acting like a submissive. It's more like she's subservient from being raised to kowtow to men. I guess that's a mafia thing. Hell, it's a biker thing, too. A frown appears on her forehead and it looks like she's struggling not to cry. Is she missing the life she had? or worrying if this is what her life will be like going forward? on her knees serving a man she hates and fears?

Foot rubs are an inspired idea and we'll definitely be making them part of our bedtime routine.

Caught

Dora

Viper has to shake me awake, just like he did late last night for that ridiculous stunt with his nasty boots, and he isn't very gentle about it. Apparently we have an important meeting to attend and can't be late. I stumble into the shower and that gets my eyes open.

"I've left out some stuff for you to wear, Poison," he calls through the door when I turn off the taps. Wrapped in a towel I cautiously peek out and seeing he's across the room I quickly snatch up the clothes before locking myself back in the restroom, ignoring his laughter.

I should have washed out my underwear and left it to dry overnight but I was just too tired to think by time we got in here. Shrugging, I do it now then drape the two pieces over the curtain-rod. The t-shirt Viper has given me is loose enough to hide the fact I'm going braless – I hope – and the fleece shorts are really baggy too. I divide my hair into two parts and pull it forward to add extra coverage to my chest.

The meeting is with the club president, Banger, the scariest man I've ever encountered. That's saying a lot for someone from a crime family. Of course I really don't meet the men who come to our house, they keep a respectful distance, but I hear the gossip and their nicknames usually tell a story.

It seems to be the norm for these bikers to be big guys and Banger is no exception. He's a bit older than Viper and Dog and a stressful life shows in the lines on his face. And according to the gossip among the club whores there's trouble with his wife.

But it's not his size or his looks that intimidate, it's the feeling of danger that emanates from him. When Viper brought me into their meeting, in a room filled with men, the only one I was aware of was Banger. He has such a menacing presence. When he focused on me everything else went blurry. I couldn't even begin to describe the room I was in or what the men sitting closest to me looked like.

I'm made to sit beside Banger and when he catches me in his pale blue gaze I'm frozen with fear. His eyes drill through my defenses and he asks me flat out *are you Loretta Spagnolo?* It takes every ounce of courage I possess to lie.

Hearing my name spoken out loud by this man is terrifying. With silent tears streaming down my face I shake my head, more of a twitch than a gesture, but it's enough. I know there are no photos of me anywhere so there's no proof.

I wrack my brains wondering how did they figure it out? Are there stories in the newspaper? If so, what's being said? Who died and who survived? Am I still a bride-to-be? Is Walter alive and is he still my *fiancé?* or has war broken out between our families?

Normally mafia business is kept very quiet but if this got out... then wow. What about the FBI? I overheard their tech guy Hard Drive? or whatever, talk about the dinner so they know that much but probably - hopefully! - think I was just a guest. After all, I'm not wearing an engagement ring.

Banger's phone is lying on the table between us and though my hands are shaking so badly I can barely control my fingers I manage to open the Notes app and type *dora*. I'd never have presumed to use his phone but it's the only one I can see.

"Dora," he says, looking at the phone, then completely ignoring me exchanges a look with Viper who pulls me out of my chair and practically pushes me out the room shutting the door firmly behind me.

Out in the hallway I see one of the young guys, a *prospect*, standing guard and beside him is a box full of cell-phones. My cousins would go crazy for it. They're always trying out different kinds of phones and downloading every app that's going. I enjoy playing with their phones whenever I get the chance. I guess only the club president can carry a phone into their private meetings.

If only I could grab one to call Angie! but even if I got my hands on one it would have a pass-code and I'm not some genius hacker.

My thoughts are wrapped up in what has happened and what will happen to me. Bad dreams every night keep me from getting a good sleep and it's hard to concentrate when I'm so tired. I need to know what's going on.

I never knew I'd be on the run but I saw an opportunity to escape and grabbed it. I've always had a long-term plan to get away from my family some day. The marriage to Walter is a joke. My cousins told me he's already got a mistress established in an apartment near his office so he'll probably go straight to her from work each day. After having dinner with his *putana* he'll come home for obligatory sex with me, the clean and boring bride, until I fall pregnant. Then I'll be stuck in his world forever.

I have one confidante, my father's much younger sister Angie, and if I can just get hold of her...

Angelina Spagnolo is only six years older than me and we've always been close. She understands the life I have and what's in store for me. Daughters of the mafia are used to forge alliances, patch rivalries, and reward loyalty. We don't get to marry for love.

Angie was married and widowed young which gives her a lot more freedom that usual. She probably wouldn't have that if my father was still around but he went missing years ago and everyone figures he's dead. Angie certainly will be married off again but she might have some choice second time around. For her sake I hope so because her husband was a bully and a brute. It was his own rash, brash behavior that got him killed and I don't think anyone ever mourned him.

I've left a good amount of cash with Auntie, as I jokingly call her, stockpiled against a future getaway from my arranged marriage. All my life relatives and friends of my father have slipped me money but I never get to go out so I've never had a chance to spend it.

My cousins and I were home-schooled by tutors and my family are my only friends. I didn't complain because I've never known a different kind of life. It wasn't until those same cousins were allowed to go to college, while still living at home of course, that I realized how restrictive my upbringing was and still is.

It's because of the feud that's going on with my mother's family pitted against my father's family for control of the empire until my younger brother comes of age. I've been caught in the middle the whole time, and Ricky is still a few years short of his majority.

I can't waste this unexpected turn of events. Yes, all the shooting and killing that happened is tragic but it's also an opportunity and maybe my only chance. I've got to be alert for any way to use this new situation to my advantage.

I've already marked out Bebe as the one most likely to help me. She was helpful – and nice, too – about the tampons, whether she meant to be or not!

That meeting with Banger was two days ago, on my first morning at their clubhouse, and I'm still stuck here. I'm used to being held captive in my own home but there's a big difference between pampered daughter and despised prisoner. There are no servants here so I have to do everything for myself and I don't know how! I've

47

never had to do stuff, and the women here won't help. They've made it clear they don't want me around.

All I can do is watch then copy what they do. Fiona figured me out and has had a great time mocking the *poor little rich girl who can't ask questions.* Of course the rest all join in hooting and pointing like chimpanzees. That Jennifer is the worst. I call them *stupid ugly sluts* to myself but I wish someone was friendly. I'm lonely and frightened, and I hate this helpless, hopeless feeling. I can't let all this crap wear me down, I have to be strong.

I spend most of my time in Viper's room because I don't feel welcome anywhere else. Not that he wants me, in fact every time he comes back to the room he just stares at me in this funny way. Funny peculiar, not funny ha-ha. It's like he forgets me the moment he leaves and then gets an unpleasant surprise on each return.

Especially when he goes in the restroom and finds my undies drying on the shower rail. The last time that happened he really yelled at me threatening to destroy everything.

"If I get slapped in the face with wet panties one more time I'll make you go around with nothing on underneath - ever!" Since then I've kept my stuff hidden, hanging over the drain pipe that runs through the cabinet under the sink.

I go to bed early and I'm always asleep when he comes back so I guess he stays away until it's late. On one more occasion he woke me to do that stupid thing with his boots and rubbing his feet which I hate doing. But we sleep in the same bed and I always waken snuggled up against him. There's no need, the bed is huge, so it's really embarrassing.

That first morning I had no idea what was pressing into me and reached back to move it out of the way but when I realized... I was shocked! The moment my hand groped him, feeling his hard length, he murmured in a sleepy voice *don't start something you can't finish, Poison* and I quickly rolled away to hug the opposite edge of the mattress.

I was deeply ashamed until I felt movement and jerked around afraid he was moving towards me but it was something quite different. Viper had rolled on to his back with one arm flung across his eyes while the other stretched down until his hand was inside his boxers. He was stroking himself in a slow, lazy manner. His erection pushed the fabric up and I caught glimpses of his fingers through the gaping slit in his underwear.

I don't know how long I watched, crouched at the far side of the bed, but I couldn't tear my eyes away. Turning his head he looked at me on my knees with my long tangled hair hanging down and my curious face staring and didn't say a word but began stroking faster and faster. My gaze darted back and forth between his hand and his eyes. His breathing got louder and color rose in his face. Still his eyes never left me. I heard the beginning of a groan deep in his chest and the spell holding me broke – I fled to the bathroom. Gasping, I leaned against the door and listened to his laughter.

My cousins told me that all guys get *morning wood*. I was so relieved once I remembered that and understand this has nothing to do with me and it isn't my fault.

Of course Viper, being the nasty prick that he is, has subjected me to repeat performances yesterday and today. Yesterday I pretended I was still asleep the whole time he pleasured himself.

He climbed out of bed right after telling me: "I know you're awake, Poison. Next time you really should make yourself useful." When I didn't reply he came and sat on the edge of the bed beside me and surprised me by gently brushing my hair back off my face. Then he ruined it by saying: "FYI at some point me and you are gonna fuck, and whether you try to fight me off or welcome me with spread legs doesn't matter 'cause I'm gonna enjoy it either way."

He stayed in the bathroom for a long time and when he finally came out, showered and dressed, I raced inside desperate to pee.

This morning as soon as I feel his dick stirring I move to get out of bed but he grabs my hips and pulls my behind tight against him. I can feel his hardness trying to burrow between my butt-cheeks. I try to get away but he has a firm hold on me and his hands are dangerously close to my private parts.

While I was sleeping my tee-shirt got twisted and pulled up leaving me almost completely exposed in just a thong. As Viper pumps his pelvis I feel confused by my needy arousal yet I'm also feeling scared and helpless. Without realizing it I'm grinding my rear-end back into him and when I feel the heat from his muscular thighs I become aware of what I'm doing. I'm so ashamed of myself. I don't understand how I can act like this. After giving one hard, final thrust he shouts *fuuuuuck* and I feel wetness soaking my crack. Then I burst into tears.

Viper grabs my shoulders and forces me around to face him. I keep my eyes screwed shut but I can feel him glaring at me.

"Look at me, Poison," he commands in a low growly voice. I shake my head and his grip tightens. "Do what you're told, Dora."

Surprise at him using my name makes me open my eyes which I'm sure are all wet and red. His expression is serious but not angry when he asks why I'm crying. I look away and shrug.

"Did I hurt you?" I think for a moment before again shaking my head *no*.

Then he asks if he scared me and I meet his gaze and reluctantly nod *yes*. Viper waits a moment longer before asking: "Did you also scare yourself?" and I don't need to answer because he sees my astonishment and smirks.

"Your ass has the softest skin I've ever felt so don't bother wearing anything to bed tonight Poison, because I'm going to touch every inch of you... and I'll make you love it." Turning away with a quiet chuckle he settles back to sleep some more.

I get out of bed quickly and spend a long time washing myself in a very hot shower. He'll make good on his threat simply because he can. I'm trapped in this room with him every night and although I'll make a point of wearing several layers of clothes to bed that will probably just amuse him. He'll still strip me down. I really hate him.

Viper

When she typed the message on Banger's phone that her name is Dora I thought *that's probably short for Adoration, a Catholic girl's name.* I couldn't help acting like a motherfucker this morning in bed but I didn't plan on making the good little Catholic girl cry. Now I'm starting to believe she's completely untouched. I've never fucked a virgin... I don't think I want to. I'd have to go slow and be gentle and I don't need that shit although... at least she'd be clean. And naive, pliable, sweet, and maybe even goodhearted but that won't last. Women don't stay innocent for long.

I've got to get my head back in the game here. Banger's trying to decide what to do with her, and Hardware's using all his skills to identify her, so I need to work on figuring out the truth of what she's really like.

For Dora to be where I found her she must have been at that party. That means she's Italian. She's fair but they aren't all dark. Just look at Casso he's got the same kind of coloring as Dora and he was actually born in Italy. He once said something about real differences between Italians from the north compared to the south. So, she's Italian and from a family with money. Yeah, that sounds like the mob.

Shit, she's got to be worth something to us.

I know the club whores are being bitches but I told Bebe to cozy up and see if she can learn anything. Bebe isn't half as dumb as she pretends to be... I mean, she's smart enough to know that her dumb act makes her more popular with us bikers.

The vicious behavior of the other club whores is becoming a problem though, and I'm positive Fiona is behind the campaign of so-called accidental pushes and tripping up that keeps happening to Dora.

I don't give a shit about her, Poison can deal with it herself, but the non-stop griping and whining is really pissing me off. Gotta say Dora's silence is a big plus although she can be pretty expressive with the eye rolls, frowns, and disgusted looks. She sighs a lot as well.

And lately Fiona is always getting in my way. I know exactly what she's trying to do and nothing's changed since I shot her down years ago. She's acting all jealous which is bullshit, maybe I should remind her yet again that nothing's ever gonna happen between her and me. Poison's got nothing to do with it.

Fiona won't believe that, she thinks so much of herself she just can't believe I would choose no one rather than her. And yet it's all fake. Fiona is only pretending, she doesn't want to be with me, how could she after everything that went down? Stupid fucking bitch.

My mind drifts down memory lane to that long-ago confrontation that ended any feeling I ever had for her. Like I would ever choose between Banger and some cunt. When King found out it was—

BANG-BANG-BANG-BANG-BANG-BANG-BANG

What the fuck! Somebody's shooting at us. I lead the dash to the front door, yanking my gun out of the shoulder holster. The prospect on the door has ducked down but our clubhouse is situated far enough back from the road to be perfectly safe from drive-by shootings. It's the guys at the gate who could be in danger.

Hardware is beside me as we race to check out the prospects on guard duty there. Thank Christ, they're in the gatehouse – which is made of cement cinderblocks – and not sunning themselves on lawn-chairs out front. They got a scare and their story is all mixed up but Hardware is already at work checking the surveillance footage.

"Two black SUVs, the kind the FBI drive... and every crime family you can think of," he says. Switching to a different camera he reports: "No plates so probably not G-men." That breaks up the tension and we all laugh too loud.

I feel my heart-rate slowing down and as the adrenaline fades anger takes its place. "Who the fuck would attack us?"

"Do you think it's anything to do with the shit Banger's got going on right now?"

I shake my head *no* because that issue is with his wife who is currently living at another MC and if they came after us they'd be on their bikes.

"Doesn't make sense. I'll talk to both Eagle and Slash to see if there's anything going on with collections, lawsuits, shit like that."

"I'll get on my computer to see if there's any chatter about what's happened here." Hardware cracks his knuckles adding: "If you need me to do something just say the word." I lightly punch his arm to show my appreciation.

Turning to the prospects I tell them to go up to the clubhouse saying they can knock off now, send their reliefs down early, and calm down with a beer. I notice they stick close to Hardware as they walk away. I call out to him to check up on Poison, not sure why she matters, but he nods that he heard me.

While waiting for the next shift to arrive I send Banger a text telling him what we know so far.

Dora

I slip into the kitchen cautiously, making sure nobody's near the stove boiling water or something equally damaging. I wouldn't put anything past these bitches.

I can only see Bebe who is doing her nails at the table which is kind of tacky but why should I care? She's the only one of them who is halfway decent towards me. I'm sure I'm right about her taking me under her wing because it made her feel good when she figured out I needed a tampon.

Going straight to the fridge I grab a bottle of cold water and holding it up give her an inquiring look. She barely glances at me before shaking her head and turning back to her phone.

As I walk past she pushes out a chair with her foot saying: "Hey Poison, you can sit. You don't have to run back to Viper's room. I know you must get pretty lonely on your own all the time. I'm just trying to take the password off my phone but I can't figure it out. Do you know anything about these iPhones?"

I shake my head even though I do know plenty about cellphones because of my cousins. I just think it makes sense for the mute girl to be clueless about them. And truthfully I've never had my own phone. Although whenever the family went out we were all given burners with trackers in them. Just in case.

"Well, I guess I'll just have to live with this. It's just such a pain in the ass to have to enter 1-1-1-1 every single time." She shakes her head and repeats, "Every. Single. Time." Like it's a huge hardship.

First World problems for idiots, I think, chewing the inside of my cheek to keep from laughing.

Then Bebe sits up suddenly and full of indignation complains that Hardware wouldn't help her. "He even got mad when I told him what my password is and snarked something about *why not 1-2-3-4?* and when I said that mine is easier he laughed but in a nasty way. Stupid man wants me to change it to something even harder to remember when all I want to do is get rid of the damn password altogether!"

I paste what I hope is a sympathetic look on my face and we sit in companionable silence. My eyes are drawn back to her phone over and over again. If I could just get my hands on it I could call Angie and see about saving myself.

I know I'd have to sneak out of the clubhouse and figure out a way off the premises but I'm sure I can manage that. The only thing is there's no point getting out until I've got somewhere to go with some resources once I get there. Angie's got everything I need. Damn, damn, damn. I can practically taste my freedom it feels so close.

I have to look away so Bebe doesn't get suspicious of me for staring at her phone so much. When I do my eyes meet those of a young teen, a boy I think. It's hard to tell because he's very thin and pale and wears his hair long. Yeah, it's a boy, but he looks nothing like my 16-year-old brother Ricky.

I can see that this young guy has been stocking food on the shelves in the walk-in pantry. The clubhouse doesn't have a cook so meals aren't provided but Fiona sees that there's plenty of snack foods, cereal, peanut butter, soup, that sort of thing, and there are microwaveable meals in the big chest freezer.

Seeing that I'm staring at something Bebe looks up and says: "Oh hey Jeremy, how are you doing?" The boy ducks his head shyly and doesn't answer. Turning to me Bebe says "Isn't he a cutie? Just turned

15 but you can already tell he's gonna be breaking plenty of hearts when he gets older."

Now the boy's face has turned crimson but he's smiling as he hurries past us out of the room.

Bebe continues telling me: "It's so sad. His father Aces was such a great guy, always ready to have a drink and share a laugh, get laid, party, he was pretty much up for anything any time. He died suddenly and when they did the autopsy they discovered he had leukemia of all things and nobody knew. He came down with a strep throat and then next day he's dead.

Jeremy's mother had left years before because truth be told Aces wasn't the faithful kind. He spent a lot of his time here so Jeremy basically lived with his Auntie, Aces' sister. She works though so while he's out of school for the summer the club is looking after him. He's such a great kid, he helps Fiona with chores like shopping and stuff.

Once he turns 18 I expect he'll join the club as a prospect and will become a brother soon after that. Unless his Auntie has something else in mind for him, I don't know the woman so I can't say."

I'm not saying anything either but I have no trouble showing interest because it shows a side to club life that I wouldn't have imagined. The irresponsible partying father sounds right but the members' care of his bereaved son is unexpected and I respect them for that.

Tilting my head back to take a deep swig of water I end up spraying it when we hear a series of loud bangs. I know the sound of gunfire when I hear it.

Bebe has leapt to her feet but I'm frozen, memories of the many, many gun shots from the massacre immobilize me with fear. She dashes from the room and I hold on to enough of my wits to snatch up her phone and shove it down my pants. Stupid thong won't hold it for long.

I'm about to follow Bebe down the hall where I can hear the voices of several women excitedly chattering about the shooting. From the corner of my eye I catch a glimpse of sunlight and realize someone, probably Jeremy since he just went out, has left the kitchen's outer door open. That's my cue to escape.

I regret the loss of my diamonds but I don't hesitate to grab this advantage while I can. Clutching the phone through my clothes I hurry through the door and run right into the club's tech guy, Hardware.

I've never seen him up close before, he's the size and strength of a brick wall. We're only inches apart so I have to tip my neck right back to look into his face. I almost say sorry but catch myself in time. I slip my hand down my behind and push the phone into a better position. I can't lose it, it's my only way out.

Hardware would make me nervous even if I wasn't trying to escape with a phone I just stole. His features are nondescript but the sheer size of him is so intimidating.

I think he's only a few years old than me, certainly younger than the other bikers. Even though he's younger than Bebe he still bosses her around. These clubs seem to work just like the *famiglia* does with men always getting their own way and treating the women like door-mats.

"You okay?" he asks and I nod, blinking and licking my suddenly dry lips. His eyes focus on my mouth but his stony expression doesn't change.

"Where are you going?" I try glancing around as if I have no idea where I am or how I got here but I'm not an actress and his deep chuckle proves it.

Folding his impressive arms across his equally impressive chest he tilts his head to give me the onceover saying: "I oughta put you over my knee for tryin' to run away."

Gasping I jump back into the open doorway and now he's really laughing. The deep rumble is strangely attractive but I'm afraid of what it might mean for me.

"Don't worry little rabbit, Viper's warned us all to keep our hands off."

Seeing my shoulders slump in relief he leans in close and his low gravelly voice vibrates in my ear. He tells me that if Viper relinquishes the right to have me he'll be sure to let Banger know he's interested in making a claim.

"Very interested in teaching a timid but naughty little thing how to behave."

It's good he doesn't expect me to talk because I can't find any words. Is this threat of his supposed to be flirtatious? Did he learn how to chat up women from Dog?

Straightening to his full height again he seems impossibly tall but I can't take my eyes away and crane my neck to see his face. His smile transforms his previously bland look and his eyes sparkle with warmth and interest.

"Everybody knows Viper has a thing for you, everybody except Viper, that is. He's so busy denying and fighting his feelings I might get a chance with you after all. He'll be down at the gate for awhile but you better get back to his room so you're there when he gets here," he orders.

I hear a snort behind me and knowing it's Fiona I don't bother looking back, I just turn around and head to the room moving as quickly as I can before the phone falls. I guess they all suppose Viper and I are having sex but despite what he did this morning we really aren't. He's mostly just in the room to sleep.

He sometimes brings me something to eat but usually he just acts like he's forgotten I'm there. I don't care because when he isn't ignoring me he's likely got a sneer on his face and a complaint about something.

So Hardware is way off-base with his crack about Viper denying having feelings for me because he doesn't. And I've read this *oh I'm afraid of caring-wanting-loving too much so I have to act like a real prick towards you* trope too many times. It's so lame.

I'm human so of course I can't help but notice how sculpted and sexy Viper's tattooed body is but I'm so thankful that he leaves me alone. I'm not sure if it's because he hates me for being such an inconvenience, or for seeing what he did to Steve, or if I'm just not his type. From what I've overhead when the club whores are gossiping Viper *isn't a horn-dog like most of them.*

Plus there was that whole discussion the first time we got into bed together. After eating with everybody Viper sent me to his bedroom while he stayed with the guys drinking for a couple of hours.

Eventually he showed up and once he locked the door behind him asked: "Are you on birth control?"

Instead of answering I went into the bathroom and fetched the box of tampons.

"You're on the rag?"

I scowl thinking *seriously? that's what he calls it?* and return the box to the cupboard under the sink. I come back and lie down on the bed, waiting for him.

"You want me to fuck you even though your cunt's full of blood?" I flinch at the word he's used but he doesn't notice. He's absolutely incredulous, a look mixed of horror and disgust on his face.

I roll my eyes and sigh loudly. He must know that I don't want to fuck him at all and am just submitting to what he wants.

"So you'll do it even though you're on your period?"

Why not? I wonder. Menstruation is perfectly natural, It's nothing to be disgusted about, and I can't get pregnant when I'm—oh shit, I forgot that I'm not actually on my period. Fortunately he's pissed off and not paying attention to my expression.

Grabbing hold of my chin he pulls my face close to his and staring deeply into my eyes growls: "The first time I fuck you I'll make you cum so many times you'll be screaming for my cock. You'll be begging for it 'cause I'll have licked your pussy till it's soaked and you're whining and vibrating. I can't do that if you're on the rag. And you sure as fuck won't be lying there like a scared virgin all shaky and stiff as a board."

I'm gasping for breath at his words, showing my true feelings with dilated pupils and nipples grown hard. He's fully aware but doesn't smirk at me. Instead, he continues in the same menacing tone: "I asked you a question and there are always consequences if I have to repeat myself."

61

My brain feels utterly scrambled but I frantically replay our conversation, thankful to recall he asked about birth control so I shake my head *no*.

He releases his hold saying: "Condom it is, next week or whenever. Come and tell me when your period is over."

How shameful will that be? My shoulders slump, already feeling the humiliation.

"And make sure you've cleaned yourself up first. Like, had a good hot soapy shower."

Bastard! the arousal I felt has dissolved into disdain at that disparaging comment. I lift up my chin thinking *I'm better than you, I'm smarter than you, and your words won't break me.*

As if he can read my mind Viper chuckles. "Next month we'll fuck through every day of your period and after you can lick me clean. In fact," he pauses and pretends to be considering something, "I'll enjoy riding you bareback so much I'll fuck you at least twice a day and I won't let up even if you're suffering from bad cramps."

I ignore him and his stupid comments but he keeps saying gross stuff, leaning close and whispering in my ear about how much he's looking forward to making me beg for his dick and then cry once I get it.

He's hateful! I flounce onto my side, turning my back to him, resolving to be long gone before a week has passed.

Turns out I'm not long gone but it hasn't been a week yet so... maybe I'll make good on that promise to myself after all.

Each morning he does more stuff with me and I can sense that I'm running out of time. I've got Bebe's phone, I know her pass-code, and Hardware said Viper would be away for awhile. This is the best opportunity I'm going to get so I dial the number I memorized long ago.

Angie's voice sounds suspicious as she answers an unknown number and her accent is more noticeable as she loudly demands to know *who is this?*

"Auntie it's me!" I cry, having to clear my throat to speak clearly.

"Dora? Dora! Dora, thank God! where are you? what's going on?"

"Oh Angie, it's been... ugh, it's a long terrible story—"

"Are you safe? were you hurt?"

"I'm fine, I'm... actually no not fine exactly. I've been taken by some motorcycle gang. Angie I saw such horrible things, I have nightmares—"

"Oh baby it's okay, it will be okay, you know? but... why were you with the FBI?"

"What? The FBI? I wasn't with them, why would you think that?"

"Tonino said he saw one of their agents guiding you away to safety—"

"No! It wasn't like that at all. An FBI guy did grab me saying I was under arrest but we both fell down and I got away before he could handcuff me. Don't you remember what it was like there? I was skidding and sliding all over the floor between the food and drinks and blood spilled everywhere... I can't stop seeing and hearing... oh Auntie, I need to get away, to get free from all of this awful life. Where can I meet you? I'll figure my way out of here—"

"Where is *here* anyhow?"

"I don't know where it is but I'm in the Devil's Tears clubhouse. No wait, not Devil's but Satan's. Have you heard of it? do you know where it is? I guess it doesn't matter, once I get out I'll grab a cab just tell me where to go."

"Dora, I need to talk to the family first. There's well... a lot of anger and grieving and bad feeling, you know? Everyone's looking for somebody to blame, there's a lot of finger-pointing going on and—"

I'm absolutely horrified when I gasp: "They CAN'T think I had ANYTHING to do with happened, they just can't! Why would I? who would I get to... I, I can't even wrap my head around this. Angie, you don't think... omigod you do! you think I was somehow involved in the killing of all those people. I-I-I just... I can't... omigod, omigod."

"Oh Jesus Dora, I don't think that, I mean not really, but there are questions and... and we need to you know talk and get everything sorted."

Her lack of trust, her betrayal leaves me numb. I'm dead inside. I coldly tell her: "That's fine, don't put yourself out. Just give me the access code to the account with my money and I'll take it from there. You don't have to get involved or associate yourself with me—"

"Dora I... I can't. Tonino said I can't give you that money because you can't run, you have to come back and face up to everything."

"You told him about the money? Why? so he and you can steal my money?" I cry in dismay.

"Loretta Antonia Spagnolo don't you dare call me a thief!" she yells, then softening her voice says: "Look, sweetie, try to understand my position. I'm being torn in two here—"

"I'm your blood and I should have your loyalty. I trusted you, Auntie. I can't believe you're doing this, I can't believe you've abandoned me."

I can't control the sob that explodes from my chest, from my heart. I hate to show her my weakness so I press *End Call* before burying my face in my hands while a storm of weeping shudders through my body.

I have nothing, no where to go, no one to go to, no hope left at all. I'm devastated and desolate.

The last thing I need to hear now is Viper cruelly taunting me as he leans against the bedroom door. He's rigid with fury and has folded his arms across his chest so tightly his biceps bulge. His whole posture is threatening and when he stalks towards me I cower, I can't help it, I'm so scared.

"Bebe sure did a good job because you took the bait. Loretta Antonia Spagnolo. I don't hear a *Dora* in there, did I miss it? or was that just another one of your lies?"

I interrupt him crying out: "No! I didn't lie about that. Everyone does call me Dora because it's a short form for Loretta."

"They don't sound the same at all," he snaps.

"Well it's like Betty being a short form of Elizabeth even though it doesn't sound the same at all..." I trail off, knowing I'm rambling but my head's in a haze. There's too much to absorb: Auntie's betrayal, Cousin Tonino demanding I give an accounting, suspicion, threats... getting caught and Viper's rage.

"Aw fuck it, I prefer Poison anyhow because it's so accurate. Now tell me the truth and don't make me ask again: you are Loretta Spagnolo, aren't you? You can't get away with playing dumb any more you little bitch."

He used Bebe, the only one I thought might like me a little, to play a trick on me. Another betrayal of stupid, stupid Dora... I should be used to it by now.

Viper

Dora is sitting hunched over on the bed with her face wet from the tears still streaming down her cheeks. The look in her eyes would break anybody's heart... well, anybody but me. I'm so angry I just want to lash out at her. She really did a number on me, playing me for a fool.

I didn't exactly believe she was unable to speak because of her calling out during her nightmares but I did believe that she temporarily couldn't talk, like from shock or trauma or something. It was all an act and I fell for it. Fucking little bitch pulled a fast one, you can't trust these cunts... not ever.

"Banger's on his way anyhow because of the shooting so you and me will wait right here and then you can explain yourself to him in person. You made a big mistake when you lied to him, Poison. Probably a fatal mistake."

I know I'm scaring her and I'm glad. I won't beat her up, I don't hit women, but if my Prez orders me to kill her then she's dead. I guess that seems like a weird distinction but it's not, not when you consider how I grew up. Killing Poison would solve a few problems – like how she makes me feel so distrustful yet I still can't help being interested – but fixing that problem might cause more serious ones.

I'll let Banger worry about that shit, and Poison can worry about Banger. Right now, I want to get some answers.

"So here's what Hardware put together: there was a fancy party at some place called Portofino's that a bunch of mafia bigwigs attended. You were like the guest of honor, right? but somehow it all went tits up with shooting and killing and the FBI involved and then you escaped."

She gives a halfhearted nod as if she's not even paying attention. Actually, she's not. It's obvious her mind is wrapped up in her own thoughts. Well fuck that noise. She's kept her mouth shut for too long already and now she's gotta spill.

Pushing right up into her space I tower over her, forcing her to look up. From this angle my focus is on her face and she looks so scared with her brown eyes like saucers and her bottom lip trembling. She looks so helpless and young. I squash renegade tender feelings and bark at her *answer me!*

"Yeah, yeah you're right. That's pretty much what happened."

"Pretty much, eh? Christ that isn't even half the story so tell me what happened. You're gonna have to tell it to Banger and he's not as patient as me so you better get your facts straight, Poison."

She frowns at me like she's already moved on from being scared and now I'm just irritating her. This girl... holy fuck. I give her a hard look and she explains in more detail.

"The party was to celebrate my engagement to Walter Vendetti. We did the purity test the day before so everything was set to go and we would have gotten married the following Saturday. Everything at the dinner was going fine and then somebody started shooting so everybody started shooting and then there were FBI pouring into the place – you know how they wear those jackets with big yellow FBI letters? and people were going crazy trying to hide, trying to get away, with lots of screaming and shouting and gunfire.

We'd all ducked down to avoid the bullets so I was on the floor and started crawling towards the kitchen. I figured I'd get out that way or at least get hold of a knife there.

Some FBI woman tries to grab my arm telling me I'm under arrest but I pull away from her. Then this FBI guy grabs hold and yanks me to my feet. He starts dragging me with him but I fight and we both fall over. We couldn't help it, the floor was covered in...in..." she huffs a deep breath and forces the words out, "Covered in blood and it's all sticky and I jump right back up and run.

I go through the kitchen and I see an open door and I don't waste time looking for a knife I just race outside. I keep running until I'm deep in the woods. I've never been out in the woods or out alone in the dark for that matter.

I have no idea where I am, I'm gasping for breath and I've never been so scared. I don't run - ever - and I don't play sports or anything like that so I've got a pain in my side and everything hurts but I'm too anxious trying to get safe to notice any of that.

I'm holding my breath so I can listen to hear if anyone's in pursuit. But there's nothing so it doesn't sound like anyone came after me.

I keep moving but slower this time and I'm still tripping over tree roots and rocks and stuff. I don't want to stop and lie down because I'm afraid wild animals will get me. I've never climbed a tree in my whole life but I have to try and I get lucky because someone has nailed boards into the tree sort of like a ladder. I take off my shoes and can fit my toes on, enough to climb up to this platform thing. I guess it was some kid's tree-house? and I can sit and wait until it's light enough to see."

I see her hand is shaking as she runs it through her hair and starts rubbing the back of her neck. I guess re-living that night has made her tense – I'm inclined to believe her but I know she's a darn good actress. Still, she seems to really be agitated and she's fidgeting.

"Okay, I kept quiet not wanting to interrupt your story but I've got questions. First off, who is Walter Vendetti?"

"He's the underboss of the Vendetti empire, Cosa Nostra from Sicily, and they're very powerful in the Mafia world. I'm a Spagnolo so I belong to the Contini Family which means I'm an asset for them to use. Offering me in marriage to Walter, whose real name is Gualtiero by the way, makes a strong alliance here."

"But you're an American and it's the 21st century so why are you letting them treat you like property?"

"Because that's what I am and I've always known it. I'm *Mafia Royalty,* a *Princess,* and this is the role I was born to fulfill. Look, I've seen two women here with *Property of* insignia on their clothes so–"

"That's different. In motorcycle clubs – we're not a gang like you said – a *Property of* patch means more than a wedding ring. It's an honor to wear."

She tilts her head and gives me an amused look saying: "Me and my family were being highly honored to be chosen by the Vendettis."

I don't get it but I have to admit MCs aren't exactly big on Women's Rights or anything so... "Okay next thing, what's a purity test?"

She looks off to the side, being evasive, but I clear my throat pointedly and she finally says "It's a test to prove I'm a virgin."

"You mean you get checked out by a doctor?"

"I wish," she huffs, folding her arms over her chest. I'm not *a student of the human condition* as our club doctor Needles claims to be but even I can read that body language. She's uncomfortable and unhappy and I don't care.

"So what does happen?"

"Well..." she pauses to chew on her lip for a moment before speaking in a low voice to describe her ordeal.

"The Sicilians are a traditional people and the Vendettis follow the old standards. It means the girl lies on a white cloth and her *fiance* penetrates her. This is witnessed by two females from her family, it was my mother and my aunt–"

I interrupt asking: "Auntie Angie?"

She gives a quick smile at the thought and says no, a much older Auntie. "And two from his. After that one thrust the man has to move away and the women check that there's blood as evidence of purity."

I can't believe shit like that happens. "What if she doesn't bleed?"

"If she didn't he'd rape her then strangle her to death."

"Fuck. So you had to do that um... test just a few days ago?"

"Yes and obviously I bled since I'm still breathing."

"I wonder if Walter still is?"

A surprised laugh explodes from her and I smile too. It wasn't meant as a joke but I can hear how it sounds. But I really am wondering. If this mafia boss *fiance* is alive will he want to negotiate for her or just destroy us as revenge. Her reaction shocked her and now she's covered her mouth as if to hold any further laughter in.

"I don't know, and I'm wondering too. I've never been close to my Mama but... I hope... I'm wondering about everyone. My Auntie only mentioned my cousin, Tonino, but other Contini family members survived because she said they want to see me."

"Yeah, I heard. She's got a loud voice when she's on the phone."

"Not just when she's on the phone."

It feels like we're getting too comfortable talking like we're friends. We aren't and I need to remember that. Banger will expect me to get as much of the story as I can before he gets here.

"Okay so you passed this purity test and wait, you said the guy *moves away* what does that mean?"

"Oh well he has to step back so the ladies can have a look–"

"And you're just lying there undressed?"

"No, I'm all covered up wearing a very full skirt so Walter could lift it, do his thing, and then his mother pulls the cloth out from under me. It's really embarrassing and it hurt too, he had to stab twice in order to break through. I don't know if the membrane was thick or if he wasn't very hard. Once they have their proof the women congratulate him, not me but him, and he walks away. We don't even kiss."

"That's pretty fucked up but at least you knew what was going to happen."

"Mostly, yeah. I mean neither my mother or my aunt had gone through that so they couldn't tell me. It's a pretty rare thing nowadays."

"What did Walter have to say about it?"

"Nothing. I mean, nothing to me because that was the first time I saw him. I'd seen his photo of course but we never met or even talked on the phone."

I just gape at her in shock. I don't know what I'd have said if I didn't heard boots pounding down the hall signaling Banger's arrival. I quickly unlock the door and when he comes in suddenly the room seems very small. Banger's a couple of inches taller than me and about thirty pounds heavier.

Moving to the edge of the bed he looms over Dora and states: "You lied to me. You *are* Loretta Spagnolo, right?"

I admire her spirit, even if it is suicidal, when she straightens her shoulders and lifts her chin to say: "I've been raised to never tell anyone my name, or acknowledge it if they ask. It puts the family at risk, it's too dangerous."

"You're dangerous to us, to this club," he thunders at her.

"That's not down to me! I never asked to come here, it's his fault," she hollers, pointing to me with a furious look, but I can hear the fear in her voice. She's terrified.

"Yeah it is. I told him he should have killed you along with that punk." He scrapes his hands through his hair and if it wasn't so short I'm sure he'd be tugging on it.

I'm so angry, really really pissed at Poison for putting my brothers at risk. I mean, the fucking mob? the Italian mafia? Jesus H. Christ. "The question now is do we tell them, the mob, that we have her?" I ask but before Banger can answer Dora speaks up. It takes balls to challenge our Prez in any way, never mind telling him what to do!

She's speaking quickly, desperate to make her point. "No! Keep my secret for your own safety. Don't tell anyone outside this room because if word gets back to my family the mafia will rain down hellfire."

"I thought you were *just property*?" I snap back.

"Exactly! I'm THEIR property and they're very possessive. Dora means nothing but a betrothed asset has great value. Even if Walter is dead I've been accepted and claimed by the Vendettis so my *title* has been transferred to them and the alliance stands and my betrothal to whoever they decide is suitable."

"So we're now in the cross-hairs of two mafia families? Fucking A," snarls Banger.

"Look, don't let on who I am or that I can speak. People talk around me because they think I'm dumb-dumb not silent-dumb so I hear stuff and I'll pass it on to you. I can help you! just keep my secrets safe and it won't be forever..." she trails off in the face of his implacable stare.

After weighing up her words he comes to his decision.

His eyes are hot and angry when he says to me: "We'll keep her secrets for now... but if anything happens because of her it's on you. And she needs to be punished and you have to be the one to do it.

Maybe like I did with Fiona way back when, remember that? I had to take my belt to her on the orders of the Club Prez. But this girl deserves a hell of a lot more than a spanking.

I'll let you decide what you want to do and how... Christ knows you get plenty creative when you're interrogating some poor slob. Well a bitch is no different. Use your brain, your talent, your skills and make sure we all can hear her suffer.

I am so fucking angry I can hardly see straight. Viper, you make sure you punish her severely. Make it memorable. Take off fingers, or an ear, I don't care what you do just make sure it fucking hurts."

He doesn't even look in Dora's direction when he goes but as he's leaving he calls back over his shoulder in a voice full of menace:

"Has she put a target on our clubhouse and a bounty on our members? If getting our place shot up turns out to be because of her she's dead," before slamming the door hard.

Punishment

Dora

Viper is going to beat me with his belt? Banger said he has to make it really hurt so... omigod, I'm so scared. Cut off my ear? He didn't really mean that... not for real. No one has ever raised their hand to me... Viper looks so, so angry!

I scoot away from him till I'm hunched against the headboard of the bed. If I'm fast enough I'll be able to spring from here to the bathroom where I can lock myself in but will a locked door keep him out? Probably not, and if he has to break down his own bathroom door he's going to be even angrier at me.

Or maybe he'll realize just how frightened I am and... and what? He's never going to go against his Club President. He's been given a direct order and I've already seen enough of this motorcycle gang world to know it's run just like the mafia: the VP was told to punish me and he will.

But I can't bear the thought... I burst into tears and launch myself from the bed to Viper's feet, clutching him around his knees I beg. I've never begged for anything in my entire life but I'm begging now. I'm pleading and sobbing for him to go easy on me. I tell him that if he'll only restrain himself, hit me with softer strikes, I'll still shriek loudly to satisfy all the listeners. He reaches down to peel my fingers off his legs but I tighten my desperate hold on him until he yells *Enough, Poison! just stop!*

But I don't want to be Poison I want to be Dora to him. He'll beat Poison but Dora's just a girl, a soft-skinned innocent girl. I release him and sitting back on my heels I look up, my frightened, tear-streaked face beseeching him, throwing myself on his mercy.

I've been biting my bottom lip and see his eyes focus there. I realize I must look so submissive and vulnerable. I wish I had the feminine wiles to use that to ensnare and captivate him but I don't know how to even begin. I'm just a pathetic and inexperienced girl.

Still staring at my mouth he orders me to take my clothes off and lie on the bed. When I gasp he speaks harshly saying: "I'm not going to beat you, Poison, but you are going to be punished. I am really fucking angry so it's gonna hurt and you're gonna suffer."

I tremble at the thought of being raped yet discover traitorous feelings and thoughts have me imagining... seriously Dora? I'm aroused? I excuse myself because rape is a common fantasy, my body is only responding to the whole dominant male thing, but I don't *really* want it to happen.

I'll choose being raped by him over a vicious belting, though. Except... I guess if I choose it then it's no longer rape? no, that doesn't seem right... maybe it's coercion? Strong-arming? Extortion?

I mean, I hate Viper and this gang and the stuff they do, but I can't deny that he's a good-looking man with a hot body. As far as rapists go I could do worse. Omigod why am I even thinking like this? It must be some sort of defense mechanism. He won't bother pleasuring me but it won't last too long. And I already felt the painful pinch when Walter broke through my hymen... and Viper is way better looking than Walter.

Sex with Viper is better than being beaten by Viper. Somewhat relieved at the thought that I'm at least *choosing my fate* I slip out of my clothes and lie on the bed as instructed.

"Just look at you with your eyes squeezed shut, your hands clenched into fists, and your knees pressed tight together. I didn't realize the thought of having sex with me is such an ordeal, Poison."

I don't want to make him angry but I have to be honest: "I know technically I'm no longer a virgin but it doesn't feel like... um, I don't really think I've had sex–"

He interrupts to tell me: "Oh you definitely haven't had sex."

"Yeah, so I'm a little anxious and well, Banger said you have to make it hurt and you agreed with that so..."

I stop talking when he kneels on the bed beside me. "Banger said to use my talent and I do have one skill I'm proud of. I'm very good at a body modification practice known as *scarification,* do you know what that is?"

I just shake my head, my mind stuttering over the words *body modification.*

"See this raised design on my left arm?"

"You drew that?"

"Yes, but I also I carved it. Into my skin. It's the club emblem—"

I scramble away from him insisting: "I don't want that!"

"Oh sweetheart," he chuckles. "You can't have it. This insignia has to be *earned.*" He's smiling and shaking his head like I've said something funny.

"Here, feel it."

I eye him with deep apprehension, no it's way more than that, it's real fear. Even though I know it's risky to argue with him I find myself insisting: "I don't want to touch it."

He pulls me closer and taking hold of my fingers presses them down over the design. It kind of feels like goosebumps but with much bigger, smooth bumps that are very hard. Like beading, but right on his skin. Or maybe in it? I can't help squealing an *ewww* sound as I tell him *it feels huge and awful.*

"Well that's because I added an irritant to grow the scars thicker, more prominent, but—" I can only imagine my look of horror when he breaks off his sentence to study my face.

"Okay, then. That answers whether or not this will be a punishment for you. I wasn't sure. I've done the emblem, and other designs, on most of my brothers. It's something different from just tattoos. A few of the girls wanted it too, but they can only get the club's initials. I do a fancy monogram of *S T M C.* Fiona was the first to ask for it," he says.

"Well scar her again instead of me. I don't want this, I don't want it at all. I don't even have a tattoo, I never wanted one." I stop abruptly recalling a memory I have of my mother and I talking about tattoos, but I was just a young girl then.

"Hey, I know what I'm doing so there's nothing to worry about. I use sterilized single-use scalpels so the cutting is always clean. It's gonna hurt, though. You see everyone's got these things called nociceptors on their nerve endings. There are a few different kinds and when you're cut it's the ones called *mechanical nociceptors* that react to the damage."

I probably look like an idiot with my mouth hanging open in surprise listening to Viper explaining with all these long words and... and such matter-of-fact confidence. It's so unexpected. I tune in again at the word *punishment.*

"In your case, because this is a punishment, I won't be numbing your skin first."

I grab hold of his arm frantic to stop him from doing this. "Viper, please do something else: have sex with me, beat me with your belt, anything else but please don't cut me with a *fancy monogram.*"

Immediately he stops being the almost-friendly man educating me in this so-called art form and reverts to being a cold, dead-eyed gang member.

"No, I've decided," he states in his *don't argue with me* voice. I whimper and plead but he's deaf to me. He just looks at my naked body from head to toe before ordering me to turn over.

I move and the bed shifts as he stands up. I hear the clink of his belt buckle and the *whoosh* sound when he pulls his belt through the loops of his jeans. It's hard to keep my face turned away, is he going to beat my ass anyhow? Will he hit me with the buckle end? Now I'm even more scared and I feel my skin tighten while my whole body shakes. Viper's silence is frightening as he studies my nude back view.

Suddenly he's on top of me. Straddling my waist he grabs my hands and yanks my arms over my head. Where his body touches mine his skin burns it's so hot or else I'm so cold.

He wraps his belt round and round my wrists until they're secured and then he fastens the buckle over the rail of his headboard before climbing off. My helpless vulnerability deepens my fear and, ridiculously, my libido sparks. I mean, I shouldn't be turned on at being laid out like an offering for him.

Extreme fear must signal the body in the same way as arousal.

When he speaks again his voice is a robotic monotone as if he's reciting instead of conversing. "The design on my arm is colored because I had Cas, the brother who does our tattoos, add ink to the wound. Your scars should end up being just a lighter shade of your own skin color. I looked, but I don't see any on your body?"

"No, I've never cut or burned myself or had stitches or anything like that."

"Good. A nice fresh canvas to work on."

Omigod, when he puts it that way... "Viper please don't do this, don't mark me or mess me up, please!" I beg. I'm so helpless with my hands secured to the headboard. I can't do a thing to stop him from doing whatever he pleases with me.

He doesn't listen... he doesn't even pause. I brace myself for the pain.

Viper

This started off being a punishment for me just as much as Dora. Banger is so pissed that I brought this trouble to our club. But now that I've got the idea of designing on her skin I'm totally into it.

I wear my scars proudly but Dora won't. Well, maybe she will in time. She'll just have to get used to it because scarification is permanent. Banger demanded that I punish Dora in a significant way so this works out.

Her skin is gorgeous. Incredibly soft, fresh and creamy. I pinch a fingerful and it's beautifully elastic and moist. And hairless. Much easier than working on a man.

"I don't want you to do anything like that to my arm!" she insists angrily.

I feel my mouth rise in a smirk even though she can't see it. "Don't worry about that. I plan to mark you in a place that isn't normally seen."

She tries lifting her head but the position I put her in doesn't give her enough movement to see what I'm doing. At the moment I'm just staring at her perfect heart-shaped ass. My delay will help build her apprehension.

My kit is stored in the bathroom. I fetch it and lay everything out on the bed, stretching the time until she's shivering with dread and anticipation. I'm getting a little turned on by my cruel thoughts but overall have to admit I'm relieved Banger didn't order her death.

When Dora starts shifting I spread her legs wide enough that I can kneel down on them to hold her in place. I need her to stay still so I can work comfortably. I've chosen the middle of her right buttock to make my artistic statement.

After cleaning the area with antiseptic wipes I apply a coating of numbing cream. I told Dora I wouldn't but when it comes to my art I am a professional. She will still suffer with each slice of the blade because the cream doesn't take effect right away but it will help ease her pain afterwards.

Unwrapping a new scalpel I begin. One hand to wield the sharp blade and the other to blot the blood.

Dora gives a high-pitched scream at the first cut.

"Jesus, Poison! I know it doesn't hurt that much."

"Yes it does, it really hurts! Please, Viper—"

"Sure, it stings like a paper-cut. Those shallow cuts are a bugger so feel free to screech as loud as you like and make Banger happy."

With my mind entirely focused on the task at hand I cut with steady, sure strokes. I'm aiming for perfection and am gentle with her tender flesh. That doesn't stop her from hollering her head off.

I realize everybody's got a different tolerance for pain. I guess the threshold changes based on how sensitive your skin is, and what you've gone through. I suffered a lot in the Group Home in lived in as a little kid but I quickly learned how to handle what I felt, and to only let them see as much as I wanted to show.

Dora's lived a very different kind of life and thinking of her pampered existence hardens my resolve. I grip her flesh in a tight hold as I form the letters. Her voice grows hoarse from screaming until it dwindles down to squeaky little cries.

"Let's see, *I* space *A M* space *A* space, that's four letters and *L I A R* is another four so yeah, a perfect balance."

I pause, waiting for her to put the sentence together, and her anguished wail is everything I could hope for. Everything that Banger needs to hear, too.

I finish soon after. Admiring the identically sized, evenly spaced letters I find myself wishing I'd written *VIPER*. A tightness forms in my chest at the thought. Shaking it off I put aside the blade for disposal.

Cleaning away the blood I smear on a thick paste of antibiotic cream. Once that's done I smooth medical grade cling film over the area and bandage it all in place.

"Don't touch any of this. I'll be cleaning and changing the dressing twice a day for a couple of days. I have to check how it's healing. No alcohol, aspirin, or illegal drugs. Avoid caffeine and you can't smoke"

Through her tears she mumbles: "I don't smoke."

"Good, don't start, it's bad for your health." For some reason those words set off a storm of sobbing. Part of me wants to cuddle and kiss her better while another part wants to smother her with the pillow so I don't have to hear another sound. I have to get out of the room.

After putting away my kit and cleaning myself up I head down the hall to the bar. The door to our meeting room is open and I spot Banger sitting with a glass of bourbon, one foot propped up on a chair, thinking his thoughts while listening to Dora scream.

Our eyes meet in a moment's wordless communication and then he gives me a tight nod. Acknowledgment that I completed the job. I scrub my hands over my face and he tells me to grab a drink and join him.

For the first time in my life I want to avoid Banger's company, and we've been friends since we were little kids, but of course I do exactly what my Prez says.

The big room falls silent when I go up to the bar and order a whiskey. Jimmy serves me a double without even needing to ask and I tip my glass in appreciation. As I head back to Banger a woman's voice mutters *the little bitch deserved it* and I stop, turning slowly, until I make eye contact with Fiona because that's who has spoken. I don't say a word, I just glare at her showing all my contempt. I despise that cunt.

Returning to the meeting room I sit down in my usual seat. Looking up at the ceiling, not at me, Banger asks: "Did I ever tell you what happened that time King made me punish Fee?"

"Well I was here for it, out there actually. You were in here and I was in the big room so I heard a lot of what went on but you and your Dad never talked about it."

He nods his head a few times then straightens in his chair, plants both feet on the floor and folding his hands on the table in front of him relates the details of the story.

"You know how it all came about because Fiona planned on using you to get what she wanted. I know you had real feelings for her at the time and coming to me and Dad with news of her plans was hard, really hard, for you but it proved your friendship to me and your loyalty to this club. Not that any of us doubted either. Never.

Ever since she was old enough to understand Fee was jealous of my favored position. I get it, it's not fair that because of misogyny in the

87

MC doors that open for me are closed to her. But that's the way it is and if she felt she couldn't accept that then she should have made a life of her own away from the club.

Instead she chose to undermine me."

My mind goes back to that time when I thought the sun shone out of Fiona Flaherty's ass. She was beautiful and sexy, passionate and smart, and at almost twenty-two an amazing catch for a teenager who'd just turned eighteen. The three of us had mostly grown up together since Des, known as King, and his wife Melva Flaherty, the Prez and his Old Lady, basically adopted me. Banger and I – he was just Pat, short for Padraig back then – spent every waking minute together while Fiona barely acknowledged our existence. She had her own interests and friends and dated guys who were several years old than us.

So it was a real surprise when Fee started showing an interest in me. Banger was already working full-time for the club and he told me flat out he didn't know how he felt about me getting together with his sister. *It's kinda weird*, he'd said, *especially since I like you way more than I like her.* We'd both laughed at that but I got what he meant because Fiona was desirable but not nice or likable.

As a horny kid I only cared about getting laid and keeping my closest friendship intact. Things were going well for me but I learned that Fiona wanted much more. She wanted to take over the leadership of the club and if she couldn't because she was a woman then she'd settle for being *the power behind the throne,* as she put it. In other words, use me to get the presidency and then use me as a front while she actually ran things.

All of these wants and wishes were confessed when we fucked and I was high with lust. Wiggling her pretty ass while I pounded her doggy-style she promised we'd have this connection every minute of every day *if only*...

Mesmerized by her bouncing tits as she rode my cock I'd eagerly agree to giving her all the support she needed. It took awhile but it finally filtered through my horny brain that giving her what she wanted meant taking away my best friend's birthright. Titles are earned in our club but Banger had been raised as the future Club Prez so long as he proved himself worthy as we all knew he would. I always hoped I'd be good enough to achieve VP status so I could work alongside him.

Fiona was whispering criticisms of Banger and praising me at every opportunity.

All of the brothers were willing to give a few minutes of their time to the President's gorgeous daughter when she wanted to chat. Most of them probably just stared at her mouth and fantasized over what they could never have rather than actually listening. But when I brought my concerns to King, Banger and Fiona's father, he spoke to some of his closest men and they backed me up.

I felt really shitty for ratting out my girlfriend but that was between her and me with nobody else being affected. Her betrayal was different. It hurt me, her family, and every single brother in our club.

King called for church and hard as it was for him he revealed what one of his children was doing to the other, to the detriment of the brotherhood we all share. The consensus was that Fiona needed to be punished and Banger had to be the one to do it.

"I know I'm bending the rules when I say the discipline will be carried out in private but she's my daughter and... well, that's the way it's going to be."

I wasn't the only one who was thankful to be spared witnessing that ordeal although there was some muttering about *bending the rules*. Up until then in my time as a club member no one had required a public punishment. I understood the rationale about the delivery of justice needing to be seen but... I think if Banger had fucked up him being the president's son wouldn't spare him but Fiona, since she was female, wasn't a member of the club so it was different in her case.

Taking up his story again Banger explains: "King forced Fiona to bend over this table and told me to spank her with my belt. After five minutes or so he declared I was being too soft and... he was right. I was holding back because shit, it was Fee.

Anyhow, he pulls her pants down, panties too, and orders me to beat her bare ass until it's properly marked and her willfulness is broken, saying he'll decide when the job is done. Well, I was uncomfortable seeing my sister naked like that but her skin is barely pink which proved his point. I glance between him and Mom and realize he isn't going to relent and she's on his side.

It's a kindness to get it over as quickly as possible, he tells me. So I listen to him and start lashing her hard, talking the whole time. I can probably repeat the words exactly as I said them ten years ago because the events of that day are burned into my brain. I said:

I hate everything about this, Fiona. I hate hurting you and even more I hate the necessity. You went behind my back badmouthing me, being disloyal, and shaming the family. I'm determined to thrash you so thoroughly this lesson will never need repeating but if it does I'll make it happen in front of all the brothers and not one will come to your aid."

As I'm saying this I'm laying down stroke after stroke and her ass is getting really red. I'm hitting hard and fast because when I slow down King just gestures for me to speed up. He shows no emotion at all watching his daughter suffer through her flesh being crisscrossed with welts, some already oozing tiny drops of blood. All I can think is *tell me to fucking stop, please!*

Fiona's really hurting and she's struggling, howling, beating her fists on this table and drumming her feet on the floor. Once she tried to reach back to protect her ass and Dad just roared "FIONA MARIE!" and she pulled back immediately.

But what I was mostly conscious of was the sound of leather painfully striking flesh. Over and over, smack-smack-smack. That's a terrible noise.

Anyhow, I wind up the beating by lashing down a hard smack along with each of three rules:

One: Don't disrespect the club with sass, gossip or back-stabbing.

Two: Accept your place by performing your assigned duties competently and without complaint.

Three: Give 100 percent of your loyalty and obedience to the club.

I stop and tell her *that's it, three simple easy-to-follow rules. I don't just expect this from you, Fiona, I demand it.*

By now Fiona's ass and thighs are bruised and striped a deep red and she's crying piteously. King steps up and demands she swear allegiance to me, our future Club President.

Stuttering out the words between sobs Fiona makes her promise. She keeps her head bowed, not looking at any of us. King pulls her pants back up and she hisses when the fabric makes contact with her tender skin. He tells Mom to tend to her and turning to me says *You gave her a good lesson, son.*

I told him I hope it sinks in because I didn't enjoy hurting Fee and I really didn't like seeing her naked, and you know what he said to me? He said *Banger, if I thought you'd enjoy it I wouldn't have let you do it.*

He was talking as our father then, not as the club prez."

We're both silent for a minute reliving our memories. I remember being in the big room and along with everybody else heard exactly what was happening in the meeting room. Banger's voice – although not his words – punctuated by the thudding of leather smacking skin and the wailing cries of a girl in agony.

Afterwards most of the guys left and those of us who remained drifted to the bar to order shots and a beer. No one said anything then but a few days later somebody commented that *Fiona went into that room mouthy and defiant but came out subdued and submissive.*

I've hated her ever since for what she was trying to do to Banger and for what she did do to me. She broke my trust and I hardened the tiny bit of heart that my mother had spared me. Fucking females. It's better this way... I'm better like this.

Banger gives half a laugh and confesses: "I've never talked about that day with anyone. It all just felt like one big embarrassment to each of us. But now that you've gone through punishing a sweet but not innocent girl on your Prez's order well, let's just say I get what you're feeling right now.

Fiona turned into a sullen thwarted woman. Let's hope your Dora doesn't turn into a dead one."

"She's not *my Dora,*" I exclaim, but he just grins at me and shakes his head.

"Did you carve her some letters?" he asks and I nod. "What did you tell her you put?"

Despite my miserable mood I can't help but smirk at his question. He knows me so well. "I told her I carved *I AM A LIAR.*"

Banger barks out a laugh exclaiming: "She is! and so are you! Fucking A, I told you she's your girl."

I dismiss that comment with a shrug.

Banger's got female troubles of his own but since we've both had enough of talking we slowly finish off the bottle, drinking in companionable silence.

I copy the number Dora called onto my phone then I wipe Bebe's phone and pull the SIM card for good measure. Replacing it I check that everything's cleared and the phone is reset to factory standard.

When I give it back I'll explain to Bebe that Poison sent out a text and I couldn't have anyone tracing it back to us. She'll probably believe that and if she doesn't well, she sure as shit isn't going to complain. Still, she did good and I'll see if I can't get Hardware to set her phone so that no pass-code is required, just like she wants.

Banger falls asleep in his chair. I manage to stagger over to a couch before passing out.

Dora

My stupid vagina is slick even though I stopped being aroused as soon as Viper got started. I rub the stickiness away, ashamed and embarrassed at myself. And I still can't stop crying. It makes me feel like I'm nothing but a little baby bawling my eyes out. So pathetic.

I have been terrified of Viper from the moment I first saw him standing over Steve's lifeless body. Then, when he shoved me down on the floorboards of his car, cramped and crowded, I added revulsion to the fear. But none of that emotion comes even close to the deep black hatred I feel for him now. I hate him the way a good Catholic girl hates the Devil because that's who he is.

He does everything he can to shame me. There was no reason to make me strip completely naked just so he could cut nasty words into my bum.

I've got to get out of here but how? I can't believe Angie cut me loose all on the say-so of that loser jerk Tonino. How can she do this to me? she's got all of the money I saved up and it's a lot. Maybe it's too much and it's too tempting.

What a family I come from! I can't trust them, I certainly can't trust the cops, and this motorcycle gang, club, whatever, is just as dangerous if not more so. I've just exchanged one prison for another but what choice did I have?

And now I'm practically branded, for life, with those stupid words on my butt. I can never ever let anyone see what he's done. My hatred for Viper stems from the very depths of my soul.

My worries exhaust me. I'm not used to sleeping on my stomach but I can't find a comfortable position to lie in. There's nothing I can do except wrap my arms around my poor hurting body and rock myself to a tearful sleep.

Banished

Viper

I wake up grumpy from a pounding headache and stiff from the too-hard, too-short sofa. Banger's gone. He must have woken up feeling even worse than me.

"Viper, hey hold up!" Fiona calls loudly, "I need to talk to you."

I've just left the meeting room but I stop in the hallway and swinging round step close up in her personal space. It's with a grim kind of satisfaction that I see her eyes widen in fear and her throat swallow convulsively. Fiona steps back but I step forward, crowding and intimidating her.

"You don't tell me what to do, Fiona."

"No, I mean yes, I won't! I just want to talk to you about Banger I'm worried about the Club he–"

"Are you really doing this again? It's not your place to be worried about the club, didn't you learn anything?"

"No! It's nothing like that, like before, no this is personal. It's well... you're his best friend and I'd like you to talk to him about what's going on with Kim."

I say nothing and just stare at her. I'm already in a shitty mood and don't feel like listening to Fiona's bullshit. I might be *Viper* but this bitch is venom.

"They've split up and she's moved into the Lightning clubhouse."

"Her cousin is the Prez there, right?"

"Yeah, that's why she's gone to live there."

This is really crap news. I mean I knew Banger had some family shit happening but him and Kim breaking up? Fuck me. This is Fiona though so I'm skeptical.

"How do you know about this? You and Kim aren't friends and she wouldn't tell you shit."

"It was Crusher who told me."

I bark out a surprised laugh. Crusher is the Lightning's main enforcer and he's a mean psycho prick. Rumor has it he's into kinky sex shit, too. "You and Crusher are back on again?"

A shudder goes through her whole body as she emphatically states: "God no! I ran into him in the mall parking lot and he told me. You know, I think he might be stalking me."

It makes me laugh to hear Fiona complain about someone else's nasty behavior.

"It's not funny, Viper. I'm serious. He's a genuine Dominant which means a possessive, controlling totally alpha-male fucking freak. I feel threatened by him... frightened. Don't you care about me at all?"

"Fuck no, Fiona, not the least little bit."

She's startled and a momentary hurt shows before she hardens her gaze and tells me I should find out what's going on. "You're supposed to be Banger's best friend so help him fix or end his marriage because people are talking."

I shrug at that comment because people can just fuck off as far as I'm concerned but Banger, as Prez, will care. So I nod at Fiona and walk away without another word. I hear her start to say something else but I just keep going.

Coming into my room I take one look at Dora's tear-stained face and decide I can't stand seeing that for one minute more. Tossing a plastic bag on the bed I tell her to pack up her stuff because she's leaving.

"Where? Where am I going?"

"You'll find out soon enough, just grab your things because we're leaving now."

I watch her scramble into the bathroom to get dressed. She comes out carrying a comb and toothbrush, her period supplies, and the t-shirt that's actually mine that she's been wearing to bed as a sleep-shirt. For some reason I like that... so I don't mind if she wants to keep it.

"Are you trading me? Selling me?" Now she freezes with a terrified look on her face.

"I liked you better as a dummy, Poison. I'm moving you someplace safer than here, okay? Now c'mon, we're outta here."

I open the door and she hustles through it ahead of me, shrinking away from any accidental touch. Neither one of us looks at, or speaks to, anybody on our way out.

I'm not sure if she could bear to sit on a bike right now so we're taking my truck. I can pick up some supplies for the club on the way back.

I've got it started but have to get out to help her climb up onto the passenger seat because she's too little to make it by herself. When I lift her she struggles then stiffens. I'm tempted to drop her back down on the pavement. There's heavy metal blaring, synced from my phone, so I don't have to talk or listen to Dora on the drive.

First, though, I pause the music in order to say: "Once you've been punished we forget the offense and the consequences. Clean slate and all that. Behave yourself and I'll never have to punish you again, got it?" I don't wait for an answer, I just crank the music back up again.

From the clubhouse to the tattoo shop is only about ten minutes and that's if we hit every light so it doesn't take long. I wish I could just drop her at the door but I've got to explain things to Casso first.

Dora enters the shop her eyes wide as she takes everything in. The samples and photos on the wall are colorful and eye-catching. The shop is small with just a love-seat and desk in reception then Casso's room and further back a bathroom, kitchenette, and storage area. Upstairs is an equally small apartment and that's where he lives.

"I don't want a tattoo, too!" she insists, her face frowning over the sound of that phrase. I bite back a chuckle preferring to ignore her.

When I reach for Dora's arm she shakes me off so I just shrug and lead the way. Casso is doing something on his laptop but he closes it to give us his attention. His eyes grow wide at the sight of Dora and I smile to myself thinking *this will be a piece of cake.*

"Casso this is Dora aka *Poison*. Dora this is Picasso aka *Casso* the club's Ink Slinger which means Tattoo Artist." I'm in a good mood now that I'm offloading her.

"Dora," Casso says, dragging out her name. "*Ciao bella.*"

"Casso I, we, need your help. Dora's been at the club—"

He interrupts with a look of shocked surprise saying: "At the clubhouse? This girl?"

"Uh, yeah and she can't stay there, those cunts will kill her, and our Prez's bitch sister will just egg them on. They're all so jealous, worried that no one will want them compared to her since she's so young and fresh."

"She is, yes. I can see why they're concerned," he says giving her a big smile. I never thought of Casso as a smoothie but the way he's acting makes me wonder. "How can I help you two?"

"I'm hoping you can hang on to Dora for a couple of days until I figure something out."

His whole body stills and the expression on his face is serious when he asks: "Who is she exactly?"

"No fucking idea, she's doesn't talk." I only decided at that moment to keep Poison's secret. At least for awhile. I'll let Banger know what I've done, he's Prez and if he wants it handled differently then that's what we'll do but for now... with the way Casso is acting? Keeping her secret feels right.

"Really? sounds perfect," he gives her a wink to show he's joking. He's eyeing her so intently, his gaze running up and down her body, and it seems to make Dora shy.

"Ha, ha yeah. A pretty woman who keeps her mouth shut – what a headline."

Casso looks at her doubtfully asking: "Is she a woman? She looks pretty young to me."

"She does, yeah. Anyhow I can move her on–"

"Sell her, you mean?" Casso's voice is flat but his eyes have narrowed.

Noticing his reaction I press the advantage continuing: "As I said, if you can hold her for a couple of days I'll owe you—"

"You already owe me for that," Casso nods at the half-sleeve he's inked on my right arm. "Tell you what, let me keep her. I'll take her as payment and I'll throw in the rest of the job, too."

Saying nothing I give him a slow smile.

"Aw, fuck," Casso swears, "You wanted to give her to me all along. And now you've got a free tat outta me, too."

I clap an arm around his shoulders saying: "I know you like them young." Turning to Dora who has been following our conversation silently I give a casual "Bye, Poison. Behave yourself and be a good girl for Casso."

She flips me the bird but discreetly so Casso doesn't see. That makes me laugh and I tell him I'll stop by again to make sure everything's okay.

Leaving the two of them to figure it out I leave for the job I've got to do thinking *No matter what he thinks I'm only loaning her to him, not trading her for a tattoo or giving her away, it's just to get her out of my hair for a bit.*

Casso

Viper's remark about me *liking them young* has stuck in my mind. It sounds kinda pervy and that's just not true, that's not how I am.

Besides, it's not a girl's age or physical development that matters to me, it's her personality. I like women who are gentle and docile, innocent and obedient, calming and restful. Like a *Quattrocento* oil painting of the Madonna come to life.

Dora does look very young. Her complexion is dewy and fresh, her limbs are rounded with soft edges, her breasts sit high on her chest, her posture and gestures are child-like. I think she's very appealing and being mute doesn't detract from her beauty at all.

Most of the girls, women, I meet are so loud and flashy. They attract everyone's attention with high-pitched giggles from their wide laughing mouths. They wear low-cut tops to flaunt their breasts and skirts that are too short and too tight. They preen in front of the men who ogle them offensively and exchange sassy, snappy words. My artist's eye always paints a picture in my mind and the images I'm imagining are so vivid it's like I can hear them.

I don't even try to keep up with their dialog, I don't want a woman like that. They smell good and it turns me on to catch glimpses when they flash their lacy lingerie, but those women are predators.

Dora is a complete contrast. She is beautiful, sweet, and unspoiled which is surprising when you consider...

Dora

I'm so glad Viper has gone, being in the same room as him makes me sick. I know I'll be much happier – and safer – here than at the clubhouse.

Casso seems nice, even if he is a bit too much with the compliments, but he's not as scary as the other guys in the club. For one thing he has a normal height and build. Lean, but muscular with it and, naturally, covered in tattoos. I bet there are stories to go with each of them. He's got an accent and I'm guessing he's also from the north of Italy with his light brown hair and blue eyes. He's a good-looking man. Great smile, with perfect teeth like most Italians since there's little sugar in our diet.

"My real name is Guglielmo Modicini," he tells me and pauses as if expecting recognition. At times like these I resent living such a sheltered life because I don't know anything current, and I don't know who anyone is. I hope my expression is friendly but it's hard. I've been so miserable and unhappy since Viper's assault last night. I hurt a lot in my body and my mind.

Casso tells me I look dead-beat and need to rest. I watch while he packs up his desk, locks it, then grabs his laptop. Standing, he gestures for me to follow him into the hallway. I watch him lock the front door then we leave the shop to walk the few feet to the side of the building where we climb the staircase to his apartment. My new temporary home is a bachelor pad. There's only one kitchen chair, one living-room chair, and one bed. It's pushed against the wall and I'm sure Casso will make me sleep on that side, hemmed in.

I immediately recognize the kind of man Casso is, I've been around guys like him all my life. Italian men who are connected. For Casso it's his motorcycle gang, not the mafia, but it's the group, the club, the family, that has his loyalty. A calm outward exterior hides a heart of ice.

Cruel, cold, and calculating but charming so long as they're getting their own way. Probably not a psychopath but the possibility remains. Like so many of these loner types he's got an artistic streak. His tattoo work shows real skill and he has a good eye for balancing color and line weight.

Still, many of this type are craftsmen. They can create but only within the parameters of their vision, no room for deviation. They live by rigid rules that set things out in black and white, guiding their behavior.

My cousins and I have spent many hours discussing and dissecting the actions of mafioso men.

I have to use his chauvinism to my advantage to gain protection for me as *his property*. I have to use that otherwise he'll view me as worthless and won't take care of me. If he was a suitor I'd already be panicking about him suffocating me with his expectations of a woman's place. Me as his possession is a concept he can get behind, and his misogyny will keep him from seeing me as anything more.

But how can I make a man who deep down is incapable of liking women like me? Well... he doesn't have to like me he just has to feel jealous and controlling. I learned plenty about sex listening to my cousins gossiping but is that kind of knowledge enough to fake it in real life? Actually I don't have to be good at sex, shy innocence will be way more appealing to a man like him. Of course once they use you you've lost your value. That mind-set is so unfair.

In order to make him feel strong and dominant and protective I just have to be helpless, obedient, and submissive. I can do this, no I *have* to do this. Playing Casso right will give me my only chance to escape.

"If I'm the babysitter then you're the baby. Time for bed, baby."

He doesn't look at me after making that pronouncement so I scoot into his armchair and curl up. It's not a battered old piece like the rest of his furniture but a form-fitting massage chair. Very expensive, but I guess he needs it. Spending his days bent over while plying his needles with precise, controlled movements must make his back and shoulders ache.

"Get in the bed," he orders but I shake my head. This oversized chair is comfy enough to easily sleep in.

Casso doesn't repeat himself, he just gives me an expressionless stare. I hold his gaze for a moment before closing my eyes and burrowing deeper into the chair. Without making a sound he steps close, scoops me up and tosses me onto the bed.

Pointing at my clothes he says *strip* and proceeds to undress himself down to his boxers. Until a couple of days ago I'd never seen a man in this state of undress and now I've seen two.

The well-defined muscles of his lean physique are breathtaking but it's the colorful ink that makes his body a work of art. I'm entranced as my eyes follow a path made up of rivers and vines and snakes.

I want to study him further but he's turned away to empty my shopping bag onto the chair. Now Viper's t-shirt sails across the room landing in my lap. I quickly pull it over my head but then Casso tells me to remove everything else. When I hesitate he makes a move towards me so I hustle to pull off my lingerie while keeping the t-shirt on.

I watch Casso pick up all of my discarded clothes as well as his own then put everything into a compact-size washing machine. He's included his boxers so he's standing with his back to me, naked, and

I'm staring at his tight bum. The tattoos on his back extend well below his waistline. Casso goes to the dresser to get a clean pair of underwear and puts them on before turning around again.

I realize this routine is all part of his daily regimen in which I've become an addition but not a distraction. Being ignored and safe should be exactly what I want but, perversely, I'm annoyed. Why is he running hot-and-cold going from *gallantly flirtatious* to being well... *totally uninterested?* I really do wish I had more experience with men.

I can't help glancing at his crotch as he stalks across the room towards me. He's got a large package. Looking up I realize he's caught me eyeballing him. I shrink back as our eyes meet in a wordless stare before I hear a click and the lights go out. I've scrambled to the edge of the bed, my back pressed into the wall, and I'm holding my breath so I can listen to his movements. There's no footboard to the bed so I plan to scoot down and escape that way if necessary.

Casso climbs in but settles himself turned away from me. He pulls the blanket over his shoulders and tells me to *sleep well, Bella.*

I slept surprisingly well and now wake up to an empty bed. I needed a deep sleep in a dreamless state to recover from yesterday's ordeal of Auntie's shocking betrayal, Banger's threats of violence, and Viper's act of cruelty.

Casso hears me stir and turns from the table where he's opened the kit Viper packed. Curious, I look at the items laid out and just as I understand their purpose Casso says:

"Go pee then come back and I'll change the dressing like Viper instructed."

My cheeks flame red with embarrassment at what he plans to do and shame over the words he will read. I start shaking my head, ready to explain that's not necessary but he lifts me off the bed and carts me to the bathroom repeating his earlier command.

Again my body fails to aid my mind's defiance as my bladder notices how damn close the toilet is. After taking care of business I try to draw out the hand-washing process but I hear the impatience in Casso's voice calling me.

Reluctantly I emerge with my head low and my feet dragging. He's quick to assure me that he'll treat me gently while cleaning up the wound as painlessly as he can. He goes on to explain that he knows everything about tattoo aftercare and this can't be too different.

I wasn't even thinking about the pain of a sticking bandage or the sting of antiseptic. All I can think of are those words. What will Casso think? How can I explain them?

I'm still struggling with my thoughts while he nudges me into position on the bed. He pulls up my t-shirt just enough to expose my bottom and pressing my thighs together I wish I was still wearing my thong.

Casso removes the bandage and plastic wrap without me feeling the slightest twinge. His touch is light and his fingers work delicately as he carefully inspects the cuts – even leaning in close to sniff at the wound – before pronouncing everything *perfecto*.

The cleansing wipe does sting but the cream he smooths on immediately soothes. I'm cringing inside, waiting for his comments, but he doesn't say a word about the phrase Viper carved. Surely he read it? Yes, of course he did. He's just being discreet.

Casso's courtesy brings tears to my eyes as a warm wave of gratitude fills me. I'm so glad to be here with him instead of anywhere near Viper.

Casso

I can't believe my great good luck that Viper has brought Dora to me. Last night I slept better than I have in... I don't know how long. A deep restorative sleep. So relaxing!

Dora was still sleeping when I woke so I just enjoyed lying there holding her. When I brushed her hair off her face she made cute little snuffling noises. Her long eyelashes sweep down her smooth cheek. Her skin is dewy and so soft. I feel so tender towards her, I never expected anything like this.

Viper is right when he says she's not safe at the clubhouse because that's no place for a girl like Dora. I guess if I hadn't missed the church meeting Banger called I'd have found out they were holding her there. The women are bad but the men are far worse. Sure, they're my brothers but I'm not blind to their faults or their rough behavior.

It's much better that Dora is here with me where I can keep her from the danger those men present. Her life is in peril and while she's probably aware of that she can't possibly know the extent. That means she needs to stay here by my side, under my watchful eye, and not try to leave or go out on her own. She has no idea what's in store for her.

It's going to be different – but nice – to have company while I'm in the shop. Especially such a pretty girl as Dora. I'm a member of the MC but I don't spend much time at the clubhouse. I've always been a bit of a loner, happy with my own company. But I've found real camaraderie with the club.

When they started calling me Casso as a nickname I thought it was an insult. I had to remind myself that since Banger doesn't speak

Italian he definitely doesn't know how to swear in my language. That's when I found out Casso is short for Picasso, Pablo Picasso.

I owe my life to Banger because if I hadn't met him, if he hadn't brought me into the club, who knows where I'd have ended up? He can call me anything he likes.

Riding with my brothers is great, I really enjoy it even if they do talk shit about my bike. They're all stuck on their American-made Harley's but my *Ducati Streetfighter* is a beauty with her curvy styling. Riding through the elements and reveling in the feeling of freedom is exquisite as a solitary pleasure but being able to share that experience with friends – brothers – is an unbeatable connection.

I look forward to having Dora as my *backpack* but not yet... for now I want to keep her to myself. I don't think that will happen though, not after the way Viper was looking at her.

I get out of bed to get ready for the day and prepare Dora's new dressing.

She's shy about showing her body and I'm glad she's a modest girl. Dora doesn't have to worry about me, though. I've put tattoos on every inch of both male and female skin surfaces. Seeing her ass won't mean a thing to me. It wouldn't anyhow.

I remove the bandage and plastic and though she fidgets and fusses I know she isn't feeling any pain, or only the slightest bit of discomfort. Viper has done a good job.

The cuts are neatly incised, the edges are smooth, and the wound is clean with no sign of infection. The amount of puffy redness is less than I would have expected. I guess he's better at his craft then I thought he would be.

Tracing my finger over the letters I can't help but imagine him doing the very same thing on Dora's naked flesh. That's a stupid thought... of course he had to touch her to carve in her nickname. He's made it quite pretty and I wonder if he'll let me add some color before the healing really gets underway?

I expect I'll get a chance to ask soon because I'm sure he'll be hanging around a lot. I don't like that thought, it puts me into a black mood.

I fall into bouts of anger or despair so easily, partly due to loneliness - I miss my family so much - and partly the artistic temperament. When Dora asks me about getting something to eat I snap at her.

Dora

Okaaaay, not a morning person, I think after Casso bites my head off when I ask about breakfast.

I guess I have a *kicked puppy* look on my face because he *tut-tuts* before kissing my forehead and asking: "Is my little *principessa* starving? That's something I can fix. Get dressed and we'll go out."

I don't have much in the way of clothes so I put on the same hand-me-downs I wore yesterday. At least they're clean now. He frowns at my baggy jeans. I think they once belonged to a boy because the label sizes them as *Husky*. Casso must think I read lips because he makes sure I'm looking at his face as he tells me he'll turn the jeans into shorts when we go to his shop.

I watch while he makes the bed and when he's done he announces that bed-making will be my chore starting tomorrow. I've never had chores and wish I'd paid closer attention to how he did it but really, how hard can it be?

Unlocking the door he ushers me outside then follows, locking up again. I make note of the fact that I can't get in or out of his one-room apartment without a key.

Situational awareness is vital, that's something I learned in my training. Not self-defense, mafioso don't want a wife who can throw hands, but more like how to behave as a hostage or what to look for as a witness. It's important that I learn about everything connected to my captivity so I can use that knowledge when I get the opportunity to escape. I have to believe that chance will come and when it does I'll be ready.

My high-heels clatter as we make our way down the metal staircase. The best part of being short is I got used to constantly wearing heels long ago. True, my feet were killing me after a night of running and stumbling through the woods but they're fine now, although I'd love a pair of sneakers.

Arriving on the ground Casso points to a back-door into the shop explaining there is no indoor access to his apartment, only the outdoor staircase. We walk around to the front of the small brick building and I see the business name *Abruzzi Ink Art* painted in fancy lettering on the door.

I see the pride he has in his accomplishment as I study him looking over his property. It's not much compared to my background but I've never achieved anything in my life so I'm impressed and think he's justified to be proud.

The shop is located on a side street in the business district. Although it's not on the main road there's a lot of foot traffic as shoppers visit the coffee shop across the road and the small grocery store on the corner. There's also a dry-cleaners, hairdressing salon, and a shoe store. My eyes are drawn to this last business but Casso doesn't notice or else refuses to take the hint. I have no money so I'm at the mercy of his goodwill. I need a change from my pricey Italian shoes, good leather shouldn't be worn on consecutive days, so a pair of sneakers would be perfect.

I deeply inhale the delicious aromas we encounter on entering the coffee shop. A few tables are occupied by people on phones or using laptops but the vast majority of orders are *to go*. The woman behind the counter greets Casso with familiarity and I get an inquiring look. I paste a small smile on my face and bite down on my tongue to keep from speaking.

Casso orders two medium coffees and then turns his attention to the glass booth filled with pastries and bread rolls. He chooses a raspberry danish and gestures with a nod of his head that I can order as well. I feel like I could eat a dozen of these treats since they all look so good! and point to a *triple chocolate* scone. I don't think I've ever eaten a scone before but it's the most chocolatey item available, and that's my weakness.

I feel the curious stares of other staff members and notice that even some patrons, probably regulars, are interested in me. I feel vaguely threatened by the attention. I'm not used to being around strangers.

Paying for our take-out order Casso calls out a pleasant goodbye without enlightening anyone. He hands me the bag with the pastries while he carries the coffees and we head back to eat our breakfast in the tattoo parlor.

Abuse

Dora

Our days are spent in the tattoo parlor where Casso creates pure magic with his needle and inks. He sees several customers per day, every day, because his work is very popular.

Viper comes by quite often. In addition to checking the healing progress of the insult he carved on my butt, he's having the rest of his *sleeve* done. Dog's having a rose with bloody thorns done on the back of his hand.

Casso didn't do the face tattoo that curves all around the outside of Dog's eye. It looks like a Nordic rune but listening to them I learn the main design is called a *Triskelion* and it's Celtic. Makes sense, from their names and the way they look, this gang is Irish or Scottish or maybe a mix of both?

Casso asks questions and Dog confirms that it really did hurt a lot. "Good thing I'm a tough guy with a lot of *big dick energy,* right Dora?" I just stare at him blankly and Viper stifles a laugh.

Dog complains that Viper never lets him come alone because *he thinks I need babysittin' or something.* Casso just tilts his head and gives Viper a speculative smile.

As I told Viper before he marred my skin forever I have no tattoos. As an adolescent I wanted to get a mermaid on my ankle but my mother was firm: no tattoos until I have children and then I can have their names inked on my arms. Like she does. But only if my husband allows it, of course.

I can only imagine what Mama would think of my scarification.

Between clients Casso's time is spent cleaning except now that he has me with him I do most of the cleaning and sanitizing. I don't mind, I have to fill my hours somehow, but he did have to teach me what to do because at home I never had to pick up after myself never mind actually clean. So I clean which frees him up to sketch out new designs. He even makes scary skulls with snakes winding through the eyeholes look beautiful.

Casso is meticulous about keeping the tools of his trade placed just so. The first time I put something back in the wrong slot he didn't yell but he did hit me. Holding my chin he slapped me open palm across one cheek and backhand on the other. It hurt and brought tears to my eyes. Even more painful was how quiet and methodical he was while disciplining me like I was a child or a pet.

"Pay attention, Dora," he says. "Do not rush, do not be sloppy. If you aren't sure let me know. Understand?"

I struggle unsuccessfully to keep from crying but the tears overflow and run down my sore face. He doesn't react to me being upset – he doesn't show any emotion at all – and he certainly doesn't apologize for hitting me.

Obviously that's perfectly acceptable behavior to him. He simply waits for me to acknowledge that I've learned my lesson. My lip trembles so much I couldn't speak even if I wasn't pretending to be mute. I nod and that movement sends more tears flowing. Casso holds my gaze for a minute or so more then turns back to checking over his supplies, acting like nothing happened.

I wish I could say I did learn properly but it's obvious I don't meet Casso's high standards because he punishes me often with a slap, a smack, or a pinch. He's always calm when he points out where I've failed and the correction occurs immediately unless there's a customer in the shop. Then I'm left waiting and worrying about what's in store. He always hits me without showing any emotion. It still makes me yelp or cry, depending on how badly I hurt.

I got a crush on Casso pretty quickly, no doubt because of our close proximity and my inexperience, but all the loving feelings ended the first time he struck me.

Sure, he's a really good-looking guy with a face right out of a Botticelli painting, but as my *nonna*, god rest her soul, used to say handsome is as handsome does and now I understand what she meant.

We sleep in the same bed every night but he never crosses that invisible line onto my half. I thought maybe I could charm him into falling for me - at least enough to stop the hitting - but that was a huge mistake.

It was all my fault. I invaded his space by pushing my bum back and wiggling against him. He didn't speak or move for a full minute and then he got out of bed and turned the light back on. Returning to the bed he knelt beside me and pulled up my nightshirt – actually Viper's t-shirt – exposing my bare body. He didn't touch me, just stared first at my breasts and then at the tight curls I have on my mound. The hair down there is a shade or two darker than my head hair.

Still not speaking a word he pulled my thigh closer to him which opened up my private place. I didn't protest, I didn't move, I didn't stop him. No man has ever looked at me there, not even Walter whose penis touched me although he never saw anything.

I think I'm about to have sex.

Casso nudges my thighs even further apart and leans in for a closer look. Now I feel self-conscious, I mean even I haven't really looked at myself, and I certainly hope there's no smell.

Without saying a word Casso suddenly pounds his fist down very hard on top of my pubic bone. The pain is excruciating and for a moment I can't get air in my lungs. When I do I wail loudly and that spurs him into action, pummeling me in a flurry of fists, and yelling at me to *shut up!* He claims I'm a nasty whoring slut who deserves to be beaten for trying to corrupt him. He slaps, punches, and smacks me until my skin is red, bruised, and sore.

I want to explain that I didn't mean to tempt him but I'm crying too hard to speak even if I was willing to do so, and he's shouting too loud to hear. I had no idea he'd feel this way or that I disgusted him so much. That thought makes me sob even more.

I hurt inside and out. These men, they get so angry and they keep causing me such pain and I don't understand why? I know I won't find out, either.

Casso rarely speaks. I don't know if he's mimicking my silence or if it's just the way he is. Regardless, it means he doesn't discuss anything that happens between us.

My days with him aren't comfortable because I'm tense and worried about making a mistake or leading him on somehow. My stomach is always tied up in knots. I've lost weight even in just a few days because I'm barely able to eat.

I find I'm constantly looking to Casso for approval and I hate that, I hate being so needy but... we're very isolated here.

Viper stops by almost every day which sucks because I don't want to see him, I hate him. I can't get over the terrible way he's marked me and yet... I never felt the need to tiptoe around his moods. I mean, before that terrible night I sometimes felt relaxed in Viper's company.

At least when he visits he never stays long. He jokes, telling Casso *it looks like you're keeping Poison in line* without realizing that it isn't a joke at all.

Viper

Banger and I drop in at the tattoo shop presumably to see Casso but really to check up on Poison. She's still playing at not speaking.

When Banger makes eye contact she shrinks back in her chair. Dora doesn't know a thing about him but because of her upbringing maybe she's got a sixth sense or something that scents out danger. She's wise to cower. Banger's operating on such a short fuse these days that the slightest show of defiance and he's sure to make her regret it.

Casso reports Dora hasn't tried to escape or send out a text or email or anything. Every day she sits in the corner of the shop while Casso works through his shift. She helps clean up afterwards then goes upstairs with him for the night. He tells us that sometimes he has to go out for something or other but he always handcuffs her securely first.

The mental image of Dora naked and handcuffed to the bed is front and center in my mind. It's only when I hear Banger's amused *hmmph* that I return to the conversation to hear Casso tell us she's been good.

He goes on to explain that this area is deserted at night because none of the businesses stay open past five. Even if Dora yelled her loudest no one would ever hear her.

Looking Dora over I can see that she's lost some weight and all of her vitality. I don't think she's sulking, I think she's depressed. Well, I guess it makes sense. She's among strangers in a completely different environment from what she's used to. And maybe she's lonely? She's not speaking and Casso isn't exactly the life of the party.

The two of them are very much on their own here. My imagination has no trouble speculating over how they entertain themselves. He's a good-looking guy and they're both young, healthy adults. Something inside me clenches at the thought of her in his bed but I can't say anything... I'm the one who brought her here.

I feel my lips tighten in a grimace as I struggle to clear from my mind a new conjured image of a naked Dora enthusiastically riding Casso's cock. It doesn't help when I look up and see my best friend smirking at me like he knows my secret. Except I don't have a secret. If he wasn't also my Prez I'd have it out with him.

Dora avoids looking at me and I suspect she's still angry and resentful but I'm not about to apologize. Pain and shame is what punishment is all about. Still... I'm sorry to see she's lost her spirit. Maybe the bright lighting or the constant whir of the machine gets on her nerves?

I guess she's bored but I have no idea what her life was like before she came to us. Before I took her, that is. But it's not like I had a choice, not after what she saw. I guess I could have killed her too. Probably would have if she'd been a guy instead of a girl.

Casso

I don't mind Viper dropping by and of course Banger, our Prez, is always welcome. Every time I see or even just think of him I remember our first meeting with gratitude.

He's the one who brought me in to Satan's Tears, before he became president, and I'll always be grateful for the brotherhood I've found here.

When I came to America as a teenager I was all alone. I had relatives-in-law here but I'd never met them and didn't know how to get in touch, even if I'd wanted to.

The weather was mild enough at that time of year to sleep outdoors but I needed to earn money to eat. I always carry art supplies so I set up on a street corner creating impromptu portraits in oil pastels. Banger discovered me there just moments before the cops arrived and he helped me get away.

With the backing of the club I apprenticed with a tattoo artist and learned a career I love. I have no idea how my life would have turned out if I'd never met Banger.

The club takes a reasonable share of my earnings and provides me with plenty of business, too. But I don't like it when our Sergeant-At-Arms comes around.

Dog never comes on his own, Viper apparently warned him not to, but even with our VP present he's constantly ogling Dora and making lewd comments. It's bullshit. I don't like hearing that kind of talk and she shouldn't have to endure it.

While working on him once or twice I've been tempted to let my professionalism slip a little and cause him more pain than necessary but I'll probably never go through with it. Unless he really pushes his luck.

Seeing him strutting down the hall immediately puts me in a sour mood. He and Viper must turn heads wherever they go because of their height and contrasting coloring. Both men are well-built and really good-looking, too. I watch Dora closely but she shows no interest in either of them and doesn't respond to any of Dog's come-ons.

I'm satisfied until he crosses the line.

"Hey Dora, can you dance?" Viper rolls his eyes saying nothing but I feel an angry growl escape me. Dog just laughs then says: "I'm serious, I want to know. I'm in charge of the exotic dancers after all. I know you can't talk but that probably means you hear better and I bet you can really get that body swaying to a deep bass beat, hmm?"

Dora is just staring at him wide-eyed.

"Yeah I can tell... you got rhythm, am I right? So, how about you becoming one of our strippers? The customers will go crazy for such an innocent look."

I see Viper narrowing his eyes and expect that my face mirrors his grim expression but Dog is oblivious to our glares.

"We could build up this whole exciting persona of *Poison the Mystery Girl who was lured into danger by the glamour of black magic.*"

He's got a huge grin as he enthuses over his idea and Dora is actually giggling, although she does it silently. I can see that Viper is amazed too because Dora's normally very stiff and wary around Dog despite him being so handsome. But now she's smiling up at him and her eyes sparkle. I feel my fists clenching.

126

"Yeah Devil worship, it's perfect, she summoned a demon who stole her voice-box but she still has a tongue... you do have a tongue, right?"

I expect her to stick hers out but instead she slowly and deliberately licks her upper lip while we three men stare at her entranced. Dora has *never* behaved like this before.

Dog groans and begs her to say she'll become his new star but she blushes and shakes her head. Viper loudly exhales his pent-up breath.

But Dog won't give up that easily. He compromises saying: "You don't even have to strip, you know, just dance in a bikini, a string bikini, and you'll still be a headliner. And if you were willing to peel it all off or at least go topless well sweetheart I could make you rich—"

"Enough!" I yell. "You shouldn't be thinking such thoughts about a pure girl like Dora never mind actually saying your disgusting words out loud. She's not one of your naked whores who flaunt their bodies for money and she never will be!"

Viper and Dog are entertained by my outburst but Dora flinches from my anger and shrinks down in her chair. Viper gets a suspicious look, like he's trying to puzzle something out. Thankfully nothing more is said about the ridiculous idea of Dora dancing on a stage and the two bikers leave shortly after.

When I return after seeing them out Dora is curled into a ball on her chair with her eyes squeezed shut. I can't tell if she's trying to make herself invisible or pretending to be asleep. Doesn't matter either way as I hiss at her: "I'll deal with your slutty flirting when we're upstairs." I'm satisfied when I see a tear escape down her soft cheek.

Dora

My body aches from last night's beating and I have my arms wrapped tightly around my middle. An incident with walk-ins helped distract me from my pain.

As usual I was curled up in my chair in the back corner of the room where everyone forgets about me and it's safe to let my mind drift. I'm unhappy, sadly feeling sorry for myself, disappointed, and hurting but I won't let it stop me from plotting. In fact, my escape plan is fully formed and as soon as the opportunity comes I'm ready to grab it. Casso banks infrequently, stashing all his cash in a lock-box instead, so I've decided that the money piling up there will fund my getaway.

Once I'm free and clear of this place I'll deal with Angie. I'm not going let her get away with stealing from me. Of course I'm planning to steal from Casso... but that's different because he never trusted or relied on me for help the way I did with her.

Each morning when I get dressed I assess my outfit to see if I can easily run in it. I don't much choice in what I wear. Every day I hope today is the day I make my dash for freedom. A little bit of inattentiveness on his part and I'll be gone. Meanwhile I'm just an obedient and quiet little mouse sitting in my corner.

Being around Casso is like sitting beside very sensitive explosive material since the slightest thing sets him off. While we're in the shop he never beats me beyond a face slap – but there's always a first time.

I don't mind keeping a low profile, it gives me the time to finalize the details of my plot.

Nowadays you need ID for everything except making purchases online. It was seeing the bus stop outside the tattoo shop that gave me the idea to make my journey by bus. A real bus, traveling out-of-state. I've never been on any kind of bus. My plan is to hightail it out of the shop running as far and as fast as I can until I can get myself to a shopping mall.

My mother took me to a mall once. It was embarrassing with our bodyguards following us everywhere, even into the ladies change-room. Other ladies complained and I never asked to go out shopping with Mama again.

Now I'm eager to go. At a mall I can buy both a cell-phone and a prepaid credit card. I can download the Greyhound app – or whichever bus line travels from wherever this place is – and buy a ticket with the card. I'll decide where I'm going to go once I see what my options are for a quick getaway.

The only thing I'll have to show the driver is the booking confirmation on the phone-screen when I board. No ID necessary, just proof of payment. Riding incognito will protect me from both the MC and my family. The FBI, too.

My thoughts are interrupted when a red-haired man enters Casso's small room and I immediately withdraw under his scrutiny. I'm relieved that his eyes only linger a moment before he dismisses my very existence. I can actually feel his coldness. It's not disdain, it's an utter lack of interest, simply a void.

I understand why once I spot the girl behind him. Done up in Goth fashion, with multiple piercings on her thin face and body, this girl exudes a hungry and lusty appetite for sex. It surrounds her like an odor or a color – is that what an aura is? The Goth's eyes glitter as she constantly licks her purple-stained lips with a split tongue. It's actually divided in two!

Casso focuses on the man, patiently waiting to hear what he wants. I find his voice pitched surprisingly high when he says: "She needs a tattoo done on her ass."

The girl turns and hikes up her skirt showing a skinny naked backside. "He wants me to get a heart colored pink—"

"Red," he insists.

"Pinky-red then I guess, so that when he paddles me he'll do it till my ass turns the same color and the heart disappears." Seeing Casso's unimpressed look she continues: "It's a thing. A really popular thing."

"I heard it on one of her books," adds the man.

"Yeah, it was on an audiobook I was listening to but it's been mentioned online and I've read about it before. I've seen a bunch of different books talk about it. It's a thing," she repeats.

Casso gets up to study the other tattoos on her body and pinches her skin in a few places before moving back to his chair and replying *No.*

The couple look at each other in surprise then she steps back while the frowning man angrily demands: "Why not?"

Casso just shrugs and answers: "I don't want to do it."

"But it's your job—" the man begins before Casso waves him off.

Casso isn't agitated but his accent grows stronger as he explains: "This is my business and I choose which jobs I want to do."

"But why don't you want to do this?" The man is sounding petulant and the girl has retreated to the doorway.

"I don't owe you an explanation," Casso calmly replies.

The man's fury shows in two spots of color on his pale face. "Well fuck you then, just fuck off you fucking foreigner. I'll take my business somewhere else."

Casso nods in agreement with that statement. Shoving the girl ahead of him the man stomps out of the room and loudly complains as he leaves the shop.

Before Casso can get immersed again in his drawing I clear my throat and when he turns his head to look at me I give him a quizzical look wondering why he refused the job.

He succinctly states: "She was high, dehydrated, unwashed, and hadn't followed the proper aftercare when she was first inked. There's four perfectly good reasons for you. Actually not wanting to do something is another perfectly good reason so that's five. But mostly it's because he's sadistic and I don't want to help him to hurt her."

Huh! He has no trouble hurting me. Of course he thinks I deserve his punishments and that he's doing the right thing. I shrug my shoulders and frown, after all the girl wasn't objecting.

"Junkies don't refuse a fix, doesn't mean I have to enable them."

My thoughts turn inward, absorbing his words. I think it's good that he acts so professionally in his career but he's such a cold man with no compassion. He's quieter than usual for the rest of the day. Something's changed. It's like that miserable couple polluted the atmosphere with more than just the stale sweat of his body and her musky scent.

That night Casso confronts me with an accusation. His voice is angry when he confusingly says: "You still don't trust me, do you?"

I start to tremble because Casso's anger generally signals a beating. I curl up to make my body as small a target as possible before his fists start flying. Why on earth would he think I could ever trust him?

Abandoned

Viper

I try not to drop in at the tattoo shop too much but Poison can't be trusted so I need to keep tabs on her. I have the excuse of inspecting her cuts even though Cas is perfectly capable of treating her.

But I like exerting my authority so I make Dora show me and she grudgingly inches her skirt up but only to the top of the dressing. I check how she's healing and tell him he's done a good job.

He nods and smiles down at the girl. I'm right to worry that she'll end up wrapping Casso around her little finger and convince him to let her go.

Banger still hasn't made any decision on her. I know he's got a lot of shit with his marriage happening right now but I need to pin him down. We're all just waiting and it's not good. As my Prez I have to give him whatever time and space he needs, but as his best friend of many years I have a responsibility to help. I can listen, I can advise, I can give him shit if necessary.

I hate to admit that anything Fiona says might actually be right but yeah, it's time I stepped up.

Right now I've got to check up on my number one witness for the prosecution.

Within moments of arriving at Casso's place I'm lounging back in a chair and ordering Poison to: "Grab me a coffee, just black, no cream or sugar or poison, Poison."

She knows it's just an excuse to get her out of the room while I talk with Casso but I can see she's very happy to go along with that. Anything to get away from me, I guess. Ha!

As I'm thinking this I push my chair even further back to look into the hallway. I can see Poison making our coffees. Not directly, but her reflection. She'd be able to see me looking at her if it was a mirror but it's only a foggy reflection from glass in a window. The first coffee is finished and she moves it to the counter while putting the second pod in the machine. Then the little bitch leans over the cup and deliberately spits into it!

I bet that's mine, I think grinning to myself. I'll know in a moment because Casso drinks his coffee with lots of milk. Sure enough she takes a container of half-and-half from the fridge and pours a big dollop into the second cup. Then, after hesitating a moment, she spits in that one too! I guess she figures Casso deserves the same treatment. The crafty little witch.

I have to stop myself from laughing out loud because if I'd met Poison – Dora – under different circumstances I'd have had no problem swapping spit with her. I like that she still has a feisty side, and I'm glad I got to see it.

Poison comes back then and keeping her distance puts my coffee down in front of me. I pick it up and give a suspicious look, tilting the mug as if I'm checking on something from a different angle. Looking up I see her watching me with a wide-eyed look of horror. As soon as I catch her eye she whirls around to Casso's desk to put his coffee on the coaster that's there.

Just as she moves Casso closes a drawer which catches Dora's skirt exposing her leg. My eyes immediately zone in and I see a dark bruise on top of older yellowing marks. What the fuck? Once again my eyes meet Dora's but she says nothing, just yanks the hem of her skirt free, and lets her gaze drift away.

Casso hasn't noticed the exchange but now I find myself studying him. Were those bruises made by a punch? Casso is very protective of his hands which makes sense because he needs them to make his living. He's artistic and shy, or at least quiet... still waters? Nah, Poison must just be clumsy. A couple of bruises in the same spot but made at different times must mean she keeps running into the same thing, something like the corner of his desk or their kitchen table.

Even if she really pissed him off I can't see Casso being violent with her. And how mad could he get if she doesn't even speak? When a woman makes me mad it's almost always because of her big mouth. Except for that wannabe club whore Julie... she didn't like what she got from me but she sure had it coming.

The memory of that incident turns me on which only goes to show what a sick fucker I am. Anyhow, I can't think about it here. Standing, I gulp the coffee down and let out a loud *Ahhh* sound.

Looking at Poison I tell her: "I think that was the best-tasting cup of coffee I've ever had. There's something about the flavor... like honey? not quite. Hmm, I'll have to try and figure it out. Thanks, Poison. Later, Casso."

Heading down the hallway I turn back to see her staring at me. I think about forcing her mouth open while I spit into it but instead I just give her a wink and my usual smirk.

Memories of the Julie incident have me hot and horny. I race back here to the clubhouse to get into the shower with my cock in my hand. I was half-hard even before I opened the throttle and between the revved up Harley and my erotic thoughts my boner was almost painful. I haven't thought of Julie in a long time and I'm surprised she's come to mind now because she and Poison are nothing alike.

Julie was an incredibly stunning girl with her huge liquid black eyes and wide full-lipped mouth. She had such a sexy body no man could look at her without thinking obscene thoughts. I can't imagine what her life was like once she hit puberty but by time she showed up at the club she'd figured out how to use her power and holy fuck did she use it. The club whores hated her because all of us brothers were drooling.

Same as everybody else I wanted a taste but I held back because that kind of woman likes a challenge. I was enjoying our banter and getting ready to take it up a notch when Julie crossed the line. I can still see the picture in my mind's eye as clearly as if it only just happened.

I never bring chicks to my room so I'm furious when I open the door and find her lying on my bed wearing nothing but a big satin bow tied around her waist. Its bright red color contrasts beautifully with her light brown skin and she gives me her bright white smile while licking those fuckable lips. She's eyeing me like a predator, like a sleek panther, that just spotted lunch. I can practically hear her purr.

"This door was locked," I state, hiding my anger.

Pulling out the thin steel clip that's holding up her hair Julie explains it was no match for her skills. "Besides, you can't avoid me for ever, not when we both know how much you want me," she states with utmost confidence. "I can make you feel soooo good."

After allowing me a good look at her perfect ass she rolls over onto her back and lets her thighs flop apart flashing the red lips of her waxed pussy.

Approaching her slowly, my eyes focused on her cunt, I ask: "You can? You're sure? Tell me all about how you're gonna do that."

Now she giggles as her hand trails over her high round tits, down her nicely rounded belly, to linger at her clit. "Oh I've got all kinds of skills, Viper, and I can't wait to share them with you. I know you don't fuck the club whores but baby you're going to be begging for more of me."

I'm close enough now to pick her up and hoist her over my shoulder. She lets out a delighted squeal until I carry her out of my room and into the main room where I toss her down on a pool table.

"Here's a present I was given that I'm re-gifting to all my brothers, use her well and make sure she learns that nobody breaks into my room without getting punished."

Stepping back I watch the men swarm her calling out comments like: *will do, boss* and *look she came gift-wrapped* and *what a pretty birthday suit*. Julie's yelling *stop* and *let me go* while being fondled and groped as the men ring round her. Big hands, some none too clean, cover every inch of her body as the bikers, young and old, squeeze handfuls of her soft flesh.

I hear Fiona's voice over the others saying *just take your medicine, bitch* and when Julie shouts *okay, okay I'll just leave* Fiona sneers at her *yeah you will once you've been properly educated*. Julie yells and swears but all those hands and mouths just keep molesting, grabbing, and invading her.

I hear Dog tell her: "School's in sweet cheeks, you crossed the line and this is what's on the other side. You're a biker bitch and you know the drill so be a good little choo-choo." He told me later that although she cursed the whole time Julie took them all, including Fiona and Bunny who each wielded a rubber dildo.

As Dog put it: "She's not only been around the block, Viper. She's got her name on the street sign."

I watch the action for awhile before fetching her clothes from my room and tossing them down by the pool table. The room is filled with the sucking sound of wet flesh, grunts and groans, the occasional slap on Julie's ass, sighs of satisfaction, and the smell of male sweat and arousal.

Looking at her face I see it's full of anger and I think *yeah, payback's a bitch ain't it?* She squints her eyes at me and I give her a cocky grin and a thumbs up.

Once the guys are done with her she scrambles into her clothes, dripping and stinking with cum but still defiant, giving everyone the finger then leaving the clubhouse never to return. I chuckle thinking *it's like the trash took itself to the curb.*

The fact that Julie broke in to my room confirmed my suspicion that she was a plant from another MC. Drop-dead gorgeous chicks don't just wander in to an outlaw clubhouse looking for a party.

That plus the way she took her punishment. She never cried *rape* and there were no repercussions which tells me she was thankful to escape with what she got. Snitches caught spying usually get maimed or killed so she must have figured what happened wasn't so bad in comparison. All Julie got was a sore cunt along with angry shame. Plus whatever reception she got when she returned to her own club empty-handed. She took a hell of a risk sneaking around our place and I wonder if she did it on a dare, a debt, or a threat?

The image of that hateful woman with her beautiful body crouched on hands and knees, head dropped down in submission, brings me to orgasm every time. In my mind's eye I can see and hear my brothers hooting and hollering as they fuck her one after the other. Real *punishment fits the crime* stuff and such a sweet revenge. Except now

I'm thinking about Dora and wondering *has Poison been planted on us?*

Getting out of the shower I immediately text Banger that we need to meet and talk.

Banger

I'm sorta drowning my sorrows at the bar except I'm just sipping. I got drunk the other night and I don't want to make a habit of it. I'm glad Viper wants to talk, that'll get me out of my own head for awhile.

Viper joins me and knocks backs his own shot then picking up his beer leads me back down the hall to his room.

"I don't want anyone overhearing this," he tells me by way of explanation. I take the only chair and he paces for a bit before getting to the point: "Do you think Dora has been playing us?"

I almost laugh in his face but I see he's serious. It is funny though that he's the only one who doesn't realize how deeply he's attracted to the girl. I thought when I told him to punish her they'd end up fucking and he'd get her out of his system but I guess that didn't happen. Now he's got himself all worked up over this stupid idea. If he'd stop to think it out he'd realize how crazy he sounds.

"Jesus brother, do you honestly think Dora somehow orchestrated you needing to stop for a piss? because that's how she came into your life. And since she'd hitched a ride on a 10-speed it's not like she was following you in the Merc, even if it is just a wagon.

You know my Old Lady is always reading, right? and she likes these romance books that have something called *meet-cute* but even the most imaginative writer couldn't come up with a plausible scenario for the rest stop and the killing and the kidnapping being a planned thing."

Now I do start to laugh and after a moment he joins me. It's really not that funny but within minutes the two of us are howling.

"Okay I admit it, I'm a fucking idiot. But I was thinking of Julie, you remember her?"

"Oh yeah, if I wasn't married I'd have been all over that. She was fucking gorgeous with a fantastic body and face, beautiful hair, lovely voice..."

"True that, everything on the outside was perfect. Too bad the inside was rotten. Anyhow, I started thinking about that whole incident and how she was a spy and it seemed like a revelation but obviously not."

"No, you just got a hard-on thinking about Julie which made your body start thinking about Dora."

"Poison? no fucking way."

This time I laugh at him right to his face which is twisted up in a scowl. "Okay bro, if you say so... but there is something fucked up about this whole hostage thing. I haven't heard from her family. Do you think the woman she called has just kept quiet about it?"

"Why though? It won't be to help Dora 'cause there's some cousin telling her not to get involved."

"Is there some benefit to Dora not coming back to them? I can't see it, it's not like she's going to take over the mafia business or anything 'cause chicks can't."

"From what Hardware was telling me it was a real massacre so maybe, if several top people were whacked, maybe they're all trying to figure out who's in charge now? But you're right, it would never be Dora. I think her *fiance* must have been killed otherwise we would have heard from him."

"So what's going on with you two?"

"What, me and Poison? Fuck you, there's nothing! No way."

I give him a skeptical look and he adds: "Maybe Casso's gonna ask you for her, I don't know. If not then yeah, sure, I'll probably fuck her eventually but just because she's cute and hasn't fucked everyone else in the place yet."

He and I both know Dora is nothing like the club whores but there's no point pushing. I take a long swig of my beer and contemplate my best friend.

"Listen I've been wanting to talk to you about something else. It's kinda awkward because you're my Prez but you're also Pat and maybe I can give some advice or maybe I can just be a sounding board but do you wanna talk about what's going on with you and Kim?"

I know he's right. Keeping it all wrapped up in my head is driving me nuts, and I'm too distracted to get anything done. The club deserves better.

I sigh deeply and admit to him: "Kim has always wanted to have a baby. I've got no objection so we've never used any kind of protection but here we are together nine years now and nothing."

"You've gone for tests?"

"She has, and everything's okay but I knew it would be. I know I'm the problem."

"What do you mean?"

"Don't you remember? when we were kids I had mumps. I figure that's made me sterile."

Viper has finally stopped pacing and now he's sitting on the bed but leaning forward to get my full attention: "Banger, that whole mumps infertility thing is a myth."

"No, it isn't!"

"Okay not completely a myth but number one, you had mumps as a kid not an adult so it's not very serious, and two, the chances are super super rare. Just go get tested, man."

"Huh, that's what Kim says. She's looked into everything and says even if the mumps did give me the side effect in my balls I would still have a ten percent chance – or maybe it's I only lost ten percent – whatever. She says I need to get tested and if I'm not completely sterile we can do that *invitro fertilization.*"

"I've heard it's really expensive, like thirty grand a pop, but Jesus man make your wife happy. You've got the money."

"Actually because it's been around so long the price has come down a lot. Kim got a quote for $12,000 but the clinic recommended budgeting for $18,000."

"Oh wow, that's way better than it used to be. So what's the problem?"

"The problem? I'm not going to go jack off in some doctor's office and have my kid created in a test-tube. Fuck that. If it happens it happens but if it doesn't then it wasn't meant to be."

"Okay fuck off right now. First of all don't use that fate bullshit 'cause I know you don't believe in it. And second, if Kim is willing to have the surgery, because it's an operation for the woman to take her egg out and then put it back, then–"

"How come you know all this?"

"You know I've always been interested in science stuff. I know plenty about cloning and DNA, too. Anyhow, stop dancing around the issue man. If Kim's gonna do all that then you gotta at least be willing to do your very easy part. Fuck, Pat."

"What?"

"Well..." He looks away, refusing to make eye contact. Now I'm getting pissed off so I snap: "Spit it out, Viper."

"You're being selfish. Look, I know you love Kim and you want to hang on to your marriage, I've always thought you two were really happy, so why wouldn't you do this for her?"

"Aww fuck, when you put it like that... but honestly what kind of a man has to—"

"Hey, I've given you my advice and I might not be right so there's no point debating it. Just think it over and make your decision. Only you know what your marriage means to you but from where I'm sitting? I think it means a hell of a lot."

Viper's always been good about not pushing things. He gives an opinion or advice or suggestion but he never follows up or puts any pressure on. He's a real *take it or leave it* kind of guy. It's relaxing. Of course I don't like him saying I'm selfish, I'm maybe a bit chauvinistic but...

"Actually I'm always willing to try stuff with Kim. I told you she reads those romance books, well they're basically porn for chicks, and when she reads about something that interests her then hell, I'm always ready to give it a go. For awhile there she seemed to be reading a lot of this BDSM stuff and she wanted me to give her a spanking."

"Seriously? You spank your wife? Shit, I don't need to hear this."

145

"No, listen, it's a funny story. So she decides she wants a sexy spanking as foreplay. It's not something I'd ever have thought of, I mean it has no appeal especially not after the old man made me beat Fee, but even though Kim was already around by then I never told her. It was club business.

Anyhow, so I'm like *sure, how do you want to do this?* and she's got it all worked out, I just have to follow along.

We go into the bedroom and she strips off except her panties. She's done that thing with her hair – you know when they bend forward and finger-comb through it then flip back and it's kinda messy but sexy-messy, all puffed out and hanging in her face. So between the hair and her naked body except for these really hot lacy panties I'm already turned on. You know Kimmy's always been the only one for me, ever since high-school and that was a few years before we actually got married."

"I remember," Viper says with a smile. "I remember when Kim arrived from Ireland and was the new girl in your class. I wasn't in high school yet so I'd never seen her but you talked about her so much it was like I knew her. Everything out of your mouth was Kim this and Kim that and I got so jealous.

Then Des started teasing you about asking her out on a date and Melva said you'd have to behave yourself with a nice Irish colleen–"

"And you said *I thought her name was Kim?*" laughs Banger.

"Yeah well, I didn't speak Irish and didn't know that colleen meant girl. But I do remember thinking *dating? ewww!*"

"I was freakin' scared to ask her out 'cause hadn't started going with girls yet but after Dad made that crack I kinda had to... and it's been her and only her ever since. I love my Kimmy even more than I did a dozen years ago.

So anyhow, she's totally into this whole scene saying shit like *ooh when you put me across your knee please don't pull down my panties* so I pick up my cue and say something about *naughty girls always get spanked on their bare bottom* and she's loving it! I gotta admit I was getting into it too. But, this is starting to get too private so I'll skip over what we're thinking and saying and get to the actual spanking."

I break out in a hearty chuckle remembering that evening. "So Kimmy's in position, I've pulled her panties down and her gorgeous ass is like an invitation. I smack one-two, one-two spanking each cheek and she shoots off my lap, clutching her ass and yelling *what the hell, Pat? that really hurt!* and I can only imagine what my face looks like because Viper, I haven't even started yet! I tell her that too, I say *honey I'm just warming you up before the real spanking begins.*"

Viper explodes in a laugh telling me I'm full of shit.

"Swear to God, she's hollering after four little swats and I was planning on giving her about forty to fifty real spanks because she described a rosy-red ass and Viper although she's whining about the stinging pain there isn't the faintest trace of color in her very white Irish cheeks, not even a fucking *tinge* of pink."

The two of us are howling and then I remember: "Oh! and then she said *it's not like this in the books.*" and this time we totally collapse in laughter.

Dora

Something's been bothering Casso but he won't talk about it. Last night he was upset but some... I don't know, intuition or something? tells me whatever is going on with him isn't about me. Or not mainly about me. I'm thankful he didn't beat me up but I'm concerned because he's canceled his appointments for today, tomorrow, and the next day. Is he going somewhere? and is he taking me with him? While I'm wondering the door opens and suddenly the room is overcrowded with Viper and Dog joining us.

Viper's gaze rakes over me with a calculating, assessing look. It makes me feel guilty even though I haven't done anything wrong. In complete contrast Dog shows plenty of interest. He makes a show of licking his lips and giving me a wink. I think I prefer Viper's cold indifference. I don't understand Dog, he's an extremely good-looking man with long hair that he pulls back off his head in a messy ponytail. He looks like a Viking with his blond coloring and having that tattoo on his very handsome face adds to his sexiness. He's tall and equally as massive and muscular as Viper. The last thing he needs to do is act like he's desperate to get laid, all slimy and horny and... and salacious. But maybe women like that?

Thinking about Dog's motives means I haven't been listening to Casso and Viper's conversation so I'm shocked to hear Casso wind it up saying: "Sorry but there's nothing I can do. I have to go, it will be a few days, so you have to look after Dora while I'm gone."

Gone? Where is he going?

Viper rubs his big hand across his mouth a few times, thinking, then says: "Fuck it, she's going to have to come back to the Clubhouse with us."

The mystery of Casso's behavior has left me unfocused but now all I can think is does he know? does he KNOW? is he going to track down... omigod, my thoughts terrify me. Dog misunderstands my look of fear thinking I'm afraid of Fiona or the club whores and says, "Hey baby, it's not the club bitches you have to worry about it's us," as he strokes my arm and leers.

Viper snorts in disgust saying: "Not *us* but *you*. *You're* the only one who wants to get it on with Poison. You know what? I don't want to take her to the clubhouse so we'll go to the safe house instead since it's just for–"

When Dog interrupts with a wolfish howl Viper shoves him out into the hallway before turning back to Casso saying: "Just for a couple of days, right?"

"Yeah, two-three maybe."

With a big sigh the VP agrees telling me to run upstairs and grab what I'll need for a short stay.

"No need," Casso tells him, "I've got her things here."

Here is the same plastic bag Viper gave me to pack up... how long ago? I've lost track. My life just keeps spiraling downward. Plotting my escape helped me fight my despair and depression but if I'm in the custody of Viper and Dog, secluded God knows where, I'll never get away and they'll want to... omigod I can't even think of what they might do to me. Dog is practically salivating and they're both scaring me to bits.

Panicking I latch on to Casso's arm my eyes pleading, He takes hold of my wrist and squeezes until I can't stand the pain and have to let go.

"Behave Dora. I will be coming back to get you," he admonishes.

"Don't worry about a thing, Picasso, we'll take *real good care of her*," Dog answers with a laugh. He thinks it's funny but it sounds like a threat to me. Especially when he tells Viper: "Brother, we're gonna have so much fun with Poison Ivy."

"You're not coming, Dog. One of us has to stay at the clubhouse and cover for Banger's absences right now. I'm taking Poison by myself."

I gasp as fear makes the color drain from my face. The three men look at me: Dog is pouting, Casso is impassive, and Viper smirks. I'm pretty sure he's going to kill me.

Casso

I hate seeing Dora leave with the two men even if it's true that Dog won't be going to the safe house with her. He might just persuade Viper to let him come after all. Fuck. Even just Dora and Viper alone is...

And what will she tell him about her and me? I know Dora can speak but does Viper? They don't actually have to talk though, she just has to lift her shirt to show him the bruises. Viper will know I put them there, who else could it be?

Fucking Tonino. Why's he demanding that we urgently meet? Him and his *it's not safe to talk on the phone* bullshit. Damn, damn, damn I forgot all about... Aw fuck it. If Viper questions me I'll just tell him she's tried to escape a couple of times and I had to restrain her and punish her for it, too.

Actually, this is a good heads-up because I've come close to losing control a few times. Thoughts of the injustice overwhelm me and then the anger takes hold. Once I get Dora back I'll have to act quickly to finish this once and for all.

I take the car to meet up with Tonino. It's perfect riding weather so taking the car is a shame but I don't want any connection between me and bikers. The bar Tonino specified is out of town. Stupid precautions... I think he just likes pretending he's a super-spy. Fucking idiot.

The rundown bar is in an out-of-the-way place and there are no other cars here so probably we'll be the only customers. No doubt Tonino will think that's a good thing without realizing how easily we'll be remembered by the bartender now. Oh well, there's no reason for anyone to be following Tonino because no matter what he might think he's really not important. If I thought anyone considered him a threat I'd have already taken him out myself.

Stepping inside the dimly lit room I'm surprised to see Tonino nursing a beer and a shot at a booth in the farthest corner. As I walk towards him the old guy behind the bar, I figure he's the owner, calls out *we don't do table service* so I change direction and order a bottled beer from him. I wouldn't trust anything else in this place.

Joining Tonino I ask: "Where's your car?"

"I parked it round back just 'cause, you know."

I stare at him while taking a swallow from my beer thinking *he's such a moron*. I don't know why I got involved with him in the first place, I already had my arrangements made and my crew sorted. But... he was in with the Spagnolo and Contini families and I needed to get closer and hoped to get useful intel from him. Nothing panned out though, so I didn't need him after all.

Didn't take me long to realize he's just an opportunist trying to ingratiate himself with the winning side.

"So, what's so important that you dragged me way the hell out here? what's going on?"

"Lots," he says, keeping his voice so low I can barely hear him. "First off, we were wrong thinking the FBI had Dora because they don't. She somehow got out of Portofino's that night and I don't know what happened immediately after but she ended up with some motorcycle gang–"

"Club," I automatically interject.

"Huh?"

"Not a gang, a club. That's what they call themselves. But never mind that, go on. How do you know this?"

He actually taps his nose like he's a wise guy in some old movie saying: "I got a source and I found out–"

"Oh Tonino quit with the drama will you?" says a woman's loud voice right behind me. I can't believe he brought someone to this meeting and decide in that moment to kill Tonino before I leave. Turning around I see Angelina something-or-other nee Spagnolo. We've never met so I have to pretend I don't know who she is as I look her over.

"I'm Angie," she tells me sitting down on the bench beside Tonino. "Who are– wait, don't tell me. I know your face... I just... I just can't quite... Oh!" she gasps. "Oh it can't be but wow, I gotta tell you you're the spitting image of my oldest brother as I remember him."

I just tilt my head and give her a half-smile as she goes on claiming: "We've gotta be related somehow. I mean, it's absolutely incredible just how much you look like Cesare, you know?"

"They say everyone has a double..." I let the statement trail off and she nods.

"You know that's so true! Anyhow, what's your name? Obviously it's no use waiting for Tonino to introduce us."

Tonino does speak up then, glad to get a word in edgewise, saying: "This is Guglielmo and that's all you need to know about our business." Turning to me he adds: "Angie here is the aunt of Loretta Spagnolo who goes by Dora. You know, the *fiancee* who escaped that night from Portofinos."

153

I'm really having to act up a storm here as I again pretend ignorance. "Escaped?"

"Yeah, we don't know how she got away or who helped her but Dora is my niece and she called me a few days ago. I almost didn't answer because the call was from an unknown number but thank God I did, you know? We talked and she told me she was being held at the... hold on, I wrote it on my phone, here it is... the *Satan's Tears Motorcycle clubhouse.*"

"And who did you pass that on to?"

"Well... I was going to tell the family but Tonino and I discussed it and decided to just sit on the information for now. I mean, we don't know who's taking over or anything and we don't want the wrong person to find out. It could be someone who wants Dora out of the way, you know?"

I nod as if considering her comment. "Why did Dora call you? are you two especially close?"

"Totally close, I'm her bestie and she's always confided in me. Tells me everything. Like that *purity test* – what a messed up thing, you know?"

"No, what's that all about?"

Angie loves an audience as much as she loves to gossip. Leaning in she lowers her voice dramatically. "The purity test is some Sicilian thing, I think, and it's done with witnesses. Dora's on a bed and Walter comes in and sticks his dick in her – just once – to bust her hymen and the women all check that there's blood and that's how she passes the test."

"That's fucked up," puts in Tonino.

"Right? You know in my opinion that doesn't even count for having sex. I mean, they didn't even kiss. In fact, she said he asked her to close her eyes and keep them shut until he left—"

"You never told me that part," interrupts Tonino.

"No way! Are you sure I didn't tell you? 'cause that was the creepiest bit of the whole thing, right? What do you think about that?"

"I agree with Tonino's assessment."

"And she never wanted this marriage and was planning to run away, you know?"

Her constantly saying *you know?* is grating on my nerves but I have to hide my annoyance. "That's stupid, how was she going to run away with no money and no where to go?"

"She has money, a lot of it too. I know because I'm looking after it for her–"

Tonino interrupts his... girlfriend? saying: "Shut up about the money, nobody wants to hear about that now," Turning to me he continues: "So, this is important shit, right? We know where Dora is, well not the exact address or anything but we can find out, and that's gotta be worth somethin', am I right?"

God does he think the clubhouse has a website? maybe with a Google map? These two morons sure deserve each other, I think but again I nod. "What's the news about Gualtiero?"

"Who?"

"The *fiance*... umm.. Walter."

"He's dead. His family didn't lose as many as ours but he definitely died."

"We lost my young nephew Ricky and his mother, my sister-in-law Toni, and–"

"Antonia Coccia is dead?"

"You know her? I mean, knew her? She's my sister-in-law. It's her husband who you look exactly like. How do you know her?"

"I don't but my parents do... did. Was she killed at the restaurant?"

"She was shot and medevaced out of Portofino's but she died *en route* to the hospital. They told us there was nothing they could have done for her. It's so sad. Both her and the cousin she was *friendly with* but he died at the scene."

I pause for a moment thinking that Dora's mother is finally dead. The American woman who took my mother's rightful place all because she had the Coccia connections.

Tired of being left out of the conversation Tonino butts in: "So here's what I'm thinkin' about doin'–" but I put up my hand to stop him saying *ssh, wait a sec.* Then I call out to the old bartender asking if there's anyone else around the place and when he answers *nope, nobody* I pull my piece and shoot him. Then I shoot Tonino and before Angie's inhaled enough air to scream I shoot her too.

It doesn't take me long to walk around the room scanning for surveillance cameras but there's nothing. I see a sawed-off shotgun under the bar beside a cash drawer. There's almost no money in it but I scoop up what there is, knock the weapon to the floor, and taking my beer bottle with me I leave. I'm happy to get out of there without having to hear Tonino's great plan. Fucking idiot.

Dora's whereabouts is safeguarded, she's my secret now.

Back outside I check for cameras and there's nothing. Good. My next stop is to check up on the surviving gang members and finish tying up loose ends. Then there's the two recent widows whose hubbies might have violated my privacy... good thing most of those guys were single.

I figure I can deal with these people quickly and get back way earlier than originally planned. I don't want Dora being alone with Viper for another night.

Arson

Viper

Our bikes are superb, noisy machines and we enjoy showing off which draws lots of attention to us so we never bring the bikes to our safe house. We keep everything very low-key here.

I park the truck on a side street in front of an empty lot and we walk the half-block to our place. Poison is looking around trying to figure out where we're going since we're at the end of the road and there are no homes in sight. Our safe house is an old, abandoned gas station surrounded by heavy-duty fencing plastered with *Danger, Toxic Groundwater, Hazardous Waste,* and *Keep Out* signs.

The pumps have rusted out, the sign has lost its color, and the building is dilapidated. Guiding her around the back of the lot I unlock a sturdy padlock and loosen the chain enough to get through the gap into the yard. There's no lock on the station's door, a solid punch could knock it down.

Entering the dark, musty and dusty room I head to a much sturdier door set in a concrete-block wall with another workmanlike lock on it. Dora leans into me shivering from the stale, damp air. Holding her by the shoulder I usher her through this last door and hear her exclamation of *oh!* once she sees the inside.

Our well-concealed safe house is a cozy space with no windows so we're able to run a small generator for heat, lights, and an air exchanger. It's small but comfortable enough for a limited time. I easily lift Dora up and onto the bed and finding the handcuff that's attached there get her secured. Of course she starts to yell but I stop her explaining I'm going on a food run. We can't risk having a delivery here and I need to know she's safely stowed away while I'm gone.

Banger still hasn't decided if he wants to ransom her or... whatever, but it might not matter anymore now that her aunt knows our club has her. He's right when he said it's funny that nobody's approached us. Regardless, I still have to keep her safe.

"I'm not hungry," she snaps but I snark right back: "I don't care." I know damn well she's gotta be hungry by now.

I plug in the little fridge and switch on the heater. Before leaving I turn to her and making sure I've got her attention I ask if she's going to behave or if I should turn the lights off and leave her to get frightened in the dark.

She quickly begs "No! don't do that, I promise I'll behave." I narrow my eyes so I look tough and she nods repeatedly adding: "I will, I will."

As I retrace my steps to leave our safe house I'm so sure she's sticking her tongue out at me I call over my shoulder: "I know a better way to use that tongue so I suggest you keep it in your mouth," and chuckle when her startled gasp tells me I was right. The little cutie is such a brat.

Dora

Viper isn't gone long, an hour or less, but the time drags. He's right about the room being small and there isn't much to see but the handcuffs attached to the bed make me wonder if this place is a love nest as much as a safe house. I mean if you're protecting somebody you don't chain them up but if you want to play sexy games then having restraints make sense.

I've read plenty of stories about that kind of thing since my cousins share their book recommendations for me to download. I have subscriptions on both Kindle and Kobo.

Is he worried I'll run away? which I totally would, or does he think my life is in danger? I scoff at that idea because why would he care? The most danger I face is from him, I'm witness to a murder he committed, he's the one I need to be protected from.

I don't trust him at all so it's best if I just ignore him. But we're going to be here alone together for days, maybe. Just me and him.

My anxiety goes into the stratosphere so despite Viper leaving the lights on I still manage to scare myself silly. When I hear him coming in I honestly can't say if it makes me feel better or worse.

When my stomach rumbles at the smell of pizza that chases away my worries temporarily. He places the box on the bed and I take a deep inhale of the delicious aroma before rattling my wrist so he can free me from the cuff.

While I pull apart the pizza slices he unloads the groceries he's bought. I can't help but notice how easily and confidently he moves. He's tall and his legs are long but there's nothing awkward about him. He has a manly grace. I quickly look away before he catches me staring. The last thing I need is another man thinking I'm leading him on.

Back in the shop I sometimes wondered if I should confide in Viper about Casso hurting me but then I realized he must already know. Why would Casso bother to hide his penchant for casual violence from his brothers in the club? and why would they care?

Viper's shopping consists of several packets of Vietnamese coffee, a six-pack of beer, a case of ginger-ale and another of bottled water. No food. Fitting as much as he can in the compact fridge he leaves the rest on the counter where there's a kettle.

"Don't drink the water from the taps, don't even use it in the kettle. Drink bottled water or soda. And use the bottled water to boil up these 3-in-1 coffee packs that have sugar and powdered milk already mixed in."

"How come you got ginger-ale?" I ask.

He shrugs saying: "I don't like cola. Do you want a beer with your pizza?"

"I don't know if I can finish a whole can–" I begin but he interrupts to assure me that's not a problem. Watching him pop a can and down half of it in one gulp I get what he means.

We eat our meal sitting on the bed. When we're finished I gather everything up and carry it over to the counter. Viper loudly belches and I glare while I chug a swallow of beer and burp right back at him. He laughs and gives me the first genuine smile I've seen yet.

Omigod he's gorgeous when he grins. Lying propped up on one elbow, his dark hair flopping forward and his blue eyes bright with amusement, he isn't *Viper* anymore.

"I can't imagine you were christened Viper so what's your real name?"

"I wasn't christened, Viper is my real name, but if you're asking about my birth name it's Gray, Gray Murdoch. It's Scottish."

"Gray? Short for Grahame?"

"No, just Gray, it's a family name."

"Oh cool. Are you close with your parents?"

His expression grows stern and I realize I've gone too far so I quickly say *sorry for being nosy*. I know better than to ask questions about family. Viper acknowledges my apology but the relaxed mood has vanished. Just as well because I don't want to be friends with my kidnapper.

I look around for a restroom and he gestures to a door I thought belonged to a closet. "Don't use too much toilet paper – and don't flush nothing else," he warns. Surely he doesn't think I'm still on my period? although I never actually was. Hmm, that means I must be due soon.

Going in I see it's literally just an ancient filthy toilet with an equally dirty sink. I barely have room to close the door and I wonder how Viper manages. When he takes his turn and leaves the door open I have my answer. Why didn't they hang it so it opens outward? I guess these bikers just don't care. They've probably all served time in jail and stopped worrying about privacy long ago. I also guess I have to stop being such a princess.

While he's occupied I grab the chance to undress for bed. Pulling on my sleep shirt I realize this is actually Viper's tee that I'm still wearing. I forgot that I'd taken it from him. Well it's mine now.

Before I put my arms through the sleeves I take off my bra but leave my panties on. Not that there's much point since I'm wearing a thong but still...

I'm sitting up against the wall, there's no headboard, with the blanket pulled up and primly covering me from toes to chest. Viper finishes up and coming to stand beside the bed yanks the blanket off me.

"That's my shirt," he says.

"Not any more," I sass at him.

"Uh yeah. Mine, mine forever."

I feel a funny twinge when he says that. I mean, I know he's talking about his stupid t-shirt but... I roll my eyes and resort to replying: "Whatever."

"And scoot over, you're on my side of the bed."

"How can you have a side when this isn't even your bed? And besides, at home you sleep on the other side."

Damn! why did that *at home* comment slip out? he noticed, too, because I saw his eyes widen. Home for me is *not* Viper's bedroom at the clubhouse. It's nowhere at the moment but that will change once I escape.

"I always sleep on the side closest to the door so you can move or you can sleep underneath me all night because my body is going to be in that spot."

He smirks at me when I roll away and pout from the safety of the other side.

Flipping the light-switch off Viper returns with the blanket to cover us both. As he punches his pillow into shape and settles into the mattress I hear him mutter *such a brat* and for some crazy reason that makes me feel good.

Viper

Dora crashed as soon as her head hit the pillow. There's so much drama in that girl's life right now it's no surprise she shuts down completely.

I can't resist... her body is so warm and cuddly and right here in front of me. I pull her back against my chest and she immediately wakes up. She tenses and goes rigid, her limbs pulling tightly to close her in.

"Wh-what?" she stutters and I hate how fearful she sounds. "Viper please don't do sex to me, please please don't."

Do sex? I bite back a laugh. Instead, I make my voice low and soothing as I lightly rub her arms and calm her with words of comfort. "Relax, Poison, like I told you before the slate is wiped clean. I'll never touch you in punishment unless you do something to deserve it. And you won't, right? Right, so there's nothing's to worry about, nothing's gonna happen."

"Then why are you touching me?"

"I'm not, I'm touching my t-shirt. I'm pretty sure I'm never getting it back so I'm just giving it a goodbye hug."

She giggles nervously but isn't reassured by my joke so I tell her: "I promise there's no punishment, no sex, there's just... this. Now go back to sleep, baby girl."

Dora loosens up a little bit and when I gently rock us back and forth her body loses most of its stiffness. I inhale deeply and breathe out warm air over the top of her head until she slips back into sleep.

Careful not to disturb I only make the smallest movements with my fingers and hands as I caress her warm, soft skin. She snuggles into my chest and my lips rest against her neck feeling the pulse in her throat. It's fucking stupid but when I hold her like this I feel so protective. That's really fucked up because I'm her biggest threat.

I thought I'd spend the night tossing and turning but instead I was sleeping soundly when she woke me by crying out: "Why are you like this?"

I'm disoriented by the sudden waking. "Wh-what? What the fuck are you going on about?"

"I don't know what you want from me, I don't how to act, you hit me no matter what I do... What do you want?" she yells.

Her shouting gets to me and I shake my head as if to clear it. I've been holding her against my body but I wasn't grinding her, I was sleeping. I'm about to yell right back when she wails a stream of garbled words I can't understand but I can make out *no more* and *please don't* and *stop hitting me*. That's when I realize she's having a bad dream although this is different from the nightmares she used to have in my room.

"Dora, you're dreaming, a bad dream for sure, but honey it's still just a dream. You're okay, you're safe now, I got you and no one's gonna hit you or hurt you again, baby girl."

I keep repeating those phrases until she stops crying and without ever fully waking she slips back into a deep sleep. Holding her close I lie awake for a long time wondering *what the hell kind of life did she used to live?*

Dora

The kitchen area is tiny so we're standing close together eating the fast food breakfast Viper brought in. I've never had hash browns before and they taste so good!

He smiles watching me eat every bite and I'm sure my face is lit with delight as I look up at him. I lick the salty grease off my lips and next thing I know I'm up in the air as he hoists me onto the counter. It feels like the most natural thing in the world when he leans in for a kiss but he pulls back at the last moment and instead nips my bottom lip.

"Ow!"

"Keep your tongue inside your mouth Poison or I'll find another use for it."

"I... oh! Oh piss off Viper. I still hate you for you know, what you did to me, but you did good with this food so let me eat in peace."

He gives me a puzzled look and when I say *what?* asks how can I have such a good appetite after fighting nightmares all night.

"No I didn't, I didn't dream at all."

"Oh right, it was the other girl in bed with us."

Now it's my turn for a puzzled frown, wondering what he's playing at. "You don't make any sense," I tell him but before he can answer we both hear a noise that puts us on alert. Viper puts a finger to his lips and draws a gun.

"Hey it's me, Casso, I'm coming in."

I let out the breath I didn't realize I'd been holding in with a sigh of relief. The only other person who knows we're here is Dog and being trapped in this place with nothing but a bed and two big men, one who is perpetually horny well...

Casso hasn't shaved and his hair is all messed up. He looks like he hasn't slept. He tells us his business was resolved quickly and now I can return with him to the tattoo shop.

Viper hesitates for a beat before saying: "Thank fuck, she's all yours brother. You can head out and I'll lock up here."

Casso picks up the shopping bag of my things and I slip into the washroom to fetch my toothbrush and box of tampons. Casso guides me out the door but I turn back and catch Viper's eye, unsure what message I want to convey and not understanding why I'm even looking at him, but he simply stares for a moment before turning away.

I follow Casso, stepping carefully, through the rundown old building and in silence we walk down the block to where he's parked his car.

We drive back to the shop in Casso's little two-seater. I like his sportscar but he's indifferent, preferring his bike. He's never taken me for a ride or a drive using either vehicle, he's never taken me anywhere. No where, other than the coffee shop across the road from the tattoo parlor.

He parks and we get out but instead of opening the shop he leads me upstairs to his home although it's not even lunchtime yet. I'm curious about why he had to go away and hope he'll explain. He doesn't. He tells me he wants to but he's beat, hasn't slept yet, and will update me on everything after he's had some rest.

He peels off his clothes and flops down on the bed, groaning when he realizes I'm just standing there looking at him. He squints up at me and is obviously debating something in his mind. With a muttered curse he gets up and drags me over to the bed. I know this means he's going to chain me there and I struggle but despite his exhaustion I'm still no match against his strength and I can't get away.

"Watch movies," he says, gesturing to the old laptop he's loaded up with movies. I discovered early on that I can't use it to contact anyone because there's no internet connection. I can't even download something new to watch. Since Casso's movies are either porn or *shoot 'em up* action flicks I decide to just think for a bit.

Last night, in the safe house with Viper, things were different between us. Almost friendly, kind of. And in the kitchen this morning I didn't mind when I thought he was going to kiss me but why did I let my guard down? I don't want anything to do with him.

Even though the pain from his assault has faded the memory is still clear as ever. I hate him and will never forgive him for what he did to me.

I can't make sense of my feelings so instead I think about my family and again find myself wondering who survived? and are they looking for me?

Casso falls asleep quickly and so deeply his chest barely stirs. Sitting propped up with my pillow in the corner of the two walls I realize I'm in for a long and boring afternoon and night.

Casso

I woke up in the early evening still tired but really hungry. Dora is beside me, she's fallen asleep curled against the wall. I'd get her up to cook me a meal but she doesn't know how. Whoever heard of an Italian woman who can't cook?

There's never much in the fridge but at least the eggs are still fresh That's good, poached eggs cook super-fast in the microwave and stale bread works fine for toast.

I look back at Dora once the meal is ready and see she's slid down to lie stretched out in the warm spot I left when I got up. I'm surprised the beeping microwave and popping toaster haven't woken her up but maybe she didn't sleep well last night?

I noticed there was only one bed for both her and Viper so maybe she didn't sleep at all... maybe he kept her up all night fucking? No, he wouldn't. He doesn't like her. He calls her *Poison*. But you never know with women, she might have been persuasive. Stupid bitch.

"Hey Dora," I shout and she jerks awake. "You hungry?"

She goes to rub the sleep out of her eyes before she remembers the handcuff. Scowling she shakes her head *No*.

It's good to see her cower when I walk over to the bed but I'm only there to free her so she can clean up the kitchen. I don't like going to bed with dishes left in the sink. I'm sure Dora wants to complain about having to do this when she didn't even eat but she doesn't dare.

I lie on the bed again to watch her at work. She's decided to make herself some toast so I guess she was hungry after all, the little liar. Oh yeah, I know all about Miss Dora's lies.

"Dora, finish up and come back to bed. We'll talk tomorrow."

I'm struggling to keep my eyes open but I wait until she's back in bed with my body blocking her in against the wall, before I can let sleep claim me again.

Dora

We're back in the shop and Casso has been tight-lipped all morning, only saying we'll go back to the apartment soon and can talk then. I wonder why he keeps putting it off?

Before he left he'd canceled several days' worth of clients so there's no work reason for us to be here, but he's been busy for the past hour sorting through his papers. He seems to be looking for something.

I just settle in to mull over my escape plan again when I sneeze loudly, twice. I smell smoke! I jump to my feet just as Casso hurries over to the door and the smoke detector sets off its ear-piercing shriek.

He snatches up his laptop and pushes it into my arms while he grabs his cash-box before hustling me out of the room. Billows of stinking black smoke roll down the hallway at us coming from the front of the building. He pushes me down the hall to the back door that opens out from the store room. Fortunately my feet obey because my mind is a muddle of *what?* and *why?* Between the horrible smell and the high-pitched alarm I can't focus.

Casso pauses to think a moment before opening the delivery door then changes his mind and forces me to turn around again to go into the kitchenette. Here he opens the window and taking a cautious look outside urges me to climb up on the sink to get out. I barely reach the ground before he's tumbling down after me.

We run through the alley to the front of the building just as gunfire rings out. Bullets strike the brick wall and sending chips flying in our faces as we race round the corner. Shouts of *they're getting away* come from behind. My heart is pounding and the sound of shooting is overwhelming me, bringing back too many scary memories.

174

Someone set the fire at the front, blocking escape, and then hid at the back door to ambush and kill us. Us? or just Casso? or just me?

Running across the street to where people have already gathered outside the coffee shop, Casso phones Viper instead of dialing 9-1-1. In this neighborhood no one is calling the cops or the fire department – cellphone calls can be traced and nobody wants to get involved. Firebombing – as I later learn it's called – occurs for many reasons, none of them good.

No flames show through the front windows so he asks the barista who serves us each day if he can borrow a fire extinguisher and heads back to investigate. The sudden roar of powerful motorcycles drowns out all noise and once the bikers arrive most of the spectators disperse.

"What the fuck happened here Casso?"

A calm Banger is intimidating but an angry club Prez is especially frightening. He strides over and kicks open the front door. The evidence is clear: we can all see and smell that the fire was caused by gasoline-soaked rags shoved through the letter-box.

"Look they were wrapped around something plastic, like a detergent bottle or even a kid's toy, to cause maximum noxious fumes."

"That was the point, the smoke would drive everyone out through the back where two, at least, were waiting," states Casso dousing the burning pile with the neighbor's extinguisher.

Viper goes down the hall to quiet the alarm. He can't switch it off so he rips it from the wall.

"Fucking thing," he snarls, looking at it dangling from its wires. "We'll get something better put in. We shouldn't even have shit like this, Jesus Christ we own the fucking building."

He goes through to the back door and opens it wide. I see him step outside and look around. With both the front and back doors open the inky smoke is blowing out of the building. The lingering smell is horrendous.

The stench, the scare of the fire, the stress, and constant fear of being beaten culminates in a sick woozy feeling. I don't know how many days I've been held captive, a week at least, and I've been through some brutal shit in that time but this is... ah, too much... I'm done... I can't think any more.

Viper

I'd already been thinking of moving Dora out of Casso's place after spotting the bruises on her leg so seeing her crumple up and hit the floor decides me. Before I can get to her Needles steps up and carries her over to a picnic table outside the coffee shop.

I don't expect the pushback I get from Banger when he flat-out vetoes my plan to bring her back with us. He's a couple of inches taller than me but I'm ready to challenge him when I stop suddenly remembering he's my Prez and I've somehow forgotten that. *Fucking Poison, she's doing my head in,* I think angrily.

"Fuck, man I'm all... I don't know," Banger just snorts at my pathetic apology. He's known me long enough to understand the words don't come easy.

"Viper I can't make the club a target if there's a chance this is because of her. If it is I don't want the people who ares coming after Poison anywhere near our place. We'll find somewhere safe for her while we figure out who's behind this. It might even be something else, it might be Casso, I don't fucking know."

Casso speaks up then saying if it was just the smoke bomb he'd figure it for an asshole walk-in he'd turned down but not with a couple of shooters lying in wait. "They'll be long gone now and the apartment wasn't affected so we can still stay here if you'll cover us with some protection?"

Banger nods, saying that's best. I see the logic but I'm worried. I guess I see Dora as my responsibility.

When Banger asks me: "Why do you care if something happens to Poison anyways?"

I insist: "I don't!" But we both know I'm lying. I'm relieved when he drops the subject and turns to Casso with the promise of a couple of brothers at the shop for a day or so.

"Hardware's making some headway hacking into the Vendetti enterprise so we're hoping for answers soon. He said there was nothing related to this on the Spagnolo machines, but he copied plenty of files with bank routing numbers, shit like that, that we'll use for leverage if we have to. We'll get this shit figured out."

We put a padlock on the busted front door and station a biker there and another round the back. Someone at the coffee shop produced a tablecloth which Needles has wrapped around Dora's shoulders. I can see she's shaky on her feet but I don't go to her, I just watch until she and Casso head upstairs and close the apartment door behind them.

Banger lightly punches my arm then calls out to the rest of our brothers: "Take a lunch break and let's ride!"

The thought of an hour on the road to clear my head sounds like the best idea ever.

Gunfire

Casso

Once we're back in the apartment again where, luckily, there's no reek of smoke I find myself eager to explain. We've got plenty of time since I canceled today's bookings. With the mess and the lingering stink of burnt plastic the shop's unusable anyways.

Bringing out a couple of bottles of wine I pour Loretta, I've always thought of her by her real name, a drink in the one glass I own while I settle down with the bottle for myself. Before starting my story I explain that getting to this place in my life was a journey that took many years and miles.

"I grew up as an only child, an unusual thing in Italy, but I didn't mind because it gave me all of my parents' attention and affection. My parents, Gino and Angela Modicini, and me, Guglielmo, had a loving home full of laughter. From an early age I showed creative ability and skills in music, languages, and most importantly to me: art, especially drawing.

Both my parents encouraged me to pursue an artistic career, and I hoped to go to Florence for my postgraduate studies. Life was good, very good, and my future plans filled me with anticipation and joy.

But just days before my seventeenth birthday everything changed and my world was destroyed... by a man called Cesare Spagnolo. And of course I know you recognize that name Loretta since it's the name of your own father. Turns out he was my father as well."

Abandoning her silence Loretta can't help blurting out: "But that means you... you're.. you're my brother?"

"Yes, I'm your only brother."

"You mean older brother, I have a younger brother–"

"No! I meant what I said. Yes, I am older but I'm also your only brother."

"My only *half*-brother, Casso I have a younger brother called–"

"Ricky is dead."

For a long moment she just stares at me before whispering in a horrified tone: "What are you saying?"

I hate repeating myself so I give her an exasperated look before answering, "I'm saying your younger brother Ricky, my half-brother, is dead."

She gasps a heartbroken cry: "But he was only sixteen–"

"So was I when my world was ripped apart," I snarl back.

"That makes it worse, you know what it feels like. Omigod, omigod, oh no-no-no-no-no." She shakes her head back and forth, so quickly the tears fly out from her eyes. "You're lying!"

"Why would I lie? I'm glad he's dead and I'm like 99 percent sure it was my bullet that killed him. Now stop asking questions and let me continue–"

But she interrupts me again wailing and crying: "Ricky can't be dead, he's just a kid–"

"I always knew you could speak, you bitch, but right now I need you to shut up and listen while I explain everything."

She childishly covers her ears with her hands and shakes her head at me. "No! I'm not listening to you, everything that comes out of your stupid mouth is hateful. I love Ricky and I hate you and I–"

"SHUT UP!!" I roar and she finally falls silent. "Forget about Ricky I'm your only brother now."

"My brother... but Casso you and I... omigod you touched me, and–"

"No! We shared a bed platonically, that's all. I made sure of that. I smacked you in anger when you tried to tempt me but I never gave in." Loretta quickly straightens up, ready to argue, but I wave my hands and tell her: "Wait until I finish, you'll have plenty of questions and we have much to discuss."

She gives a tight nod and I know she'll revisit my statement but now the frown leaves her face as I see her eyes traveling over my face, looking for similarities in our appearance.

Several customers at the shop commented on the resemblance between us but I always explained that's because of generations' worth of intermarriage in Abruzzo, the region our families come from. We both have the fair coloring of light eyes - mine blue hers brown - sandy hair, and only average height – neither of us is tall.

"When Cesare was a young man living in Italy he got my mother pregnant. Already a rising star in the mob there was no place in his life for us. He was to go to America where the Mafia's plans included an arranged marriage for an alliance with the Coccia family. They found an unimportant husband and father for the unwed mother and her bastard son. Luckily for me he was a wonderful man called Gino Modicini who loved my mother and raised me as his own child.

Because of a blood feud in America a contract was taken out on Cesare's life. There are always threats but this danger convinces him he won't have long to live. By now he's married with two legitimate children so he travels back to Italy to bring his firstborn – me – home for the job of body-guarding his youngest son until the boy comes of age.

I have a one-way ticket for him and a passport in the same name. I can get him out of Italy safely but we have to go now, he states.

He knows nothing about me, my life, my wants, my dreams... and he doesn't care. He just figures since I'm blood I can be trusted and since I'm his son he can do as he pleases with me.

I'm reeling from the tremendous impact of discovering my father isn't my father and that my mother kept such a monumental secret from me all these years.

Cesare's roundabout journey has been difficult as he's had to travel incognito and take evasive measures for his safety. He arrives at our home exhausted and short-tempered and my parents are shocked to see him.

I ask my mother *who is this man?* and he immediately gets angry demanding to know why I don't know about him. Mama accused him of being the one who turned his back on us. *We were nothing to you then so you are nothing to us now,* she insists.

He swears a bit before saying *was he at least taught to speak English?* And I answer in that language saying *I'm right here and I can speak for myself.* Mama chimes in bragging that I learned English quickly because I have an ear for languages and an eye for drawing.

He dismisses her words saying *the boy needs to have a different skill-set for America. Can he even shoot a gun?* That's when she loses her temper and starts screaming at him asking *why has he come back after all these years? and why now?*

Cesare tells her not to be stupid, he has to get me out of the country before I'm taken for my mandatory military service. Mama protests *that ended years and years ago, back in 2005* but Cesare accuses her of lying. She starts to laugh at him saying he's the stupid one and in a fit of temper he shoots her. Right in front of me he kills her, my mother. Gino puts up his hands, he knows Cesare's reputation and is full of fear, but me? I'm stunned and enraged.

The whole street must have heard that shot, I think to myself, *because everything has stopped. No squeal of brakes, no children shrieking with laughter, no barking dogs...* I can only describe it as a thick sluggish slo-mo kind of silence as I grab for the gun, twisting his arm just as he fires a second time. The bullet meant for my adopted father goes wide.

Still struggling my fingers find the trigger and the third bullet kills my *real* father. No, not the bullet... me. I killed him. I committed patricide. Cesare falls and the gun goes clattering across the floor.

The noise wakens Gino out of his shocked stupor and he immediately takes charge. *This is an unsanctioned killing,* he says. *Even worse Cesare Spagnolo is – was – a Capo. You have to get out of here, son. They will kill you for this.* I try to argue, after all Cesare killed my mother, but Gino just repeats urgently that what Cesare did doesn't matter and I'm the one who has to get away quickly.

Act the part Cesare planned for you. Fast! go pack while I check his pockets for your papers and money. Then you'll have to head to the airport. When your father doesn't show up you say he told you that might happen and you need to follow his instructions and catch your flight to America.

I do what he says. He's told me he'll dispose of the body. When I cried *No Mama needs a proper burial* he hurries to explain he meant

Cesare's body. Then he'll go to the police and tell them about the visit and Cesare giving me money and telling me to meet him at the airport for a flight out that night. Then he'll say he saw Cesare shoot Mama, which is true, and that he took off taking his gun with him.

The police will go to the airport to stop us but they'll be too late. I'll have left on the afternoon plane while they're still searching for two men called Modicini or Spagnolo.

Gino also tells me that I've always been his son, that he is my true father, and he will always keep me in his heart. I think about his words repeatedly on the long sleepless flight and that's when I decide to make my own plan.

At US Customs I say I'm visiting family and give my father's address but I don't go to his home. I make the choice to enter the United States and disappear. Not far though, because I need to keep an eye on my enemies: my father's family... oh by the way your mother's dead, too."

"What? My mama was killed in the massacre?" Her brown eyes are huge in her ghostly white face.

"Uh, yeah. So you're an orphan like me. Anyhow, I was telling you how I've been keeping watch on Cesare Spagnolo's family in order to exact my revenge against my half-siblings."

"Your r-r-revenge?" she whispers in a shaky voice and I simply smile.

Dora

Casso has told me his story full of things I never wanted to hear. I just stare into his eyes that are the same shape as mine although a different color. Our hair is nearly the same color so based on our looks it's easy to believe he's my brother.

I can't react, I'm frozen because thawing means letting something nasty in. His cold and casual delivery of devastating news leaves me numb. He hates me. He's hated me from the moment he learned of my existence, well before we ever met.

I don't question a word Casso says because it has the ring of truth. I was a kid in grade school when my father went away on a trip and didn't return.

My mother never knew if he was alive or dead. The uncertainty this caused put the organization's affairs into turmoil. My two Spagnolo uncles wanted to run the family businesses until my brother grew up but my mother didn't agree. She allied with her Coccia cousins who insisted on getting involved and we've all lived with the ensuing distrust, feuding, and even violence, ever since.

All I remember of my Papa is a big man who swung me up to sit on his shoulders while calling out *everyone come see the bella principessa [beautiful princess]*. I heard plenty of bad stories as I got older and while those tales were probably true all I ever did was hope he might still be alive. Now I know he truly has been gone all this time and I never got to say goodbye.

I regress back to my seven-year-old self and pointing my finger at Casso – he will never be Guglielmo to me – shout: "You killed my Papa!"

He gives me a wicked grin saying: "I did, Loretta. And almost definitely your brother as well, just as I'm going to kill you, too."

"You already tried at the engagement party, didn't you? It was you who started all the shooting at Portofino's, not some rival family but my own family. You bastard, you... that's right! you are a bastard in every meaning of the word!"

"Yes, you're right, I am! Why do you think I started the fight? because it *is* my family and I'm taking over. Ruling the Spagnolo family is *my* birthright.

You know I had some inside help..." I pause, waiting for her complete attention. I'm eager to explain about the double and triple betrayal by her own family.

"Our Aunt Angie, yeah she's my aunt too even though I'm a year or so older than her, hooked up with a cousin called Tonino and he's using her to strengthen his connection to the Spagnolos. Between the two of them I learned everything I needed to know to infiltrate and then destroy your engagement dinner."

"A-A-Angie helped you?"

"Well, to be honest? she didn't realize what she was doing. She was just making conversation, and maybe bragging a bit about her position, to Tonino and he passed it all on to me. I didn't trust him enough to enlist his help beyond sharing gossip so I put together my own crew. I didn't expect him to survive the night but I guess I should have realized that he'd be one of the first taking cover under the tables. Huh!"

"I talked to Angie and... and she made it sound like Tonino was saying it was on me because I was with the FBI..." her voice drifts off in confusion.

"I know, I heard all about it. He's the one who colluded – with me – but it was you he was blaming. I also heard how they stole your money. You really aren't loved by anyone, are you Loretta? oh excuse me, *Poison*. You're getting betrayed from every side.

And they didn't report your phone-call or your whereabouts, either. She might have, I mean maybe she didn't totally hate you..." I say doubtfully, mocking her. "But Angie listened to Tonino instead. He told her to wait while he tried to figure out a way to profit from the knowledge. And she agreed. Your Auntie Angie chose her boyfriend's scheming over the chance to save you from these dirty bikers."

I don't want to let go in front of him but I can't help myself. I'm sobbing because the shock and the sadness are just too much. Gulping a deep breath to steady myself I ask "How do you know all this? Is it something to do with where you went?"

"Clever girl, aren't you? You're right again, I had to go out and meet Tonino. I didn't know what he wanted – he wouldn't say over the phone, more of his cloak-and-dagger nonsense - so I had no idea what my next steps would be. Turned out it was all taken care of quickly once he told me everything he knew. Too bad he brought our auntie along with him, it meant I had to kill her too."

I'm no longer shocked by his words but I am in shock, traumatized, and only reply dully: "Angie and Tonino are dead?"

"Yeah, I did you a solid there."

He thinks he's done me a favor? I wonder, closing my eyes to escape for a minute.

"Dora!" he calls loudly to bring back my attention, "I haven't told you the best part of my plan."

188

Tears streaming down my face I just stare at this monster who shares my blood.

"The best part will be killing you," he states with a maniacal grin.

"Fuck you, you piece of shit!" I scream throwing my wine in his face and racing for the door but as usual he locked it as soon as we came in.

Terror makes me clumsy as I scramble for the key and he catches me with a blow across my temple hard enough to make everything fade to black.

Casso

Oh great, now I gotta wait till this bitch comes to, I think, frustrated and annoyed. *Might as well do what I can while she's out.*

Her body is pliant as I strip off her clothes. Running my hands over her arms I marvel at how soft her skin is. She's smooth as silk, too. Hairless, except for the places where hair belongs, but with no pimples or birthmarks or anything like that. I had planned on tattooing my ownership but never got around to it.

In fact, I'd love to mark up this smooth flesh with an intricate colorful design but I'd just be wasting my time. Besides, all she deserves is having her biker nickname carved into her ass.

Pulling her wrists together I wrap my belt tightly around them. Glancing down at her long thighs makes me wish I was using the belt to whip painful stripes across them I really want to hurt her. So far she's only had a taste of my anger but I'll unleash the full might of my rage when I beat her to death.

Loretta will wish she'd taken the bullet meant for her at that party.

I don't handcuff her to the bed because I'm going to need to move her body into different positions while I'm using and abusing her before the killing. I won't rape her, that would be sick, but I will torture her for maximum pain.

When I pull her into an upright position on the bed her head lolls forward. I lift it by yanking on her hair and my hand comes away bloody. I've heard that head wounds bleed a lot but I hope she isn't concussed. She can't slip into a coma, she needs to be fully aware of what I'm doing to her.

It's only right. Her and her brother destroyed my life so now I'm destroying theirs. That's justice. Once I avenge my mother's death I will take my rightful place as head of the Spagnolo family. When they see that I'm the one who stepped up they'll realize I'm my father's true heir.

Young Ricardo died quickly but Loretta won't. I'm going to take my time to cause maximum pain for her and maximum pleasure for me. Torture and torment, beating and slicing...... *WAKE UP!!!* I shout in frustration at her unresponsive body.

Dora

I wake up woozy and with a pounding headache. From this angle on the bed I can see a bit of the window and it shows a darkening sky. Twilight? We got home about noon so we've been back for about five hours? Ugh, trying to figure this out only makes my head hurt worse.

Then I remember.

All the horrible truths Casso has revealed, the losses I've suffered, the complete devastation of my family, his cruelty...

Casso is ranting in Italian and while I understand the words I can't grasp the meaning, the sounds are annoying gibberish. *Damn this man! I've got one nerve left and he's pressing on it,* I complain to myself.

I try to push up off the bed only to discover my wrists are tied together with his belt. The same belt that he's been using on me for days now. That's when I realize I'm naked. Naked, bound prey.

He turns to me with a horrible expression on his face. His lips are flattened so tight the glimpse of teeth looks like he's grinning but there's no humor, his look is feral. His excited state shows in the glittering of his eyes. It makes me so scared. My throbbing headache still exists but pure terror focuses me on the danger posed by my captor, my half-brother.

"Casso, listen!" I plead desperately. "No one cares about me, they haven't tried to rescue or ransom me. There's no one to stop you from taking over the family. You don't have to do this—"

He interrupts me with a hearty laugh, long and loud, like I've said the funniest thing ever. The sound sends me to the edge of panic and I can hardly catch a breath. How can I choke on air? No, it's not air but the lack of it. My throat is closing. I'm going to die of fear, of a heart attack or a stroke.

"You're right, Loretta, I don't have to kill you... *but I want to.*" Casso flicks open a switchblade and it's like a light switch goes on behind his eyes making them sparkle and shine with his mad blood-lust.

Gasping to drag air into my lungs I cry: "No, No! NO!"

His gleeful laughter is cut short by someone pounding heavily on the door.

I recognize that the curse words Casso spits out in Italian are very bad swears. Furious at the interruption he angrily stalks over and flings the door wide. His belligerent demand becomes a garbled gurgling when a bullet catches him in the throat. He falls outside, and the second gunshot misses him to hit me in the arm, but the third shot goes through his eye into his brain.

It all happens so fast I can't move, I can't even blink. I haven't felt the pain of my bullet wound yet. I'm hyperventilating, paralyzed with fear, but the unseen gunman goes clattering back down the stairs and I hear the roar of a car's engine and squeal of its tires as it peels away.

There's a perfect moment of absolute silence and then my loud harsh breathing shakes me out of my shocked state. Casso told Viper and... and someone, I can't remember – I can't think! – but just the other day he said that I could scream my head off here and no one would ever hear me. That means there's no one heard the gunshots. No one will call the police.

I can't stay here but I can't run. I'm tied up and naked, plus it's dark now and I don't know where I am. I don't even know what city I'm in. Freedom doesn't mean much when there's no where to go.

The light from the room must be shining out into the night, spotlighting the crumpled body fallen at the open door. Even if the risk of discovery is very low I can't take the chance of attracting yet another predator.

I flick the switch off and grab hold of Casso's foot to drag his body inside so it's hidden from view. It's a nearly impossible task for me. He's not an especially big man but that expression about dead weight is true! but so is the super-human strength we can find through adrenaline-fueled desperation.

I only have to haul him far enough to pull the door closed. Thank God he tied my hands in front.

Once I've got the door locked I flip the light back on and find Casso's phone in it's usual spot. It was only a few hours ago that he placed it there and now... now he's dead. My teeth start to chatter from the cold that's emanating out of the very heart of me.

I don't even hesitate when I make the call.

Risk

Viper

I'm just thinking about getting some dinner when a call comes in and Casso's name shows up on my phone. All I hear is a girl crying *he's dead, he's dead* but I know it's got to be Dora and that sends me running to my ride.

"I'm on my way. Don't do anything and don't call nobody," I say and disconnect. You can't talk on a mobile while racing through the streets on a bike with loud pipes.

Her choked sobs keep replaying in my head. Damn, I should have brought the pick-up because I'll need to bring Dora and her stuff back with me... I didn't think about that. I always go for my bike when I need to get somewhere fast.

It looks like she listened because there are no emergency vehicles or cops in the parking-lot. In fact the whole street is dark and quiet, with only a faint glow through the window of the upstairs apartment. There's no sign of either of the two prospects we left on guard here.

I hurry up the stairs but come to a quick stop when I see blood splattered over the door. I'm sure she's heard my bike and she must have heard me on those metal stairs but I still call out *it's me, Viper* and the door clicks when it's unlatched. I use my phone to push it open.

Casso's body is right inside the door and Dora's hands are bloody so I figure she dragged him inside. One shot tore open his throat and the other shattered his eye. Seems like there might be a message in that, maybe? All I know is he died quickly but not without pain.

I look at Dora and see that her always pale complexion is now dead white except for a bruise forming around her eye and a trickle of blood dripping down from her nose. Her eyes are staring at nothing until she realizes I'm in the room. Then she brings her hands up to stifle her cry and that smears the blood over her lips and streaks her chin. Her shoulders are hunched and her movements are awkward and unbalanced.

I can see her trembling from six feet away. She's in shock but I can't coddle her, I need answers fast.

"The guy beat you up too?"

"Shot," she answers and now I see she's cradling her arm against her chest. Reaching her quickly I have a look at her upper arm and see where the bullet tore through. A graze, but fucking painful and bleeding like a son-of-a-bitch. Taking off my bandanna I tie a tight tourniquet to stop the flow. When she yelps *hey, that hurts!* I just stare until she loses the attitude.

With her head tilted up at me I see another streak of blood where it streamed from her scalp. I figure she took three different hits to her head and wonder if she's concussed.

"Did you call 9-1-1? Police? Anyone?" She shakes her head and I yell at her to talk now that we all know she can. I can't be soft with her or she'll fall apart and I need to know what's happening.

"He was gonna kill me!" she shrieks.

She's on the verge of a total meltdown and I should slap her but instead I get close up and take her face in my hands and stare into her eyes.

"Deep breath," I tell her calmly.

She obeys but with shudders and gasps.

"I didn't call because I don't know the address here. Where would I tell them to come? and they'd want to know why I don't know and why I'm here and who Casso is to me and isn't that a fucked-up story all on its own? and then they'd ask what's going on and—"

Now that she's started she can't stop yammering on, swearing even, so I reach out to shake her but end up drawing her in for a hug. That seems to help anchor both of us until I realize the girl in my arms is naked.

Holding her away from me I notice that her wrists are bound with a belt. Pushing her long hair out of the way I can see red welts and bruises on her body. I also see her nipples, her full breasts, the curve of her belly, and the pubic hair nested between her round thighs. I've seen her naked body before, on the day Banger made me punish her, but at that time sex was the last thing on my mind.

I draw a deep breath and tell my brain to ignore my dick. I force my thoughts back on track and automatically rub her sore wrists once I've got the belt off.

"What the hell happened here, Dora? some guy shoots Casso dead then strips you and beats you up?"

"No, that was Casso, and he's the one who tied me up," she answers shaking out the pins and needles in her arms now that they're free. This jostling makes her breasts jiggle and I have to force my eyes away. Looking up I spot more bruises blooming on her face.

Suddenly her emotionless calm deserts her as she gasps: "Casso said he was going to hurt me, cut me, and kill me! He had his switchblade out and he was grinning like... like..." She starts hiccuping and panting for air.

"Casso?" Now I'm the one shaking my head trying to make sense of this, sense of calm and quiet Casso acting and talking like... "Hey, we'll figure it out but we gotta get some help here now."

I call the club and ask if anyone's heard from the missing prospects before I explain what I need here. I don't want to leave Dora to go looking for them, or more likely their corpses. I can't understand why I feel angry and protective about the blood on her arm and her beaten body because I hate her, right? Fucking Dora... I mean Poison.

When she starts talking about the shooting I tell her to wait until Needles and the clean-up crew arrive so she only has to tell it once.

"No!" she cries out, "I don't want anyone else to know I can talk."

"The secret's gotta come out now, Poison."

"No, my family and the police, and the FBI are all looking for me. I don't want the wrong person hearing anything about me." She clutches at me drawing my eyes down and my voice is sharp when I tell her to get dressed before the guys arrive.

"But no sleeves, otherwise Doc will have to undress you." For some reason that idea doesn't sit right with me.

Dora gets some sweats out of a drawer but she can't manage to put them on one-handed. I have to put her feet in then draw the fleece pants up over her legs. I'm not wasting time trying to get her into underwear.

I see marks on her back and lightly rubbing my fingers over the red stripes I feel the swollen edges where a strap or belt cut in. There's nothing on her ass except the bandage. I'm relieved to see that it's clean.

I'm gentle as I pull the elasticized waistband wide so it doesn't rub over any damage I can't see. Not sure why that feels necessary but, well, it just does.

She doesn't have a sleeveless t-shirt so I get out my knife to make one noticing that she flinches when she spots the blade. Of course I'm carrying a weapon, more than one actually, but I say nothing and she doesn't comment - just gives me her wide-eyed stare.

The belt marks all over her torso are from a vicious beating, it was abusive and I can't help but wonder what Poison did to deserve it. My face must give away my thoughts because she turns away from me looking ashamed.

It's only afterwards that I realize she's only been hit in the places that nobody sees.

We can't manage to get her into a bra but the shape of her tits and her stiff nipples show very clearly through the altered tee. Taking one of Casso's hoodies I slip it over her good arm and pull it around her. I stand back to look her over and it does the job of covering her fully. Something feels wrong. I take off my cut and remove my own hoodie, exchanging it with Casso's, before putting my cut back on.

Pocketing a switchblade I find on the only armchair I sit down and pull her onto my lap. Her whole body is vibrating and I figure being in a state of shock is making her shiver. I pull her against me to warm up.

Tucking Dora's head under my chin so she can't see Casso's body, I say: "C'mon baby-girl, tell me everything that happened today."

Dora

When Viper trades Casso's hoodie for his own I wonder if it's something to do with DNA evidence? My eyes are drawn to the bulge of his biceps then drift across his chest to the defined abs I can see through his tight white t-shirt. Just because I despise the man doesn't mean I can't appreciate his perfect physique.

Time and place, Dora I admonish myself but yeah, I need a distraction from the pain of the gunshot wound in my arm, the throbbing in my head, and the heartbreaking news from Casso. I have to ignore the fact that I was almost killed otherwise I'll start screaming and won't be able to stop.

I'm not sure why, of all people, it was Viper I called. I just knew I needed him, and I was sure he'd be in Casso's *Contacts*. *Banger* was the first name on the list but I'd never willingly call him!

Viper is scary but... his presence reassures me. Why do I trust him? Maybe I figured I might as well have the tough guy on my side. And thankfully he is tough and hard and mean because I think any show of kindness would do me in right now.

We're sitting in what would be called a cuddle with any other two people but I'm not complaining. The heat I feel emanating from his body comforts me.

In this position I can talk without having to look at Viper or Casso. "Will you talk to the police for me?" I ask.

"No, no way, we never talk to cops," he states firmly.

"But we have to explain—" I begin before he interrupts.

"No, we don't. We just leave Casso here and they'll find him. Eventually."

"But... but that's horrible! and he's a member of Satan's Tears so they'll come to talk to you anyways."

"Don't matter, I won't talk to them."

Now I'm worried. Thinking aloud I say: "The cops will find Casso's body, maybe when someone reports him missing or maybe," I shiver in disgust, "from the smell—"

"We'll place an anonymous 9-1-1- call."

"Oh! That's good. So he'll be found right away and the police will start to look for clues here and in the shop, they'll check his papers and his bank accounts and his phone records. They'll look for his associates, friends, family and someone - probably that woman from the coffee shop - will tell them about me. My fingerprints are all over here and at the shop since he made me go and sit down there with him every day."

"Are your fingerprints on file?" I have to pause a moment to think which makes him tilt my chin up to look at my face, his narrowed his eyes showing that he's wondering why that is.

"No, no I'm good," I hasten to reply, "But people saw us together, people who can describe me. I need to talk to the police otherwise they might think I killed him. I need to explain and—"

"No. I already told you, we don't talk to cops."

"Maybe you don't but I have to clear my name."

"Oh yeah? and what name is that exactly?"

My mouth falls open and I'm left staring.

"You're right," he continues, "You will be a person of interest to the police. Missing, and with no gun left behind? Hmm, you're fucked, sweetheart. I guess I'm gonna have to hide you but I'm sure you'll be happy to pay back the enormous debt you'll owe me, right?"

I can't believe he's actually talking about sex stuff at a time like this. His cruel laughter rumbles right through his chest but I can't fight him because he's absolutely right - the very last thing I want is for the cops to come to me asking questions.

"But I've been shot too and okay you tell me it's just a graze but it hurts like hell, you know."

And although I struggle to contain the emotion overwhelming me I can't hold back the tears and now I'm crying like a baby. I can't bear Viper's contempt right now so I try to pull away but he has a firm hold on me and swear I see a flicker of sympathy cross his face. He quickly smooths his expression back into his usual stern gaze.

"You have motive, Poison."

"What? What are you talking about?"

"You were being help captive in his apartment—"

I interrupt to exclaim: "Only because you put me there!"

He ignores me and continues with: "And he... assaulted you just like a battered wife, a domestic incident."

That comment stops my argument. Of course he saw the marks from Casso's belt and bruises from his fists. It's not right that being beaten embarrasses me, it's not my fault, I'm a victim, but still...

"What did you do to make Casso hit you?"

Anger dries my tears and indignantly I sit up straight so I can look him right in the eye. "What did *I* do? I didn't do anything! He's just crazy."

"That's not the Casso I know so tell me, why did he hit you? "

"Huh! You know nothing about him and I know far too much. He was nasty and vengeful and violent and... and twisted. He's a killer!"

Viper's face changes when those last few words slip out. I do not want to discuss any of that, not with him, not with anyone.

I can't reveal the truth about Casso and me although I see Viper wants to know much more, everything in fact, but the thought of that conversation exhausts me. Everything about today has just been too much.

I let out a big sigh but manage to give him a brief outline of the events leading up to Casso's death... his murder.

Needles

Casso is a mess and beyond any help I can give but I still look him over. I don't know how he scraped his knuckles unless he managed to get in one punch before the shooting started? It's not my job to speculate, just observe and note the factual information. The girl is holding up really well considering the physical and mental trauma she's suffering. Maybe she's in numbed shock after witnessing the killing of her captor? boyfriend? and getting shot herself.

The damage to her face is superficial, just a bloody but not broken nose and a black eye, but I'm concerned about a heavy blow she took to her head.

The bullet's done some damage and she'll have a fair-sized scar. Shame, she's a pretty little thing, but she can always wear long sleeves.

I've specifically noticed her arm because it's so smooth and unmarked. It's also the only part of her body I can see since she's drowning in an oversized hoodie and sweatpants. Normally I wouldn't think twice but when I held her at the waist to angle her into the light she squeaked a yelp of pain and her body flinched.

After giving me a frightened look she refuses to meet my gaze so I get Viper's attention - easy enough since he hasn't taken his eyes off me - and tell him I'll be examining her back at the clubhouse where I have a basic clinic set up. He's royally pissed at me and scowls at her. I'm sure there's a story here.

I was curious about this girl and her state of mind long before I met her. I'd seen glimpses of her at the clubhouse, and heard stories about how Viper came to pick up a mute girl. I'm very conscious that he's watching my hands intently as I deal with Dora's injury. His intensity is revealing but I'm careful to keep my thoughts, and the slight grin I feel tugging at my mouth, hidden. Viper has a vicious temper.

Why is he so protective of this girl? is it a Hero Complex since he rescued her? from what I heard he's the one who was a danger to her in the first place! However, complexes and fantasies aren't grounded in reality but in perception. He probably couldn't, wouldn't, acknowledge that this girl means something to him.

I'm going to enjoy watching how it plays out. All human interactions interest me, and, happily, despite my forty-six years of living I can still be surprised.

When I scooped her up after she fainted at the tattoo shop I was struck by how tiny and lightweight she was. Barely an inch over five feet and weighing about a hundred pounds. Casso was a short man compared to the rest of us but even so he would have towered over her.

Now I find myself wondering about the shadows under her eyes, her timid nature, the abrasions on Casso's knuckles, and this girl's apparent physical pain... am I adding 2 plus 2 to get 5? or is there a secret being covered up?

I'll be able to study her better when I get her on my examining table but for now I see a very frail and feminine young woman with her pretty face and waist-length hair.

I think I'm starting to understand Viper's protectiveness.

Viper

Seeing tears stream silently down Dora's face almost did me in. Luckily she found the anger she usually feels for me and got herself over that weak moment. Now it looks like Needles is finally finished pawing over her. Thank Christ! I was just getting ready to say something.

The prick is saying he's not done yet and will check her more thoroughly back at the clubhouse. Asshole is yanking my chain... fucking doctor. He is a real doctor although he lost his license to practice. That was for fraud, double billing or something, there was never any complaint about his medical skills. Banger brought him into the club and he's been a good addition. Still... he's getting a little handsy with Dora.

I leave him to clean up the scene a bit before the cops come around investigating. Needles had to bring another two prospects because it turns out the idiots who were left here to guard the shop left after their so-called *shift* was over. Fuckheads. Seriously, how could anyone imagine for one second that it's okay to leave your charge unprotected?

If there's anything left of them after Banger's finished his shit-kicking I'll have a go.

I've told these guys to remove anything pointing to Dora: clothing, toothbrush, hairbrush, the sort of thing cops use for evidence. God knows what they'll bring back to the clubhouse. And I said they need to drag Casso back out into the doorway with Needles to set up his body in as close a match as he can to the blood splatter on the door.

Casso's keys lie tossed on a table in the entrance so I take them to check out his office in the tattoo shop. I bring Poison along to show me what, if anything, is missing. So far I've honored her request about the talking thing. I'm not committing to it, though. That's Banger's call. She was still clutching Casso's mobile when I got here so I pocketed that.

Having had ink done in Casso's workroom I already know it will be clean and sterile so it's no surprise that his office desk at the front is just as tidy. I guess it can't get cluttered when there's so little stuff. I take his laptop, check-book, and cash box.

I think about wrecking the place so it looks like a robbery but decide that will take too long. There's a filing cabinet that I eye with consideration but there's no lock so I figure it won't have anything private. No, I'll have Hardware look for whatever secrets Casso has hidden on his phone and computer, and in his bank account.

When we leave the shop the guys have just finished their work upstairs. Casting a critical gaze over the placement of the body - it's no longer Casso to me - I give a silent nod of approval. The prospects get back into their cage, a beat-up old Dodge Neon, and I tell Needles to pass on a message to Banger.

"We're going to stop and eat something now so I can just put her straight into a room when we get back. We can check her out tomorrow."

His eyes flick up at me when I say *we* but wisely he doesn't comment. "Tell Banger I can talk to him tonight or tomorrow, whenever he likes."

I don't like the way Needles' eyebrow twitches when I mention a room, it's not like I said my room or anything, but when I squint at him his face has no expression. He doesn't reply, just imitates my earlier silent nod before climbing on his bike.

I hand Dora my helmet and ask if she's ever ridden before.

"You mean on a motorcycle?" I don't even bother answering that stupid question and she doesn't say anything more, just struggles with the helmet until I take over and get the strap buckled properly.

"You press against my back and hold on to me as tight as you can. When I lean you lean with me, don't fight against me, I'm not going to let you fall off. These pipes get hot so keep your feet on these foot-pegs all the time, even if we're stopped. You're probably too small to unbalance me but let's not test that, okay?"

I mount the bike and she slips on behind me. Checking that her feet are properly placed I grab her wrists and pull her much closer although I'm careful not to yank her injured arm. Her reach isn't long enough to wrap all the way around me but I can see her small hands gripping my cut. Under the circumstances I'll allow it this time.

Smiling to myself I decide to race and weave and scare her until she's clutching me with her hands white-knuckled. Of course Poison ruins that plan. No matter how fast I speed, or how much I dip and swerve, or how many horns honk at us for cutting them off this girl shows no fear at all. In fact, I feel her thighs pulsing where she's pressed in to me as the fingers of her hot little hands massage me.

When we arrive at the diner she's starry-eyed and breathless and simply says *wow!*

Dora

Wow! I don't ever want to be driven in a car again, not after that ride. No wonder they like their motorcycles so much, such a thrill and that's as the passenger! What would it be like to drive the bike?

The excitement overcomes all the fears these last couple of hours brought and I'm happy to let it.

Viper helps me take the helmet off and although his face is wearing its usual hard look there's a distinct twinkle in his eye. I'm pretty sure he was showing off for me and I can tell that he's pleased I enjoyed the ride.

"That was exhilarating!" I exclaim.

"Oh *exhilarating* is it? Fancy word, Poison."

"Fancy ride, Viper."

He blinks at me after I say his name and wondering if I've overstepped I ask: "Is that okay? me calling you by—"

"It's fine," he cuts in. "Or call me VP. Either is fine. But even better? don't talk to me at all unless I ask you a question and then all I want is a yes or no answer."

Hmmph, that moment of joy was short-lived, I think but keep the thought to myself. Instead I follow him into this place called *Pancakes Plus!* full of curiosity. I've never been inside a diner and it looks just like I'd expect from TV. A standing sign tells us to seat ourselves and we slide into a booth facing each other.

I'm relieved to see that the tabletop isn't sticky and the cutlery is perfectly clean even though the serviettes are made of paper.

A moment later an overly made-up woman with a tight perm in her too-dark hair simultaneously puts down glasses of ice-water, hands us large plastic-laminated menus, and gestures with a coffee pot.

Following Viper's actions I turn over the cup in my saucer and she expertly pours without a splash. No one has spoken a word yet. I feel her eyes studying me before she says she'll be back to take our orders.

Suddenly, I'm conscious of my black eye, gauze strip on my forehead, and bandaged arm. I didn't feel any pain while riding on the bike but it's throbbing now. The headache never did go away. Viper seems to remember my injury as well because he says I can get a pain-killer back at the clubhouse and I tell him thanks.

I want to read every item on the menu but Viper, after a quick glance at the contents, tells me we'll be having the All-Day Breakfast and takes it out of my hands. That signals the waitress to return and I answer all her questions: eggs scrambled, bacon for my meat selection, whole grain toast, and hashbrowns instead of pancakes. Viper must hear the hesitation in my voice because he tells her to bring me both and I grin happily at him. Of course he just narrows his eyes at me and makes an odd sound behind his closed lips.

Our meals arrive quickly, before I've even finished my coffee, and there's so much food! I grab the salt shaker and immediately dig in. After shoveling a few mouthfuls down my throat I catch Viper's look and am amazed to see he's smiling. Of course my cheeks are puffed full of food so I probably do look funny. I cover my mouth and ask *what?*

"When's the last time you had a meal?"

I have to think for a moment before answering: "Yesterday morning when you got that take-out breakfast. It seems like that was so long ago! Oh and I had a piece of toast late last night. Today we didn't eat, we drank some wine but never got around to having any dinner..." My voice trails off when I remember why not.

"Well eat some more and when you're ready to slow down enough so you can talk without choking on your food finish telling me everything about today."

Nodding, I follow Viper's instructions.

He takes me through the part about the gunman again and asks a bunch of questions.

"So you can't describe him because he was wearing a ski-mask or had his hoodie pulled way down or something? Is that why?"

"No, I told you, I never saw him at all. I don't even know if it was a him. Casso opened the door and bullets came through. I didn't see who did the shooting and have no idea what he looked like, or how tall, or if he was a white guy, or what kind of a build.

I do know that there was only one person on the stairs because I only heard one set of footsteps but someone else could have been waiting at the bottom or in the car."

He leans in, interested, saying: "Yeah, you mentioned a car. Tell me about that again."

"Tell you what? I didn't see it and I don't know much about cars. I heard the door slam—"

"Just one door?"

"Oh, yeah, just the one slam. That's right. Then it raced away and it was loud."

"Loud? Like revved up with a powerful motor or noisy from a damaged muffler?"

I just shake my head at him saying: "I have no idea."

Viper doesn't scowl at me but he isn't happy with the scant amount of information I can provide. At some point our waitress had come by and placed the bill facedown on the table. Viper turns it over and standing up fishes several bills from his pocket that leaves them with the check. I get up as well and see him catch the woman's eye and nod.

As we walk to the door she hurries over to collect her payment. I guess he tipped well because she calls a *Goodnight and thanks, Hon* after us.

The ride back to the clubhouse is over all too quickly.

Viper

I'm not sure why but everything is irritating me. It must be because of the talk I had with Dora. I know she's holding back but not about the shooting. It sounds like the killer didn't even know she was in the place.

She was pretty graphic about the beating Casso laid on her. But I could tell she was skirting around the truth when she talked about her conversation with him. So what's she hiding? It must be something about her and Casso and why he hit her.

I don't understand how any man who calls himself a man could beat up on a woman. I mean I was an enforcer so there were times when I had to inflict pain, like Poison's punishment, and I could kill a chick if I had to, but to punch and kick somebody so much weaker than me? Why hit when they'd be so easy to subdue?

We're back in my room at the clubhouse and I'm watching her unpack that stupid shopping bag. She has practically nothing in it but there's that fucking tampon box again. She tries to hide it when she catches me looking.

"What's in this fucking thing?" I demand, striding over and snatching it up.

The box doesn't weigh anything but I dump the contents on the bed anyhow. Several wrapped tampons fall out along with one opened packet. Opened? I pick it up and yeah, there is a tampon in there but when I stick a finger inside I feel something hard. I pull it apart and a ring with a huge diamond tumbles out. Matching earrings follow. Caught in the beam of the overhead light the three stones shine brilliantly.

I'm shocked and when I look at Dora I see she's got a scared look on her face.

"What are these worth?" I growl at her.

"My freedom?" she asks tentatively.

I just stare, getting angrier by the second, and she talks fast.

"Viper, these are really expensive jewels. They're my *insurance policy* but if you help me escape they're yours. They're worth a lot—"

"So am I," I interrupt.

She stops, surprised at my words, then starts chewing on her lip again while reaching to grab my forearm, stroking and massaging, anxious to persuade me.

I fling her off, she's only trying to capitalize on the friendliness of the last couple of hours. This little cunt thinks she can manipulate me. That fucking pisses me off so much. Why would she think, for even one second, that I'd just let her leave? Keep the diamonds and sneak her out? like fuck! what kind of man does she think I am?

This is what happens when you act nice, the bitches always take advantage, not caring who gets hurt in the process, just so long as they get what they want.

"You're not going anywhere and I'm taking these anyhow," She grabs the jewelry but I'm stronger and it doesn't take much squeezing to force her hand open. It's not her injured arm but she still starts to cry.

"Viper, please, please don't take my diamonds," she begs. Even if you don't let me go now well someday you will and I'll need them to live on."

I feel my lip curl in contempt as I tell her *don't worry about that 'cause there's no guarantee you're gonna to be living much longer.*

That comment chokes off her sobs so I continue, rubbing it in: "I have a ton of money. I earn plenty as VP of this club and I don't spend on anything except my bike. You, on the hand, have nothing and the only way you can earn money is on your knees."

She gives me such a confused look I spell it out: "Sucking dick, Poison. That's how a chick like you pays her way. So, are you still anxious to leave?"

I reach in the pocket of my jeans and pull out a couple of twenty dollar bills. "Tell you what, I'll give you this cash if I can fuck your throat and I'll give you more if you swallow my cum."

She backs away from me with her hands going to cover her mouth. Every bitch in this clubhouse will blow me without needing payment of any kind but fucking Poison looks like she's gonna heave. *We'll see about that,* I think *but not right now.*

I give the door a good slam when I leave to go find Banger.

Banger

Hardware and I are sitting in the meeting room drinking coffee. I'm not sleeping well so caffeine isn't going to be a problem, and I've been putting away too much booze lately.

Hardware is really into health and fitness so he's never been much of a boozer.

Viper comes in with a face like thunder. It looks like he's barely hanging on to his temper which isn't great at the best of times. He marches over to the fridge and I'm surprised to see him grab a bottle of water instead of beer. He chugs down half of it before joining us at the table.

"So, Poison's back with us again, huh?"

He tries scowling but that just makes me laugh. "Needles told me. He said he needs to check her over, there's something wrong, something more than the gunshot wound, I guess. Anyhow, Casso shot and killed? what the fuck is that all about? First the fire and then a shooting but who is the target? was it Casso? or is it Poison?"

"That fire was just to flush them out. The shooting of one or both of them was gonna happen one way or the other. But I think they were only after Casso because the killer didn't go into the apartment to look for Poison."

"Yeah well it shouldn't have happened on our watch. If our prospects weren't such fucking retards... what the hell were they thinking? that this is a nine-to-five job for fuckssakes? If Casso wasn't already dead I'd let him kill them. Do you think Poison might want to take a shot?"

I'm joking but Viper answers seriously saying he's pretty sure Poison is glad to get away from Casso. His face gets a closed-off look so I guess he's not ready to tell me about that yet. The two of them have been living in very close quarters and, well, things happen and I'm guessing Viper's not too happy about that.

In the silence that follows Hardware opens up his laptop, the iPad is already on, and starts showing us what he's found out.

"I finally got through the firewall protecting the Vendetti's files and learned a lot. Both mafia families have their hands full struggling to rebuild after the loss of so many among their leadership. That engagement was a really big deal which is why all the top people attended the dinner.

It really was a massacre and Dora's lucky she escaped because not many did. The end result is she no longer has a position with either the Spagnolos or the Vendettis. Her *fiance* is dead and there's no one suitable to take his place - yeah, that's actually a thing with these people. Plus, from the Spagnolo side her brother and a bunch of uncles are gone so there's no one to take charge of her. Neither family wants her.

Believe it or not there was some back-and-forth arguing over the dowry that was paid but the Vendettis claim the heirloom jewels she was wearing are missing—"

Viper interrupts by opening his fist to drop a diamond ring and earrings that he was clutching. Even though none of us are experts we can tell these are the real deal. Each of the three pieces contains a big diamond and do they ever sparkle!

"When I discovered them with Poison's things she tried to bribe me."

"Good thing you're such a stand-up guy," I crack and Hardware laughs along with me. Even Viper's lips twitch.

Hardware continues saying: "The families are going to call it even financially. The important news is they've pieced together enough intel from the guys they caught and tortured to know it was staged by a gang, not a rival family.

These young punks thought they could take out the competition and they were led on by some Italian guy called Guglielmo who planned to claim his birthright as one of the top Capo's successor.

These Vendettis are cold as ice because their emails show that they're waiting to see how it plays out. If this bloodthirsty son is victorious taking over the Spagnolos they *might* kill him as revenge for Walter but they're also thinking *such a man would be a ruthless and worthy ally*. I guess that's how they became the most powerful mafia family in the region - by acting with their brains instead of their emotions.

Anyhow, most of the gang was also killed that night at Portofino's. I mean what were they thinking? every person in the place was probably armed to the teeth plus they all have bodyguards following them everywhere. The conclusion is that the gang started shooting, the families turned on each other, and the FBI were forced to move in from their surveillance position. It was a bloodbath."

"So as far as we know this *Google-mo* guy hasn't been killed yet?"

"No, he got away but they're looking for him—"

I interrupt asking: "What's Casso's real name? I knew it but I forget what it was."

Viper pauses a moment to think then says "Will, well I guess it's William? or maybe not, maybe Will is the short version of an Italian name."

"Oh, okay forget that. So, the mafia hoods are going after those gang punks, right?"

"Yeah, they're taking out everybody and that includes killing the gang members' wives and even their kids."

"Fucking mafia, they're fucking animals."

"Which is why we're happy to keep quiet about Dora, right? I mean, they've known for what, two weeks now? that we have her but thank Christ nobody's reached out."

"She phoned her aunt who's involved with some guy, some cousin, who maybe decided to keep quiet about it? Dora said she left a bunch of money with this woman so probably him and her decided to keep the cash and cut her loose."

"Motherfuckers..."

Viper explains: "From what Dora told me the family won't want nothing to do with her now. She's been living here with us bikers which means she's *tainted goods*. She said Walter won't marry her now, but of course she doesn't know he's dead. She thinks her younger brother will want her back but maybe just to kill her - she doesn't know he's dead either. You're right, they are all motherfuckers.

Anyhow, we know the FBI was involved too, but I guess you can't get in to their shit, huh?"

"Welllll," Hardware draws it out and tells us we don't want to know how but he did manage to access some pertinent stuff.

"And you owe me for a laptop because I had to buy a throwaway for one-time use but it didn't cost that much. Anyhow, I intercepted a cryptic message referring to the date of the party and stating that *the asset no longer has value* so they've decided *not to pursue that option*. So it looks like everything's being swept under the carpet."

"And to hell with the girl who got caught in the middle? That sucks... and you know what's worse? that *we're* the best thing that happened to her." I shake my head to think of the little mafia princess cut loose by everyone in her world and our government as well.

"Hell Viper, that means she's all yours. You figure out what you want to do to her, with her, whatever. I'm letting you make this call."

He gives me a surprised look and I chuckle before saying to Hardware: "We should probably get popcorn for this shitshow!"

The huge enforcer is surprisingly handsome when he laughs, no longer intimidating. "Prez I'm gonna take a pass on that. Needles dropped off that stuff from Casso's office so I want to get started on breaking into his computer."

"You got his phone, too?" Viper asks.

"Yeah and his checkbook so I've got everything I'll need to get into his bank account too."

"Well, let us know what you find out once you dissect Picasso's life."

Hardware nods and gets up to go. Giving Viper a hearty smack on his shoulder he tells him: "You're a lucky guy, VP."

Viper

I curse loudly when I see Fiona lurking in the hall waiting for me, it's getting to be a habit with her.

"Here we fucking go again, eh Fiona? What do you want?"

"I'm not the problem Viper, that girl is. It's way too risky having her here, she puts us all in danger."

"Really? and what do you know about it?"

"I know that her family hasn't come for her and the mafia doesn't appear to be pursuing so—"

I interrupt her angrily demanding: "How do you know about this?"

"I heard you guys talking—"

"Eavesdropped, you mean. Like a nosy spy!"

"No, I was just next door—"

Again I cut her off, sneering: "Well you shouldn't have been anywhere near us."

"I can go where I want, I'm a daughter of this club!" she retorts.

"You were... until you tried to become its queen."

"Oh for crissakes I was punished already, aren't you ever going to forget that?"

How can she even ask me that? "No, of course not. I will never trust you, never."

"Fine then, forget about me and think about the club. If nobody's after that little bitch you can cut her loose. That story you told sounded like she was already running away so just let her go so she can keep on running. Viper, listen, the FBI's involved and the club can't afford a RICO investigation. She's going to bring all kinds of heat on us."

"That's not your concern, Fiona. so stay in your own lane."

"It is my concern, this is my club too and it's my family too. Have you got a thing for her or something?"

"Again, not your concern if I do but you seem to be forgetting that she witnessed me commit a murder."

"Then kill her if you're worried about that."

"You've always been a cunt Fiona but you've gotten nastier as you age."

"Oh fuck you, Viper!" She yells, before whirling away.

Seeing her give in to anger and frustration makes me feel better but I can't ignore what she's said... and Banger's put the decision right on me.

Exposure

Viper

The painkiller Needles gave Dora last night knocked her right out and she was already sleeping by time I finished arguing with Fiona and got back to my room. I let her sleep.

She must have needed the rest since she was still sleeping soundly when I woke up. Having her warm body cuddled against me again felt good, but I left her alone and went to shower and get dressed for the day. By then it was ten so I woke her up.

I like seeing her smooth young face looking so serene while she sleeps. She'd put her long hair into a braid but it loosened during the night and now long strands are spread over the pillow.

She's a beautiful girl and I don't know how Casso could bring himself to hit her. The marks showed that he didn't just slap he actually punched. Her explanation about why wasn't very satisfactory but I'm sure the whole story will come out.

"C'mon Dora, Needles wants to check you out so let's go get it over with."

Her expression is slightly dazed when she blinks her eyes open. Her delectable mouth widens in a yawn as she rubs her eyes like a little kid. I have to think of her as a child, otherwise I'll be tempted to shove my cock down that wet, pink throat.

She sits up and swings her legs to the floor then pats herself down checking if she's still fully dressed.

"You slept in yesterday's clothes but you can just come as is because Needles said *don't shower*, remember? He wants to change that dressing first."

She nods and gets up. I follow her down the hall noticing that my hoodie is way too big but I like seeing it on her. I direct her to Needles *clinic* – two rooms we knocked together – where he does his thing and, if necessary, can keep a patient recovering on a cot under supervision.

As we walk through the door Dora stops and turning to me says: "You don't need to be here." So much for keeping her secret.

Needles looks up with a grin agreeing with her: "Yeah, Viper you can leave, Dora's in *real good hands,*" and he chuckles. He's deliberately trying to piss me off but I keep my cool.

"You can't needle me, Needles. Actually I'm here 'cause I'm keeping tabs on my property."

Dora narrows her eyes at me and snaps: "Your what?"

"Oh didn't I tell you? Last night Banger gave you to me."

"What!? He *gave* me? He can't do that, I'm a person!"

"Well yeah actually he can, and did. That means I can – and will – do whatever I like with you... to you..." I let my voice trail off hoping I sound sultry and threatening. "This whole time that you've been under our protection–"

"In your custody, you mean."

I ignore her interruption: "You've been Banger's property to dispose of how he likes and he likes the idea of dumping you on me. In fact he likes it so much he thinks it's hilarious."

"You mean my fate is in your hands?"

I smirk at her and confirm: "Yes, my little slave girl."

"Doctor don't bother to fix my arm, let it get infected so it kills me. That's better than the alternative."

"Oh are you bringing me into this conversation now? I've just been patiently sitting here enjoying your banter," he says as we both interrupt him by her squawking *banter?* and me saying *fuck off and just get on with it.*

Needles

"Much as I enjoy watching you two fighting your obvious attraction I've got a busy day and we need to move this along. However, I will just say this one thing: Viper it's great to see you treating a woman with compassion instead of anger or indifference."

Before he can voice his complaint I turn to Dora saying: "Dora hop up here and slip off your... well *someone's* hoodie, so I can take a look at your arm."

Pointedly ignoring Viper the girl complies with my request and I'm pleased to note that no blood has seeped through the bandage. Unwrapping the gauze I gently probe the torn flesh checking for discoloration and seepage, then lean in sniffing for any bad odor.

Even before I pull back I can feel Viper's hot gaze silently urging me to keep my distance. Although I've pressed my lips tight together I know I've failed miserably at hiding my smile.

He clears his throat loudly before coming closer to look at the wound with his own eyes. Dora bears it all with calm stoicism. I smear a thick amount of soothing gel over the area then wrap it up again.

"It's looking good, and I'll check it each morning to make sure it stays clean. I don't like prescribing antibiotics for young women on birth control because it can mess up both their gut bacteria and cause yeast infections." I explain.

She states in a very matter-of-fact voice: "I'm not on birth control. I'm supposed to get pregnant as soon as possible. Or at least I was... with Walter, like."

I'm sure it's reflected in my expression that I have no idea what she's talking about. I begin with *Walter?*

"My *fiance*. But he might be dead. I don't know... when the shooting started I just ducked my head down and ran." She drops her voice down when she says: "I was so scared I peed myself a little bit. And when those agents grabbed me I fell and there was blood on the floor so I got it on my legs! but I twisted away and ran for the kitchen because there's always a door outside from the kitchen because, you know, all the garbage to get rid of."

I still don't have a clue what she's talking about but hearing that girlish voice reciting such gruesome details is chilling. I meet Viper's gaze and neither of us is smiling. It's obvious this story isn't new to him but I don't think he's heard these details before.

Now that I've finished bandaging her arm he puts her hand back in the empty sleeve and pulls the material right up to her neck. Then he lifts up the hair that got caught and gently smooths it down her back. She tilts her head back so she can look in his eyes and the zing of their attraction ripples through the air like a tangible thing, even though she shudders and he sneers.

I interrupt their moment by asking Dora to lift up her tops so I can take a look at her stomach.

"Why?" demands Viper but I just wave him off while waging a battle of wills with the blushing girl. She doesn't want me to see which makes me all the more determined.

"It's okay..." she says quietly.

"Dora, when you fainted yesterday and I picked you up you flinched and groaned in pain. Something's wrong so I want you to show me."

With great reluctance she takes hold of the hems of both the oversized t-shirt and the hoodie and slowly pulls them up. Although I'm only seeing what I expect – bruises – the severity makes me suck in a breath. Viper actually growls at the sight of her marred skin. The older bruises have reached the technicolor stage with new, deep purple discolorations lying on top.

Drawing on my professional training I keep all emotion out of my voice when I ask: "How high up and how far down does it go?"

Dora gestures to the top of her chest, just below her throat, then down to mid-thigh. I tell her to lie back and I gently tap on top of her clothes over the area she indicated. She winces even though I pass lightly over her groin and I can feel Viper crowding me, watching every move my fingers make.

"Okay sweetheart, you can sit up. I don't believe there's any organ damage or serious internal injuries. There's been no blood showing up in your urine, right?"

Her voice is barely more than a whisper when she confirms that's right.

"Make sure you tell me if that changes and Dora, look at me." I wait until she drags her eyes up to meet my gaze. "Dora, there is *nothing* for you to be ashamed of. You've been victimized and none of this is your fault. Do you understand?"

I want to comfort her like a hurt child but instead this time I make my voice stern so she knows I'm serious about what I'm saying. Her chin trembles and her face crumples in tears and suddenly Viper is between us holding her in his arms while she cries deep sobs.

His willingness to help her prompts me to speak out: "Since Banger has decreed Poison to be your property it's up to you to provide Dora with pastoral care. Soothe and comfort this girl, she's endured horrific events at least half of which are down to you."

Being Viper he just curls a lip at me but then he scoops her up in his arms and carries her out of the room.

I didn't realize I'd clenched my hands into fists until I go to lock the door. I shake my head at the thought of anyone battering a young girl – any female, actually – like that. I go looking for Banger to make my report.

Dora

Viper Murdoch is the last person I should want to be with right now but I just can't bear the thought of pulling out of his embrace. From the first moment I laid eyes on him his size and strength frightened me... until now. Right now I feel comforted, not intimidated, by his unsmiling face and hard body.

The ordeal of the carving is still fresh in my mind. I'll never be able to forget what he did since that horrible phrase will mark my skin forever. Even though I have trouble reconciling the cruel biker with this man who sometimes looks at me with such tenderness.

Thinking that way is dangerous to my sanity but I'll allow myself to accept that for this moment I desperately need him and need to be in his arms to feel safe. I do feel protected by him, I just don't feel protected from him.

He doesn't speak as he carries me back to his room laying me down gently on the bed. I'm embarrassed about crying so much and I gulp big breaths to choke off my tears but that only makes me hiccup. I'm such a mess. Now he's patting my back and I feel about twelve years old.

Viper carefully pushes me back and when I curl into a ball he gentle straightens me until I'm lying flat. Thankfully he avoids looking at my streaming eyes and blotchy face. Last night I noticed he looked away from my nakedness although he did spot the belt marks on my back because I felt him gently running his fingers over the welts.

He also checked out my bandage which he now tells me can come off and let exposure to the air do its work.

Lying under this overhead light I feel every mark, mar, bruise, and cut is completely exposed to his scrutiny.

His gaze is focused on my bared stomach and his fingers lightly trail over my bruised skin. The waistband of the too-big sweats is loose enough for him to slide it down with just one finger. He strokes the marks on my hips before uncovering me to the top of my pubic mound. I'd forgotten how Casso had marked me there until I hear the sharp hiss of Viper's indrawn breath. "What is this?" he demands, obviously trying to tone down his usual harsh speech.

Propping myself up on my elbows I see the black ink from Casso's marker. I remember when he wrote it. He told me he'd eventually tattoo the words but never said what they were. Afterwards, when I was alone, I studied what was written. I couldn't read it upside-down and using a mirror was no help but by writing down each letter I was able to piece it together. I didn't understand until I'd written it all out because he wrote it in Italian. I speak our dialect fluently but I'm not very good at writing it although I can read some words.

Casso wrote *Proprietà di* which translates to *Property of.* I figured he was going to use a different font for the rest but now I realize he wasn't ready to reveal his real name. Or his secrets, which is why he didn't finish.

Breathing loudly through his nose Viper strokes the lettering and though he's speaking out loud I think he's really talking to himself: "Oh I like this. But in English, of course." He can't stop staring. When a sudden thought occurs he lifts his head to ask: "Who will do our ink now?"

Then he surprises me with an unexpected question: "How come you never said anything to me about Casso beating you up?"

I shrug and reply: "You wouldn't care."

"Fuck Dora of course I would. How can you say that?"

I give a sarcastic laugh explaining: "Well because why would you care about Poison? I mean you knew what Casso was like, right? That's why you took me there—"

"No! None of us had any idea... in fact it's so hard to wrap my head around quiet loner Casso actually hurting you. On purpose."

Another surprise. I shrug again saying, "I thought putting me into Casso's care was just more of my punishment."

"Oh sweetheart no. Didn't I tell you that after a punishment the slate is wiped clean? there's no such thing as *more punishment*. If I'd had any idea..." he pauses for a moment then looking into my eyes with determination confesses that he did spot a big bruise and wondered if I'd done something to deserve it then figured I'd just been clumsy.

"I can't believe I thought that way I, I'd take everything back and fix it if I could." His expression is concerned and earnest as if he really does mean it but that can't be right.

I refuse to let him off the hook although I do think most people, women too, do think that way. I just make a disbelieving *hmmph* sound.

He tries again saying in what I can only imagine is his weird way of offering comfort: "I might execute a woman but I'd never hit one."

I expect I'm looking totally perplexed at that statement and decide we need to move on. "Nobody expects someone they know will just lash out for no reason, I guess nobody wants to believe stuff like that does happen."

"Well it's never gonna happen to you again."

"You can't say *never* because you don't know what the future holds."

"The future... hmm," he says before leaning in and placing the most gentle, tender kiss first on my cheek then on my lips. I'm dumbfounded.

This close I can smell his earthy, woodsy scent. I remember my cousins passing around the different colognes they bought their brothers for Christmas presents and Viper smells like the Dior.

I already know what his shampoo smells like because I used it before in his shower. I reach to touch his long brown hair which is smooth and silky under my fingers.

He holds the back of my head with one hand while the other strokes my face from forehead to chin. All the while his lips are caressing mine in a swoon-worthy kiss. His mouth is warm and tastes delicious. His tongue probes delicately. We kiss for the longest time.

I sigh and he hums in response, a deep and rumbly tone that thrills me. I can't believe this masterful kisser is Viper of all people. I wonder what Needles meant about how he treats women? But I better remember it as a warning.

Viper

Dora tastes so good. I love the feel of her soft lips, warm mouth, and darting tongue though I'm not usually big on kissing. This girl is full of surprises.

Her touch is timid when she reaches up to run her fingers through my hair and she gives a soft, girlish sigh. She's so sweet I have to fight the urge to take a big bite out of her. Not literally but... I want to run my stubbly chin across the tender skin of her inner thighs, I want to mark and scratch and claim her. But I can't.

The evidence of Casso's fists on Dora's body gives me a grudge against the prick who killed him so quickly. He deserved a much harder death. I tamp down a surge of anger knowing Dora needs a gentle hand right now.

Actually I shouldn't be touching her at all. It's too soon. I'm not turned off by the bruises but I am worked up about their cause. There's a really large one just above her hip with a yellow interior that still has a burgundy ring around it. Casso must have stomped down on her with his boots on to cause such a lasting deep tissue injury. Fuck, I wish I'd known...

I just want to kiss everything better, like she's my little girl to tend to and take care of. Fuck me, how did we get to this place? Why does Poison bring out my protective instincts? I've only ever looked after me. I love Banger as my closest friend and the brotherhood I share with the guys in the club has always given me enough of a social life. Until now. With Dora I feel... I feel like I have to keep touching her all the time.

Needles pushed up her t-shirt exposing the damage done to her rib-cage and belly, and I pushed her sweat-pants below her hip-bones but I need to see the rest of Casso's handiwork. And I told her I'd be removing the bandage.

I know she doesn't have underwear on because I'm the one who dressed her. I don't want to break off kissing her but I need to see her face when I strip her because I don't want to hurt or frighten her.

I've done enough damage to Dora. Killing that boy, kidnapping her, handing her over to Cas... I find it hard to meet her eye.

Then I feel her hand lightly rest on my shoulder. I lean my face against it and her fingers caress me. It's crazy that she's the one reassuring me. I give her another kiss hoping she accepts it as an apology.

Then, taking hold of the hem I slowly lift her top up over her naked tits my eyes never breaking contact with hers. Dora assists by raising her arms so I can slide the material over and off. Now that she's topless I hold her gaze for a long moment until I feel her chest heave with a deep breath.

Finally I look down at my girl's breasts and they're beautiful. Round and full with hard rosy nipples. I don't know how long I stare but when I murmur *you're perfect* she exhales loudly and I realize she'd been holding her breath.

With the lightest of touches my fingers skim over her skin. So warm, so soft, such firm young flesh. I want to fill my hands and squeeze but I hold myself back. This isn't just about me guarding Dora from pain, it's about me worshiping her beautiful body.

I've entertained many, many naked women but this moment outshines every experience I've ever had. I am fucking in awe of her beauty, I'm just overwhelmed. Blowing a warm breath over her skin I use just the tip of my tongue to flick her nipple. Her boob swells so now I swirl my tongue around her nipple before taking it in my mouth. I feel it grow even harder as I graze my teeth back and forth. I love her little sighs and gasps.

Moving my mouth to her other nipple I caress the sides of both her boobs to make her shiver with goosebumps. Her pretty tits are thrust forward begging for attention. Now I move just the palms of both hands up and down to skim over her nipples, barely touching them. She arches her back to push her tits up into my hands but I draw back teasing her.

It's a relief to see that other than some redness, probably from slapping? there's none of the damage I'd see if Casso had been punching her beautiful rack.

I already knew her shoulders, arms and throat weren't marked. Casso was cunning enough to keep the injuries hidden. Motherfucking psycho.

How come I didn't see anything that night we spent in the safe house? I think back, trying to remember how she looked and what she was wearing... and the memory makes me smile. Dora was sleeping in one of my t-shirts that came down to her knees and only left her forearms bare. Places Casso was careful to leave untouched.

Yes, I remember now. I liked seeing Dora wearing my shirt to sleep in and we argued over who it belong to and when I insisted *mine* it seemed like we were talking about something else.

Leaning on one elbow I let my eyes roam all over Dora's lovely torso while I lazily trace delicate patterns over the undamaged portions of her super-soft skin.

I keep my fingers away from her bruises but I do trail fluttering kisses over the marred area. Her eyes follow every move I make. She watches my hand then looks into my eyes, watches my mouth then again meets my eyes. She's entranced and her wondering, trusting gaze stirs something inside me, something more than sexual attraction.

Something in her look is saying *I'm yours* and weirdly I feel like I've been entrusted with something fragile and special. *What the fuck! Where did all this tenderness come from?*

Dora

He's got me mesmerized, that's the only possible answer, I tell myself. Just moments ago I was reminding myself that I have to keep the hate alive and now...

Viper is caressing and fondling me with such lightness I can barely feel it except all the visible and invisible hairs on my body are standing to attention. I'm in a pleasant lazy haze of relaxation with the occasional shiver of electricity running across my skin.

I know I'm staring but I just can't believe this is Viper. This calm, smiling man with the sparkling eyes is really Viper the motorcycle club VP: Steve's killer, my abductor, my future something-or-other. My mind can't reconcile this lover with that monster.

What happened? and did it happen to him or to me?

Now he's carefully lifting me over onto my stomach. He scoops my long hair out of the way, spreading it over the pillow and baring my back. I was never able to get a good look at any marks Casso left because I was always too stiff after a beating to be able to twist my head over my shoulder.

Closing my eyes I re-live Casso's vicious rage when he stomps his foot down before kicking me and dropping all his weight on top of me. Viper's growl as he runs the pads of his fingers in lines across my skin tells me I have welts or stripes still left from the belting I took. He doesn't speak but he runs his lips over the whole area, kissing it better. His warm breath soothes at the same time it stimulates me.

When his hands move to the waistband of my sweats I tense up. I experience a flash of memory from the last time he touched my bottom, but he's so considerate in the way he eases the pants down my legs.

Viper gets up and just stands there for a long moment staring down at my body. I don't know why I find it arousing to be naked before him while he's still fully clothed. Viper goes into the bathroom and comes back with a bottle he tells me is *Witch Hazel.*

"I've had one or two black eyes," he says as he smooths the cool, soothing liquid over my punished flesh.

It feels so good, but even better is when he stretches out beside me, pulling me against him with his arm across my undamaged shoulders and his lips whispering sweet promising words in my ear. *Sleep now, sweetheart, I'm here to watch out for you.*

Viper

Today Slash, our club treasurer, is working with me in town so I reluctantly leave my sleeping girl to head out and do my job. The two of us are taking the cash I brought back and depositing it into various businesses that we own or are involved in.

We have to get the money into cash-based enterprises to clean it. Businesses like nail boutiques, tanning salons, coffee shops, and convenience stores. Used to be everyone paid with cash at the hairdresser but not now that the cost of all the fancy treatments keeps going up. The barbershops are still good, though.

We don't want to carry too much cash on our bikes so we've brought a prospect along to drive the car. He got a drive-thru order and is killing time in the parking lot of the fast food joint while we make our deliveries then return to stock up again.

It's not a difficult job but it is time-consuming. Unfortunately for me it's something only top executives of the club can handle because of the sheer amount of money involved. We trust our members but we're not stupid enough to put that kind of temptation in somebody's way. I'm frustrated because I don't want to be here, instead of with Dora, today.

A couple of other guys, maybe Dog and Hardware, can handle the night-time venues: bars and strip joints, a diner, a bowling alley... All-night gas stations would be great but with all the environmental regulations they're a real pain in the ass with inspectors popping by all the time.

Most of us double-up in our duties. As VP I handle a lot of tasks for the Prez to free him up but I'm still on call when another enforcer is needed. I like doing that job and missed it when I first moved up.

I heard plenty about my anger issues when I was a kid and maybe some of that was true because yeah, gotta admit that I do love a good punch-up.

Slash has been a friend for years and I always like working with him. For a number-cruncher he's very laid-back and not fussy or finicky at all. He does have a tidy, groomed look though. Like Banger he wears his hair short and his beard is neatly trimmed.

We're dressed in a similar style but I feel rumpled compared to him. Probably has a lot to do with the fact that I put on clothes that were picked up off my bedroom floor whereas Slash has an Old Lady to look after him.

I never plan to tie myself to a woman. Trish, Slash's wife, is good people so far as I know but that's the thing: you never really know. When life is good the relationship is great but as soon as shit hits the fan then all kinds of truths are revealed.

Fiona's betrayal really hurt but it was nothing compared to that bitch who birthed me.

Women don't value honesty, honor, or loyalty so they aren't capable of providing it. Thank fuck for the club. It gives me both brotherhood and good times.

"Something on your mind, VP?" Slash asks in his mild voice.

I grimace and confess to letting my thoughts get away from me. "I think I'm just feeling a little antsy or something. Between the problems Banger is having, along with Casso getting killed, and then there's Poison to deal with... no wonder I'm feeling fucking stressed."

"Yeah we've all seen that there's something between you and the girl."

"What? No! Why do you even think that?"

244

He huffs a laugh and replies: "Because of the way you look at her, like you're assessing and trying to figure something out - like maybe your feelings for her?"

I categorically deny any such thing.

"Okay, sorry man, forget I said anything—" he apologizes but I stop him.

"No Slash it's me, I'm the problem today. I.. I've got a lot of stuff in my head right now and I'm not good company."

He nods in understanding suggesting: "Once we finish our distribution do you want to ride for a half-hour or so?"

I quickly agree hopig a ride will clear my head from the crazy thought that I'd rather be spending my time at the clubhouse right now.

Dora

I'm completely engrossed in a paperback about English spies that I found on the bedside table so I'm startled when I hear the key turn in the lock, followed by the sound of birdlike twittering.

I expected Viper so I don't know who is more surprised: me or the two girls staring from the doorway. For a long moment the three of us just look from one of our faces to the other, three pairs of brown eyes all wide circles of surprise.

The girls have light brown skin, black hair, tiny noses and bright white teeth in small full-lipped mouths. I think they're Asian. I don't know what language they're speaking. In broken English they say *sorry sorry ma'am* and start backing out the door.

"No wait!" I call. I've noticed keys in one of the girl's hands so Viper must want them to come in here. I spot an upright vacuum cleaner in the hall behind them as well as a cart like hotel maids use. While the key-holder is busy saying *no, no, is okay, sorry* the other girl, who looks like her twin, is chattering away in their own tongue with the occasional English word like *the Mister* and *never* being thrown into the mix.

Seeing that they're about to close the door I fling back the duvet and jump out of bed but now their mouths are as round as their eyes as they gasp. It takes me a moment to realize they expected I'd be naked. I feel the heat of a blush flooding my cheeks. Viper's tee practically reaches my knees so I know I'm suitably covered. I grab the arm of the closest girl and drag her in saying "Come, come in and do your work," and they do.

Immediately they enter a well-practiced routine of dusting, vacuuming, and changing the bed before moving on to clean every inch of the bathroom, taking away the towels and leaving clean ones behind.

I didn't like to interrupt them when they're busy but now that they're on the last chore – emptying the bedroom and bathroom garbage bins – I point to myself and say *Dora*.

The sisters, because they must be, giggle at each other before the leader points to herself saying *Trini* and at the other girl saying *Mexi*. We all nod and smile at each other and then they grab their gear and back into the hall right into Viper.

More apologies and exclamations and Viper just nods and smiles back at them before giving each girl a twenty and sidling past them into the bedroom.

"So Poison, now you've met the house mice."

"The what?"

"That's what the females in the club's *no-sex domestic relationships* are called," he says using air quotes around the phrase. "Usually there's just one living with a biker and taking care of him so it's really house mouse."

"Oh! well that's a different kind of thing, isn't it? These two are sisters, right?"

"Yeah, at least we all think so. None of us speak Tagalog and their English isn't good."

"Neither is yours," I begin but quickly morph that criticism into the question: "What's Tagalog?"

"A Filipino language. We were told everybody learns English at school in the Philippines but I guess our girls didn't get much education."

"I would have expected them to speak Spanish which I can mostly understand because it's close to Italian."

"Well I don't recommend you practice on them if you still want to keep your secret because they report to Fiona and I'm sure she'll be quizzing the mice."

"Omigod I didn't even realize! I've done so well at keeping quiet in front of everyone else—"

"Except you talked non-stop with Needles," he interrupts to say but I brush that comment aside.

"Doctors are different, they're used to keeping confidences, but with these girls it just seemed natural to talk to them. They're so nice, how on earth did they end up working here?"

"It's none of your business but I don't want you asking and upsetting them so just know that they're rescues and we don't talk about it."

"Rescues? Okay. I was so surprised when they came in but Trini had a key so–"

"You already know their names?" he's giving me a peculiar look that I can't interpret but it's Viper, I can't expect him to make sense.

"Yeah Trini and Mexi, she's the shy one."

"They're both shy but you're right Trinidad, the oldest at twenty-seven, does most of the speaking while Mexico, who is twenty-six, just hangs back and nods. I only ever knew their full names."

"Well you're the boss, *the mister* as they call you, so naturally they're more formal around you. I can't believe they're that old!"

"You think that's old? I'm twenty-eight," He seems slightly offended which is entertaining but I'm careful to keep my smile at his vanity in check.

"No, I don't think that's old but I'm twenty-one and I thought they were like fifteen-year-old twins!"

Slightly mollified he agrees saying: "Yeah, they do look a lot younger. Partly because they're so small. I mean you're little but I think they're even shorter."

"I'm not that short, I'm almost 5-foot-2 and that's taller than they are."

"Oh that's too bad 'cause if you really are twenty-one then you've done all your growing so you're stuck being a shrimp for the rest of your life."

I'm wracking my brain for a snarky comeback when I realize he's just pushing my buttons. "Omigod you're teasing me! Jeez Viper what are you, twelve?"

"I guess you're hard of hearing as well as being mute, eh Poison?"

"Oh ha-ha. By the way, they were very surprised to see me here..." He knows I'm fishing for information about how often he has women for sleepovers but he only smirks at me. Flinging my hair over my shoulder I march, not flounce, to the bathroom.

Just before I close the door he makes a *tsk tsk* noise and sends me his parting shot: "When they inspect the sheets the sisters are going to be very disappointed in you, Poison."

I whirl around asking: "What? What do you mean?"

"Well, there won't be much of a mess so they'll probably think you're not doing your job..." He gives an exaggerated shrug to his shoulders and when his meaning becomes clear I squeak an *oh, you!* before slamming the door on his laughter.

I stay in the restroom for a long time and it pays off because Viper is gone when I finally emerge. I'm hungry and head down to the kitchen to get some cereal or something.

I'm surprised to see so many of the club whores hanging around. At first I didn't like referring to them that way but Viper told me that's what they call themselves. They don't consider the label insulting.

These are women with outside jobs who like to chill at the clubhouse in their free time. They're attracted to the biker mystique, I guess. I don't see it myself.

I suppose it's like going to a bar or a casino or a dance hall. They come to socialize and have sex. Now a lot of these men are drop-dead gorgeous – most notably Dog – and they're well-built with muscles on muscles, messy long hair, scruff, and of course all that black leather *hmm*, where was I going with this thought? Oh yeah! There's also the older guys, balding with stringy hair and straggly beards and potbellies and – ugh – they want girlie action too. Double ugh!

Usually the club whores ignore me and I'm happy to stay out of their way. They all stop talking when I come into the kitchen but seeing it's just *Poison-the-Dummy* they aren't worried and resume their conversation.

Peg is speculating about who Banger's wife is shacked up with at the Road Lightning clubhouse but Bebe puts her wise explaining she's not with a guy, she's visiting with her cousin who is the Prez there.

"For this many days? that's some visit. There's gotta be more to it than that."

"You wouldn't be shooting your mouth off like this if Fiona was around," taunts Jennifer. She's a very pretty brunette and seeing her cute pixie cut and big blue eyes you could easily be fooled into thinking she's the sweetest girl but I've watched her in action and she's a sly back-stabber.

Peg isn't bothered, she just flips Jennifer the bird and takes a long drag on her cigarette. None of the women would be smoking in the kitchen if Fiona was here – in fact she'd probably chase them all out regardless.

"Fiona needs to get laid, seriously. I know she's got this love-hate thing going on with Viper but she needs to accept that he ain't interested and get herself some other guy."

"It's got to be hard though when the club Prez is your brother. I mean, no one's gonna fuck her and dump her without any consequences, right?"

"Well then she should be the one hanging around at Road Lightning's place, not Kim," states Peg.

"Oh give it a rest willya? Most likely we'll never know exactly what's going on with her and Banger and who cares? it's none of our business," insists Bebe.

"It will be if Banger is suddenly single..."

"Oh you're right and I call *dibs*. He is one hot hunk of man and he's never been with anybody here–"

"But that doesn't stop him looking when some chick's putting on a show!" giggles Bunny.

Their sniggers sound dirty-minded but maybe that's just me overreacting.

"Fiona won't hang around the Lightning's clubhouse because of Crusher—"

Bunny interrupts Bebe saying: "Can you blame her? I mean we've all heard the stories..."

"Like what?" prompts Jennifer, always hungry for gossip.

"Oh he's into all this S and M stuff, you know Master and Slave and—"

"I don't think that's necessarily S & M, Bunny. I mean, it's like a lifestyle thing for some people."

"He's an enforcer so we already know that makes him a tough guy, plus he's the Road Lightning's interrogator so that makes him a mean guy—"

This time Peg interrupts saying: "And he and Fiona were together for ages so that means he's gotta be a psycho guy!"

The women all cackle with laughter.

Bebe picks up the conversation again stating: "Fiona acts like she's afraid of him – or maybe she's not acting, I mean he is a truly scary guy – but damn if he isn't super-hot." Fanning herself she smiles and adds: "I can't help wondering just how kinky his kink is?"

"You're such a slut," laughs Bunny, giving her friend a shove.

Peg asks: "Who broke it off?"

"She says it was her but nobody really knows for sure."

Having women around seems to be a club necessity but Fiona doesn't like it. I've learned that the members who have *Old Ladies*, a term they claim is the highest honor, don't like the club whores mingling when the wives are around. Worried about tales being told? or is there just too much nudity and public sex on display? apparently that's a club necessity as well.

I fix my bowl of cereal and slink out of the room with my head down. No point inviting trouble. I just get into the hall when I hear the slamming of car doors which means Fiona is back. She probably took Jeremy out on a shopping trip. With my free hand I rap on the kitchen wall and when Bunny looks up I jerk my head towards the outside wall.

"Fuck guys, Fiona's back!" I hear her whisper-yell as I scurry down the hall.

Moments later I hear Fiona's piercing voice demand that "Everyone get the fuck out of my kitchen now! and who the fuck was smoking in here?"

I'm thankful to escape the drama of too many women with too much time on their hands. Unfortunately Viper's back in the room when I return.

His eyes light up when he sees the food. "Oh good, you got me a snack."

"No, it's for me."

"Hmm, maybe it was but it's mine now," he says as he effortlessly relieves me of the bowl.

I fume but I can't exactly fight him over it. He takes a big spoonful and makes *mmm-mmm* noises as he crunches noisily. "So good, but don't pout baby, come and sit on my knee and I'll share it with you."

I try to turn away but it's no use, he easily lifts me onto his lap and makes a big deal out of feeding me.

"C'mon baby girl, open wide for the choo-choo," which makes me laugh. It's so silly but also... kinda cute, kinda nice. I guess he's trying.

Abduction

Needles

I find Banger sitting at the bar eating a late breakfast with Hardware. Our enforcer has been mostly in his tech role lately and spending a lot of time with the club Prez and VP.

"I think we're going to need another enforcer since you're doing so much IT work Hardware." I say by way of greeting.

"It will take at least two guys to replace me, Needles, but I still like getting out there for a workout you know." He gives me his menacing look and I pat his bulging bicep.

"Besides, Viper is always quick to ride along for a job if he's free."

Banger asks me: "So how's Viper's girl doing, Needles?"

"Viper's girl is right. The sparks going off between the two of them is...wow. But someone has been systematically beating Dora for days. I only saw her stomach but it's in technicolor with bruises on bruises. It looks like the goal was to cause maximum surface pain with no lasting damage. They made an effort to keep the marks hidden."

"Casso did that?"

"Someone who had close access to her. I can't prove it was Casso but I did notice abrasions on his knuckles. Based on his gunshot wounds he never had a chance to fight with the shooter so I'll leave you to draw your own conclusion."

Banger mutters a quiet *cocksucker* in disgust, but Hardware is really angry. He lets loose a virulent string of nasty curse words. Misogyny, contempt, and disdain is prevalent in outlaw MC culture but as I've seen time and again that the harming of women or kids brings out the protective instincts in these men.

Then Banger asks *what's happening now?* and I explain that I've told Viper to look after her.

"Having the truth come out is a huge relief but also a huge embarrassment to the girl. Like many victims she feels guilty as if she was somehow to blame for *making* him hit her. Plus the girl's undergone incredible trauma since that night at Portofino's and maybe even before. We don't know that she was a willing *fiancee*. The arranged marriage, the bloodbath of an attack, escaping through the woods at night–"

"Then witnessing her would-be rescuer get strangled to death by a big stranger who abducts her to the clubhouse of a motorcycle gang. Fuck, she's probably got PTSD."

"She probably should but no, she doesn't. From the bits of information she dropped I've pieced together a picture of an extremely naive and sheltered girl. No formal education, no exposure to the nasty underbelly of life, and no contact with men.

Dora's recent experiences must feel like a scene from an action movie. Something on-screen that is dramatic and gory and exciting but leaves her untouched inside. It's really quite fascinating."

"Oh quite," mocks Banger and Hardware snorts a laugh.

"Sorry! I forgot to dumb-it-down for you Neanderthals," I quip back.

Just then Viper returns and we all look at him with questioning glances.

"Dora has finally fallen into a real sleep, not passed out like last night, so I'm going to stay with her. Hopefully she'll sleep for a while."

Banger and Hardware exchange knowing glances but Viper doesn't notice, he's looking at me. After fidgeting a bit he bursts out: "I don't know what to say or do, Should I encourage her to talk or forget? I don't want to fuck her up worse."

Now they all turn to me expecting I have the answer. Of course I don't, I can only go with my gut feeling. "Don't encourage or discourage. Just be there. If she talks, hold her hand. If she's silent give her a hug. Establish non-threatening physical contact but don't make any demands. Can you do that?"

He nods and when he meets my eye I see a look of... shame? and without thinking I blurt out: "Did you know about the abuse?"

His jaw juts out because he's clenching his teeth so hard and a nerve under his eye twitches in a tic. Finally he spits out that he saw one bruise, on her thigh, and thought she was clumsy. I can tell he's furious at himself for doing nothing about it. There's no point beating himself up over something that's already done but there's also no need for me to be telling him that.

Hardware breaks the tense silence by telling us he's made headway on Casso's laptop and the contents are revealing. Banger tells Viper he can go back to Dora while we move from the bar to a table where we can listen to Hardware in privacy.

Hardware

I look from one man to the other as I explain what I found on Casso's computer. I see tense, serious faces intent on what I'm saying. I know I'm stalling but it's because the words I have to say won't come easy. Casso not only played us all, he managed to hide his true nature and a sick secret.

"Banger gave me the first clue when he asked *what's Casso's real name?* Viper knew it was *William* but we all know Casso was from Italy so it would be an Italian version of William. I googled that question and the answer is Guglielmo. Same as the name of the guy who led that rogue gang against the two mafia families.

Then I checked in my paid searches for a link between Guglielmo, Spagnolo, and Vendetti. The connection I got was totally unexpected. Ten years ago a Guglielmo Spagnolo entered this country on an open-ended air ticket from Palermo, Sicily for a family visit. There's no record of him after that. Certainly no exit stamp or return trip was ever recorded. Guglielmo Spagnolo effectively disappeared once he arrived in this country.

Checking for that name in Italian records from back then I learned that a Cesare Spagnolo flew into the same airport and also disappeared but in Italy this time–"

"Wait, are you saying that this Cesare became Guglielmo who became Casso?"

"No, no this Cesare was a man somewhere in his late thirties ten years ago. And it looked like he only came in order to kill a woman he'd been involved with many years before. Cesare shot her to death in front of her husband who called the cops right away but Cesare vanished without a trace.

I don't have a name for this woman but I figure she's got to be Casso's mother. He wrote... well I guess an autobiography or a diary or something. He made several attempts but they all come together to form his life story.

Seems he grew up in Italy, an only child, with his parents Gino and Angela Modicini. Casso came to America on a plane ticket his father bought for him but it was using his birth father's name, and his father is, was, Cesare Spagnolo.

"That story hangs together," comments Banger. "This Angela and Cesare have a fling, the result is Casso – Google-oh – and x number of years later Cesare comes back to Italy to... claim his son?"

"Maybe he never knew about the boy and killed the mother in a rage when he found out?"

"Or she put up a fight when he wanted to bring the boy home with him?"

"Since the mother, the father, and the son are all dead now I don't think we'll ever find out the truth there."

"No, but it's an interesting story," begins Banger before I interrupt him.

"It's more than interesting, Prez. Cesare Spagnolo was married to an American woman, a Mafia Princess, and they had two children the oldest being a girl named Loretta."

"You mean... Dora is Casso's... sister?"

"Half-sister, yeah."

"Oh fuck, that explains a lot.." Needles starts but stops when we both turn his way. "I need to figure it out first, give me a few minutes."

"And I think Dora was also his target."

"What?"

"The witnesses from the Portofino's massacre report the first shots fired were aimed at Ricardo Spagnolo's bodyguards and once they were down he was killed. Ricardo was Dora's younger brother, only sixteen."

Banger adds to that telling us: "When Dora first confessed who she was to me and Viper she said when gunfire broke out she immediately hit the floor and started crawling to an exit. She said *it was really loud with the gunshots and the screaming, swearing and yelling in English and Italian, dishes and glasses breaking, furniture being overturned and the FBI shouting out commands. It was too noisy to think or feel anything.*"

"Poor Dora, what a terrifying experience," Needles shakes his head over her ordeal. "So she came away from the restaurant without knowing who survived or what had actually happened."

"Yeah, shit. She said she got outta there and straight into the woods. She's in high-heels, tripping and running around in the dark until she climbs a ladder nailed into a tree and sleeps in a hut. I think she meant that she'd found a hunter's blind. As soon as it was light enough to see she just kept going as far and as fast as she could in the opposite direction from Portofino's. Needles, you're gonna have to tell her about her brother's death."

"No I won't because Casso already did. And yeah," he turns to me adding: "You're right Hardware. He told Dora she was going to be his next victim."

"So who set fire to his tattoo shop?"

"Probably someone from the Spagnolo family, they're the ones actively pursuing the remaining gang members."

"So they didn't go after him because of Dora?"

"No, it looks like nobody cares about what's happened to Dora."

One of the club whores comes over to us then bringing a platter of sandwiches for our lunch.

I ask if we should get her to take some to Viper's room but Banger shakes his head saying: "No, let's just leave them alone for now."

Viper

I covered Dora with a blanket when I left but now I pull it off her to get an eyeful of her sleeping body. I've been thinking about what Slash said and I have to admit that yeah, maybe there's some truth to it, some attraction, but since when? Sure, Dora is young and pretty but... she's Poison!

She's also lush with rounded womanly hips, thick curvy thighs, soft shoulders... and her tits, ass, and cunt are gorgeous. I know I'm taking advantage but I need to peek at the prize between her legs.

Another look at the bruising on her back reignites my burning rage against Casso but I have to push down on the angry thoughts. Instead, I roll Dora over and her legs fall splayed open. The movement doesn't wake her up so I nudge her thighs even wider apart.

Her pussy is a pink slit of thin folds with a glisten of her arousal. I lean close deeply inhaling her spicy scent. I ache to taste her sweet cream and decide just a quick lick won't do any harm. Sliding my tongue between her outer lips I slowly draw it up to the hard nub hiding beneath light brown hair. Now there's a tangy taste added to the sweetness.

I hear of squeak of surprise and looking up am caught red-handed. Dora's big brown eyes are staring. Propped up on her elbows she can see exactly what my tongue is doing. Her beautiful sweet honey-filled cunt is drawing me in with the delicious aroma of her arousal.

My cock is so hard it aches and my balls are pulling tight. I haven't felt this turned on since my very first fuck at age fourteen.

"I had to taste you," I explain. Her eyes flick from mine to her pussy and then back to my mouth. She flattens her thighs which lifts and opens her cunt for me. My mouth is drawn in before I can even think. My lips suck, my teeth delicately nibble, and my tongue swirls in a frenzied whirl.

Dora gasps then moans and those sounds make me groan with need and desire but my goal is her pleasure. She cums quickly, to her obvious surprise, then falls back flat on the bed but I'm determined to bring her to ecstasy at least two more times. When my tongue keeps up it's assault on her sensitive clit she shakes her head crying out *no I can't, not again* but of course she can and she does.

"Viper ahhh, ohhh... no stop!"

I pull back and smile at her. "You want me to stop doing this?"

"No! Yes... ugh, I don't know. I don't like being all like, um like this..."

"Like what, sweetheart?"

She's just adorable with her face scrunched up in a frown while her body squirms.

"I don't like being all... all wanting... and... oh, Viper."

Bending close to her ear I whisper: "All desperate and needy and begging?"

Her back arches as my words penetrate and her thighs open wider. I know what my girl needs.

"Is it scary, Dora?"

"Yes."

"Why, baby?"

"Because... because I have no control. Because it feels too good. Because I want it too much and that's wrong because I hate you."

I love to hear her beg but I need to capture her mouth with mine once more. While pressing a deep kiss on her lips I add to her pleasure by pushing a finger inside to curl up against her g-spot. That makes her jerk and she's soon pumping her hips to make me rub it hard.

"Please Viper, please-please-please do all the dirty stuff that feels so good."

When she cums this time it's with a loud drawn-out cry of *oh! oh! oh!* and I see tears shine on her cheeks. I kiss them repeatedly then scooting up to the top of the bed I cradle her in my arms and pull her into another passionate and lengthy kiss. Her lips are sweet and I know mine are salty from her slick. Everything comes together exactly right as I assure her that I hate her too.

Her eyes are almost shut but she rouses herself enough to exclaim: "I've *never* felt anything like that!" I tell her she's such a good girl for me.

"No really, you could teach a Masterclass on cunnilingus."

I splutter out a laugh telling her: "I can't even spell that word! and what do you know about it and Masterclasses?"

"My cousins got their homeschooling with my tutors but those girls taught me so much more. All the computers in my house had restricted access, parental controls or something? but my cousins could get the Internet on their phones. I never had a cellphone of my own, but I learned an awful lot from theirs."

She yawns hugely and curls up against my chest ready to fall back asleep. A conscience I thought I'd lost years ago nudges at me and I sigh deeply. Dora turns back towards me questioningly.

"I have to confess something but it's not a bad thing, um... it's just well... teasing, I guess you could say."

I blow out pent-up breath and figure it's best to just tell her the truth. "Dora, I didn't carve I AM A LIAR on your butt, I carved the word POISON."

I watch as conflicting thoughts chase across her face. Her eyes widen in surprise, narrow in anger, then a wondering look fills them: "You carved my nickname?"

When I nod she smiles, a brilliant happy smile. "But you spoke out loud naming each of the letters as you cut and you said I AM A LIAR."

"Well I am, and so are you. But yeah, I was lying when I told you what I'd carved."

Dora suddenly pulls back with her eyes darkening and a frown pinching her brow. "Wait a minute! Are you lying now? Is this a joke to make fun of me?" she accuses.

"Sweetheart no!" I chuckle as I lift her off the bed and holding her against me walk into the bathroom to stand in front of the big mirror. "Look, you won't be able to read it clearly backwards - and it's still red - but you can see that there's just one word."

She swivels round in my arms and looking over her shoulder focuses on the new scars. Watching her reflection I see her lips mouth the word she's reading: *POISON*.

With a relieved sigh Dora snuggles into the sheltered spot between my neck and shoulder and I nuzzle her hair. Returning the both of us to bed I hold her close as she drifts off. Sweet, innocent Poison. All mine.

Sweet, innocent Poison. All mine.

Needles

Once the server has left us I lean in to confide what I've figured out but didn't want to discuss in front of Viper. Banger and Hardware both nod at me to continue.

"Okay, this is just surmise but here goes. Casso knows that Dora is his sister but I think he comes on to her, sexually, regardless. Then he gets all mad and disgusted with himself and takes it out on her. Classic response of victim blaming and shaming. He beats her up for tempting him, something like that. The thing is she didn't know about their blood relationship so she was just acting and reacting like a normal girl.

Maybe she did flirt and maybe that's why she never said anything because he convinced her she deserved the abuse. Victims very often do take the blame. He probably told her she was evil and bad and she took it to heart."

"Did they fuck?"

"I don't think so... she mentioned that she wasn't on birth control because her marriage was expected to result in children arriving as soon as possible. She certainly isn't worried about being pregnant but maybe Casso wore a condom?"

"Ugh, he couldn't have fucked her, right? I mean he knew what their relationship was... you said that's why he hit her."

"And you don't think she knew about them being brother and sister?"

"No, I'm sure she didn't. I don't think she could have kept quiet about that and–"

Hardware jumps in saying: "Hey! Was it the shock that let Dora get her voice back do you think?"

Before I can comment Banger smoothly states: "That's a good point, Hardware. I think you're probably right."

Okay, so that's how we're going to play it? Fine by me, it's not my concern.

Out loud I continue: "I think it was just one more sickening revelation from Casso and she probably hasn't even begun processing it on top of everything else that's happened."

"Fuck, Viper will want to kill him all over again," says Hardware shaking his head.

"He really has fallen for her, hasn't he? I wasn't here when he and Fiona were together so I can honestly say I've never see Viper romantically involved with anyone."

"Oh fuck yeah and him acting like he isn't crazy about her is fucking hilarious," laughs Banger with glee.

Dora's presence has changed all of us to some extent.

Viper

I didn't plan on sleeping when I went back to my room but curling up beside Dora felt like a good idea and next thing I know I'm waking from a nap feeling hungry.

I don't think Dora's ready to face anyone yet but she should get up. Digging through my dresser I find a Henley that she could wear as a dress but I add a pair of flannel boxers as well. These clothes are made of soft material so they won't irritate her sore skin... and they're mine.

Dora wakens as I'm stroking her long hair away from her face. Her exposed neck draws me to run my lips in feather-light strokes up and down that slender column. She smiles so sweetly I can't resist smothering her with kisses. A small part of me is wondering *who the fuck am I?*

After all, Dora is the only witness to me killing that boy. It would be a manslaughter charge but me being who I am I'd probably get a life sentence. Especially if I told the judge to go fuck himself which, yeah I figure I would. I have before. I got a problem with authority, big fucking deal.

Dora stands between me going free or living the rest of my life in prison. I should be... damn, I can't even think the words. But this little fawn with her light brown eyes is so innocent and fragile and fuck... I really want to be with her and I'm willing to risk everything for that.

The first time Dora was staying at the clubhouse I told Fiona to get her some clothes and a toothbrush, shit like that. Fiona dug out some old jeans that looked like Jeremy's discards. They hung off Dora which I'm sure was intentional.

Fiona never gave her any make-up but that didn't matter because Dora is a natural beauty. Probably because her lips are bare is the reason why I like kissing her so much. Lipstick can make a girl's mouth look really sexy but I hate tasting it. No, she's lovely without any additions and her skin is... what's the expression? petal-soft. And it is, her cheek is smooth like a rose petal. *Thank Christ she can't hear my thoughts! Fucking rose petals??? Banger is right, I've got it bad for little Poison.*

"I'm starving and I know I ate more than you did yesterday so I thought I'd get us something to eat."

"You're leaving?"

"No, I'll just go to the kitchen see if anyone's cooked anything. We can order out too, if you like, but if there's a meal available that would be quickest."

"Okay, but... do I have to come?"

"No sweetheart, I didn't think you'd want to. But you should get up. It's probably time we talked about everything that has happened and what we plan to happen. I found you some of my stuff that you can wear. So you get dressed and I'll head to the kitchen."

"Do I have time for a shower? I'd like to wash before I put clean clothes on."

She yawns and I agree that a shower sounds like a good idea, it might wake her up. I hesitate though, because I want to be there to help her. She can't move her arm much. But we need to eat so I remind her: "Just remember to keep that dressing dry or we'll hear about it from Needles."

Dora goes straight into the bathroom and I tidy up our things, clearing a space so we have room to eat. I pause before locking the door and decide not to because Dora's no longer a prisoner. Besides, I'll have my hands full with our food when I return.

I hear women talking in the kitchen but there's no cooking on the go. Fiona snarks about me *wanting special treatment for the princess* so I tell her:

"Stop being such a cunt, Fiona."

"Really, Viper? This girl of yours gets a brother killed and all you do is give me shit?"

"Just fuck off, you don't know what you're talking about."

Her face is twisted in an ugly sneer when she spits out: "I know Casso is dead and that little bitch is alive. What else is there to know?"

Taking a deep breath I hold my rage in. Fiona doesn't deserve the truth and the rest don't need me putting on a show. So I ignore her and thank Bunny when she offers to make us pancakes.

Fiona flounces out without another word, thank Christ, and Bebe leaves as well saying she's got clean linens coming out of the dryer.

Sitting down at the table to keep out of Bunny's way I stretch out my legs and watch her prepare batter for the pancakes.

She moves with ease and efficiency in the kitchen and I'm reminded that our club whores aren't here 24-7. They've got jobs, working for us in one of our businesses usually, and they have family and friends outside of the club. I think Bunny has a kid, too. While she's waiting to flip the pancakes Bunny observes that she doesn't really know Poison but it looks like the girl is good for me because I'm more relaxed than she's seen in... forever.

272

I chuckle and say I'm just catching up after a busy time with lots going on.

"I know the Prez made you punish her and we all heard the screaming but you guys have got past that, eh? I mean, you don't mess around with us but you've got something going with her, right?"

Bunny's crossing a line here but it's not a secret or anything and I do appreciate her making us a meal so I tell her the truth that no, I'm not fucking Poison but I am looking out for her. Bunny will spread the word so everyone knows Dora is under my protection and off-limits. Not so sure they'll believe her about the not fucking part because she's looking pretty skeptical herself.

"Oh okay, that's um, kinda sweet actually. I'm going to put this on a tray cause you need butter and syrup too." I thank her as she loads it up.

My stomach's rumbling as I head back to my room and I'm grateful the food prep only kept me away about 20 minutes, tops.

Banger

Hardware has gone to log onto his desktop computer so he track something without leaving a trace, he said. He'll but back but meanwhile this is a good opportunity to pick Needle's brain and get some information for me and Kimmy.

I speak up asking "Hey, can you tell me how to get some of that *intrivo* stuff?"

Needles replies: "It's *invitro,* actually it's *invitro fertilization* but just call it IVF, and does Kim know you're looking into this?"

"Of course she fucking knows," I snaps back. "It's her fucking idea."

I pause while Viper walks by us carrying a tray of food. Looks like pancakes and now I'm wishing I'd had that instead of a sandwich. I always find a hot meal more satisfying.

I'm quizzing Needles because of what Viper said about me and Kim and our marriage. It made me think about what matters to me most, and how I can get there. With Kim.

Not that I'll ever let on to Viper, but last night I phoned Kim, even though it was pretty late, and told her I'm willing to do what she wants. Wish I'd known then about these initials because I'm sure I was calling it by the wrong fucking name.

Of course being a woman my wife had to turn things around demanding *don't you want this too?* and I was honest saying *yeah, but not as much as you do but that's okay because you're everything to me so whatever you want I'll give to you.*

I've always been open about my thoughts and feelings, and I never lie to Kim. If there's something I can't or won't tell her I say so or I don't say anything at all and she figures it out. We've been together since we were teenagers.

Then she started blubbing and we made a few promises of love and fucking as soon as she gets back here. She needs to talk to her cousin first and he won't be around until after lunch today. I'm happy to know I'll be picking her up on my bike, and having her back home by tonight.

"I don't want to waste time Prez, so tell me what you already know on the subject."

I then proceed to tell Needles everything Kim has passed on to me. Maybe it's because he's a medical man but he doesn't think it's unmanly at all. When I ask if I can even produce any *viable sperm*, as Kim calls it - jizz to me - because of having the mumps he just laughs. When did that stop being true?

I see Hardware is coming back so I shelve the conversation for now. Kim can ask Needles any questions she has now that I've clued him in.

Hardware sits down and tells us: "I've got my searches running, doing a deep dive this time into Guglielmo Spagnolo matched with Guglielmo Modicini and Cesare Spagnolo, and we'll see what comes up."

Viper

As I cross from the kitchen through the main room into the hallway I hear Banger's raised voice and and it makes me chuckle. It looks like he's pulled his head out of his ass if he's talking to Needles about Kim. I'm still smiling when I walk into my room.

Dora's not on the bed or sitting at the table. I set the tray down and since the restroom door is open I stick my head in but she's isn't there either.

Where is she? Going back to the main room I see the guys huddled close while Needles is telling them something. They break apart with another laugh and that's when I ask where Dora went. She didn't come to the kitchen but she must have walked by them.

They shake their heads at me and Banger states: "Dora never came out of the hall at all, Viper."

"Yeah, we would have seen her for sure if she did."

I don't recognize the wave of feeling that explodes out of me but it's all about Dora. Dora who is missing.

"She's gone!" I yell.

"She can't be gone, bro. She didn't come out this end of the hall and you need keypad access to get out the other end. Only we have that, well us and–"

"And your fucking sister Fiona. That cunt! I'll kill her Banger, I will fucking kill her if she's hurt Dora."

"Remember who you're talking to VP and why the fuck would you want to kill Fee because of Poison?"

"Because fucking Fee has taken Dora."

Rescue

Needles

Viper's face has gone from red with anger to white with worry. He doesn't answer Banger, just turns on his heel and runs back into the hallway. The three of us join him. After the bedrooms the hall doglegs to a smaller stretch that houses our laundry facility and a door to the outside.

As the four of us go crashing into that cramped space we're forced to a stop by the sight of Trini or Mexi – I can't tell them apart – on the floor clutching a bloody nose with Bebe kneeling by her side. They're surrounded by scattered bedding and an overturned laundry basket.

The guys are all hollering at once but I rush to kneel by Trini, it must be her because she never lets Mexi go anywhere alone, and I tilt her head back while pinching her nostrils shut. She's always hard to understand but even worse now that her voice is thickened by blood. Her meaning is clear when she points to the outer door saying "Gah! Gah!"

"I don't know what happened," cries Bebe. "Everything was fine when I was here fifteen minutes ago. I came back a second before you got here and found her like this."

I wave the men on to pursue Dora while I stay behind to attend to Trini. After a quick inspection I determine her nose isn't broken but it's already swelling and hurting like hell, I bet. I'm more concerned with the damage to her chin but when I gently rotate her jaw back and forth she says there's only a twinge of discomfort.

"Good thing you've got such a tiny nose," I tell her and pointing to my own explain: "If it was my size it would have taken all the impact from the wall and be broken for sure!"

She's not ready to laugh yet but she does find a smile for me.

I hear cursing and looking down the short hall see that Banger has to elbow Viper out of the way because the younger man can't manage to enter the key code.

When the door is pushed open the three of them crowd outside but all I can see are their dark silhouettes against the bright summer sunshine.

Banger

I have to keep my cool because both Viper and Hardware have lost theirs. Hardware's fingers keep flexing into fists, anxious to find a target and release his anger. Viper is just stunned.

It's just around lunch-hour which means only 24-hours ago we were at the tattoo parlor dealing with the fake fire. A lot has happened since then and even more has come to light. Who would have believed Casso... but I have to put those thoughts out of my mind right now and concentrate on finding Poison. I mean Dora.

Viper's rage against Fiona is nothing new because he's never gotten over her betrayal of him, me, and the club. I understand but I can't allow him to hurt her. It's my job to determine if punishment is required, and to choose who will deliver it. I can't actually kill Fee but dammit... the way I'm feeling right now? I'm fucking close to it.

Needles steps outside to report what the house mouse told him. Her arms were full carrying a basket of clean washing when Fiona came down the hall dragging Poison by her hair and yelling *get outta my way.*

The girl couldn't really take in what was happening until Fiona was practically on top of her and then some big guy came up from behind and shoved her into the wall. She hit it face-first, dropping the laundry, and hearing Fiona shout *I told you to wait outside.*

"Who was this motherfucker?"

"Trini never saw his face but he was really tall, wore a Road Lightning patch on his cut, and had a long brown ponytail."

I realize Fiona must have expected him and also that she must have given him our door code since he got inside. No sense saying any of that out loud, but it's one more nail in my sister's coffin. Now I have to fucking remember to change the access.

"He picked up Dora and tucked her under his arm like a football then the three of them left. We showed up before Trini could raise the alarm.

"Brown ponytail? Sounds like that motherfucker Hammer!" declares Hardware.

I nod in agreement but keep my mind on what Needles is relating. "So only a minute, is that right?"

"Something like that. They must have had a car because she didn't hear a bike."

"We all would have heard a stranger's bike."

"Fucking Fiona planned this, Prez. She hated Dora being here and... aw fuck I'm going to their clubhouse."

"Wait a sec Viper, you can't just go barreling in there or you'll get shot. We don't even know for sure that their club's got her–"

"That club's into sex trafficking! I'm not letting them sell Dora on!"

"They don't do that shit, not anymore," I begin but then Hardware speaks up too voicing his agreement with Viper's plan.

He continues: "Trini saw the Lightning patch so if Hammer didn't take her to the clubhouse somebody there should know where he's at."

My phone goes off with my wife's ringtone so I swipe to answer but before I can speak Kim is screaming at me wanting to know why I sent my bitch of a sister with a girl for the club to traffic. Kim starts going off on me about how I know they don't do that sick shit. I disconnect in the middle of her rant, one more thing she can be pissed off about, so I can call Goblin, Road Lightning's Prez. He has to talk to me since we're related by marriage. At least that's what I always tell him and he tells me to go fuck myself. I give him a heads-up that me and my men are on our way. "Make sure my sister and the girl she brought don't go anywhere." I warn. He starts saying the same thing as Kim but I cut him off as well as I run to my bike.

Needles will spread the word and I know our membership will turn out as back-up. This can easily turn into a bloodbath and it's up to me to prevent that from happening.

Poison has brought us nothing but trouble from the moment Viper dragged her into his car. I know I'm being unfair on the girl but right now I don't fucking care. I care about getting everyone safely back home.

Dora

I really wish my mother had let me take that *Krav Maga* self-defense class. My cousins were allowed to attend but I had to settle for their second-hand accounts of what the instructor taught. Unfortunately none of those lessons included a how-to on breaking the hold of a bigger, stronger, mentally-deranged person who has wrapped a chain around your throat.

Fiona burst into Viper's room and has me incapacitated in seconds. Grabbing a fistful of my hair in one hand and yanking the chain up around my jaw with the other she propels me down the hall and into the rough grasp of a big sweat-stinking biker.

He tosses me in the back of a four-door sedan where an equally large man is waiting to hold me down. I'm trying to pay attention to all these details so I can tell them to Viper when he asks but I have no idea what kind of car it is.

Fiona gets in beside us and the stinky guy gets in the front. I never do see the driver. No one speaks until Fiona snaps *shut the fuck up* to my questions of *what? where?* and *why?* and we travel in silence after that.

The car races away from the clubhouse and at that speed it doesn't take long to reach our destination. Once there I'm manhandled out of the vehicle and half-carried into another motorcycle gang's clubhouse. I'm hollering and screaming which attracts plenty of attention but of the wrong kind. I get dumped on the floor and am immediately hemmed in by a circle of big men whose laughter sounds nasty to me, threatening and intimidating. The few women present look cowed. They won't be any help.

I can hear Fiona's voice raised in argument with another female, someone not browbeaten like these washed-out women. Will she be willing to help? Tuning out the lewd comments of the men I concentrate on the two women's loud words. There's certainly no love lost between them.

The air is pierced by a high-pitched whistle and a man with fiery-red hair shoulders his way through the crowd. He's not a big man but all of the bikers make way for him. He has an air of authority and menace that reminds me of Banger... ahhh, I understand when I see the word Prez on his vest, what Viper calls a *cut*.

"A crew from Satan's Tears is on the way and their Prez is pissed so somebody better tell me what the fuck is going on right fucking now," he demands in a voice with a strong accent.

In the momentary silence that follows I somehow find the courage to speak up. "I was abducted from their clubhouse and brought here."

The Irishman looks down at me sprawled on the floor. I thank God that I put those boxers on after all, I had thought of just wearing Viper's shirt. Praying my knees aren't shaking too badly I get to my feet and look into his freckled face.

"And who the fuck are you?"

"Loretta Antonia Spagnolo, but I go by Dora. Except Banger and Viper, and I guess pretty much everyone else at the club, call me Poison." I frown over that last statement and the man's bright blue eyes twinkle at me.

A woman, obviously his relative, comes to stand beside him to give me the onceover. "That Banger's me husband so who are you ta him?" she asks loudly.

I have to listen closely to understand her heavy accent which I suspect she's putting on extra for me. It's the same voice that was shouting at Fiona.

"Well apparently he *gave me* to Viper so I'd have to say I'm nothing at all to him and thank God because ma'am I think your husband is really scary."

Both the woman and the Prez laugh heartily at my comment and most of the club members join in until the Prez interrupts demanding: "What I want to know is who brought you here and why?"

The man who grabbed me out of the clubhouse steps forward now saying: "I did, Prez. This girl was offered to me, to the Lightning, and I know you said the club was getting out of the trafficking trade but I figured we could make things right by passing her on to the cartel. There's a fuckload of money to be made if we work with them."

A few bikers murmur their agreement but most stay silent with their eyes fixed on their club president.

He responds in a calm voice that is all the more frightening for its low tone: "Oh *you figured*, did you laddie? Well, well, well," and before I can blink he's hit the much-bigger man hard. First in his solar plexus making him hunch over in pain, then an upper-cut that catches him under the chin snapping his head back, and a final jab straight to his Adam's apple that drives the huge biker to his knees. The Prez is dancing with his fists up ready to go another round but his opponent is finished.

Amid the applause and cheering it takes me a minute or so to recognize the word the crowd is chanting – *Goblin* – and another minute to realize that is the name of their president. He looks more like a leprechaun to me but I'm keeping that thought to myself.

Making a show of cracking his knuckles he motions for quiet and asks: "Who offered this girl to Hammer?"

The men step back until Fiona is left standing alone. She lifts her chin and tosses her head defiantly.

"Fiona Flaherty, hmm? What are you doing involving yourself with this racket? You know what these sex traffickers do to their victims, right? You know the girls don't survive for long which is after being' a bloody blessing, truth be told."

Although Goblin is several inches shorter than Fiona she shrinks before his implacable gaze. There is no justification for what she's done but she opens her mouth as if to explain until the roar of motorcycles racing full throttle drowns out anything she might have said.

Banger's wife comes to stand beside me, only stepping away when Viper rushes forward. Hardware is right behind him, followed by Banger. More bikes arrive carrying Satan's Tears members and soon the room fills up with macho bullshit and testosterone and lots of male shouting and posturing. The very air vibrates with violence.

Thank God for Viper's lack of sentimentality. It keeps me from breaking down in front of these people. I never doubted he'd come for me but I was still scared and I fold my lips inward and press down hard to keep from crying.

He looks closely at my face before stating: "You're okay, right Poison?"

I nod and he turns to look for Fiona. Spotting her at the back of the crowd he growls: "You're not."

Banger steps forward then with a greeting to Goblin. The two club presidents are almost toe-to-toe but without animosity. No friendship, either as far as I can tell.

"I'll deal with my sister," he states and turning to the red-haired woman adds: "And my wife. Kim, you're coming back with me. Needles has some info to discuss with you and then we'll go get that thing you want done."

I don't know what he means but his wife does and it pleases her. She grins at her husband and loops her arm around his elbow. He pulls her in close then calls out: "Is Crusher here?"

A tall man steps forward. His lankiness on a big frame is deceptive, he's obviously a hard, tough man. He doesn't speak but when Banger says he can have Fiona for *a dirty weekend* his eyes glitter with pleasure. I can't repress the shiver that runs down my spine. I meant it when I said Banger was scary but this guy is utterly terrifying.

Fiona shares that fear crying out in protest that Banger *has no right to give her away* but he shouts her down saying *arrogance must run in the family then*. He's right, Fiona thought she could pass me on so I guess she's being handed over to this man as her punishment.

Viper gives my back a rough push which makes me stumble but he scoops me up before I fall, hoisting me over his shoulder. Hardware is right behind us and his rumbling chuckle tells me the tension has broken so I can safely relax into Viper's hold.

Out in the parking lot he slides me down his body but still hangs on. I look up into his eyes and his expression is very serious as he tells me: "You're safe now."

I can't stop myself from blurting out "With you? Huh!"

289

He snorts a genuine laugh and pokes his tongue into one cheek giving me a wry smile. "That's right Poison, safe with me. Go figure."

Once again he has to buckle me into his helmet before he straddles his bike and pulls me up behind him.

"Do you remember what to do?" he asks. I nod but realize he can't see me so I quickly answer *yes*. I get a grunt in reply.

I'm not sure why Viper is mad at me but he's sure acting different then he did when it was just him and me on his bed. I guess that this is the public biker versus the private man.

All I'm certain of is that when I flatten my front against his back and wrap my arms tightly around him, as far as I can, I hear a vibration that signifies he's humming. The hard, tight feel of Viper's abdominal muscles has my core tingling with awareness. I snuggle my cheek against the soft leather of his cut and sigh contentedly.

This bike ride is even more thrilling than my first was because now I'm part of a convoy of motorcycles. The powerful racket they make vibrates right through me. Ahead of me I see Banger's wife Kim holding on to her husband. She and I are the only two women here.

I'm part of something much bigger than just me and I'm not riding with just anyone, I'm riding with the club VP. It almost feels like I belong.

Revelations

Viper

Kim has gone to their suite so Banger's taking this opportunity to talk to me privately. He follows me and Poison to my room explaining they're going ahead with *the baby-making shit* so he'll have to be away from the clubhouse for appointments and testing and stuff.

"No problem Prez, that's what I'm here for. But if we have any more under-the-radar car trips can I appoint someone else to step up? because after the last trip..." Poison had run into the restroom as soon as we walked through the door and when she comes out we both look at her.

She stands there holding the door handle and suspiciously questions: "What? Why are you looking at me?"

"Oh we're just reminiscing about how eventful Viper's last road trip was since it resulted in you being here now."

"Huh, not by choice... and hey! what did he mean about you *giving me* to him? What's that all about?"

In the dead silence that follows even Poison must realize she's overstepped big time. I'm ready to make excuses for her but before I can open my mouth Banger's across the room with his hand wrapped around her throat. I can't see his expression but from the look on her face it must be terrifying. I'm poised to intervene which is a really bad idea but even I'm worried.

In a quiet, menacing voice he says: "Nobody speaks to me like that, little girl. Not. Ever. Got it?"

She nods as much as she can around his big hand, her eyes shiny with unshed tears. She's barely drawing breath.

He relaxes his grip but still holds on. Looking her up and down he comments to me: "She's a pretty little thing, Viper. I did you a solid when I made her yours. You'll enjoy yourself when you finally get around to fucking her."

Banger looks sideways at me trying to act all casual and shit before he huffs out a laugh saying: "Yeah, I knew you'd hold back until I made the decision about what to do with her. You're a good brother, man."

He finally releases her and Dora's hands fly to her throat. I can see she's struggling not to cough so I tell her to get a drink of water. The look she shoots me is pure hatred and I think *Hey! I'm not the one who just choked you, bitch.*

Banger watches us closely and I can see he's laughing to himself. He moves towards the door then stops, slaps at his pockets and produces a business card. "I almost forgot to give you this. Take her diamonds to this address and bring the card too, there's a note on the back from our referral. Can you do that now or at least in the next couple of hours?"

I nod and read the card. The location isn't far and it won't take me long to get there. I pull the jewelry out of my pocket and we both study the sparkling diamonds.

"Poison, these things look real shiny but are they worth much?"

She tilts her head thinking a moment before clearing her throat and explaining: "I can't say what you'll get from a jeweler or pawnshop or whoever you use, and of course we don't have the necklace–"

"Right, you figure the cop grabbed it off you?"

"Yeah, well not intentionally like, but yeah the FBI guy did grab me and we both fell to the ground. I think the chain broke then.

Anyhow, I can tell you the set is insured for 10 million so since of the value is lost when a set is no longer intact I would guess... hmm, 3 to 4 million for these stones."

I just stare at her in shock, I've had these things lying loose in the pocket of my cut ever since I took them off her.

Banger slaps me on the back saying "Shit, if the fence offers 10 percent – even half that – we're still sitting pretty. Good job, VP."

After a few more instructions on how to negotiate Banger leaves and then I put on my leathers and head out as well. Looking back into the room I see Dora sitting on the bed chewing the side of her thumb with a worried frown. Is she going to get into a lot of shit for not returning the diamonds back to her in-laws? I feel a momentary twinge of guilt thinking 10 million is a hell of lot of money before deciding that losing the diamonds is the least of her problems.

After all, so far as we can tell her in-laws aren't even looking for her or the jewelry.

The wind has really picked up, maybe about 25 miles per hour, but it will have to get a lot stronger than that to be a problem for an experienced rider like me. Actually, it's loose objects being lifted by stronger winds that become the problem. If necessary you have to be able to dodge without dropping your bike.

Because of the wind and the roar of my engine I don't hear Poison and don't see her until she's right in front of me frantically waving her arms. She's run out in a hurry because she's still just wearing my tee-shirt and boxers – no shoes.

"You can't go, don't do it, don't go!" she screams trying to be heard. I shake my head at her but she drapes herself over the front wheel and starts sobbing. *What the fuck now?*

I turn my machine off and get ready to yell at her when she cries out: "It's not safe, you'll be killed. I'm so sorry."

"Explain," I growl, and she does.

"The diamonds are marked, laser etching that needs a powerful jeweler's loupe to read but believe me anyone handling diamonds of this quality will check. They'll identify the markings because for many decades the word has been out – even internationally – to hold onto whoever tries to sell these and contact the Vendettis. It means a big reward to the informant and torture and death for the seller. For you. I'm really, really sorry," she adds tearfully.

I stare at her for a long time but it's like I'm only now seeing her for the woman she is. Poison, no Dora, who I've terrorized, held captive, mentally and... yes, physically abused, who knows I'm a cold-blooded killer, yet still saves my life with a warning.

She's run out here to protect me despite everything that's happened. Even after all the shitty things I've done to her.

She doesn't use me or betray me because Dora, my poor little rich girl mafia princess, has a good heart. *Wait, why calling her my girl?* I ask myself.

But when I look into her light brown eyes I know the answer, it courses through my blood and floods every inch of my body from my brain to my heart to my hardening cock. Dora is mine.

Needles

I can see blood staining the white bandage on Dora's arm as she goes racing through the main room of the clubhouse. Shaking my head at the antics of those two I hurry after her and catch up with them in the parking lot. I can feel the magnetism of their attraction crackling like electricity in the air between them.

"Dora, your arm!" I holler and both of them look down there where a lot of blood has seeped through.

Viper hits the kickstand and jumps off his bike in one fluid motion before scooping her up. He holds her gently in his arms instead of flinging her over his shoulder like he did before. Dora's bloody arm lays across her chest but the other has snaked around his neck. He carries her as I lead them to my clinic.

"Put her on the examining table and then leave us alone." He opens his mouth to argue but I silence him by forcefully saying: "No! Dora and I need to have a chat and if she wants to share our conversation with you that's her decision but for now I need to have a one-on-one talk with Casso's victim."

That statement makes him still and I can see his thoughts chasing across his face. He gives a curt nod and steps out of the room but not until he's given a kind and reassuring glance to the girl. She's very clearly his girl.

Once we're alone I get my gauze and antiseptic ready and start unwinding the soiled bandage while I begin our chat.

"Dora, there are some things Hardware found out about Casso... bad things, but I think you might already be aware of at least some of them." I don't look at her but I know I've got her full attention.

"For example, you know that Casso was actually your older brother, right?"

Her correction of *just a half-brother* is almost inaudible.

"Look sweetheart, this isn't an easy conversation for me and it must be pure hell for you but the words have got to be spoken out loud. If the very worst happened then we need to deal with the consequences, we can't bury everything no matter how tempting it is to hide the truth."

Tears are running down her face in a silent stream and a renewed anger towards Casso ignites inside of me.

"Did Casso have penetrating sexual intercourse with you?" I ask. I'm blunt, but I need to be explicit enough to avoid any misunderstanding.

She shakes her head furiously back and forth.

"Oh thank God. He tried though, didn't he?"

"No!" she insists, then adds in a stutter: "B-but he said I was t-trying t-t-to..." She closes her eyes and her cheeks flame with a blush of shame. I stop cleaning the gunshot wound and taking hold of both her small hands I rub some warmth into them.

"Look at me Dora, because it's vital that you understand this." She opens her watery eyes and focuses on me with a scared look.

"You have the perfectly normal appetite of a healthy young woman and when you were in close physical contact with a good-looking and equally hormonal young man it was natural for an attraction to form. Why do you think parents go to such trouble to keep their daughters from being alone with a guy? Because it's natural, normal behavior exactly as Mother Nature intended.

You did nothing wrong and any thoughts you had about him weren't wrong either. You only knew him as Casso, a club member and tattoo artist.

He was definitely in the wrong because he knew about your relationship. He should have kept his distance but he deliberately chose not to do so. And, I suspect, it was Casso's guilty conscience that made him blame you and lash out hitting you – but you are not at fault."

"He was so kind to begin with especially compared to... well..."

"Compared to Viper, yes, I understand that. I know Viper punished you under Banger's orders and you were moved on to Casso next day. I don't know what Viper did but the whole club heard your screams. Both Hardware and I were heading to Viper's room to intervene but just then he came out, slamming the door in a rage, so we knew your ordeal was over. I don't know if it's any consolation but his face bore a look of pain like I have never seen before. He was very determined not to discuss anything."

"Viper really, really hurt me," she whispers in a choked voice. I'm deeply curious about the details but I don't feel I can probe. "Casso hurt me too."

She hesitates for the longest time then taking a deep breath she very bravely tells me everything. It seems Casso would slap her for the slightest mistake in the shop but she said that seemed more like an annoyed reaction rather than anger. He saved up using his fists for when they were alone in the apartment.

She knew if he was in a violent mood by the way he'd shove her through the door, or fist a handful of her hair and drag her into the room. Sometimes, though, they'd be calmly interacting when he'd just boil over as she put it.

"He really hated me. He admitted it when he told me he was my brother and he was the one who killed our father and my brother and he tried to kill me at the engagement dinner, too. Since then he's killed my auntie and her boyfriend. If that gunman hadn't shown up Casso would have killed me for sure.

When he beat me he pretended if was some kind of punishment for being sexy but it wasn't, it was his evil hatred of my family."

The beatings included having her clothes pulled or torn off her body before he'd whip her with his belt while she did her best to curl up and roll away from the lashes. Eventually he'd toss the belt aside and start punching and kicking her all over screaming insults and threats and calling her dirty names.

"Not all over, though," I comment, pointing out that he kept the parts that the public sees bruise-free. "He was aware enough to protect himself, Dora. He might have seemed to be gripped in a berserk frenzy but he acted with cunning and self-preservation. Now you must do the same."

At her curious look I explain that I won't make her tell Viper but that my advice is she should.

"If the two of you are going to engage in any kind of relationship, and it's pretty obvious to everyone that that's where you're headed, then start with honesty. Don't keep secrets that will end up festering and shaming you, especially since you have nothing to be ashamed of."

She chews on her bottom lip while thinking over my words and the gesture is adorably sexy. I bet Viper gets hard every time he sees her do it.

"Should I call him to come back in? and would you like me to stay, to get the conversation started even?"

Her hopeful look gives me my answer and I go to fetch our VP.

Viper

I ignore Needles raised eyebrow when he sees me lounging against the wall beside the door. Of course I'm waiting here, where else would I be? When I straighten up and walk into his clinic he suddenly slams me against the wall.

I'm younger than Needles by about 20 years but we're the same size and he's still a strong man. His rage holds me in place as much as the hand he's got pressing into my chest.

Pushing his face up close he hisses: "I know about a lot of the shit you've done as Club Enforcer but don't you dare hurt that child. I'm warning you now that I will come after you. I don't give a fuck who you are. I don't even care if you kick the crap out of me so long as I get some shots in first."

I know he's kept his voice low for Dora's sake so I don't yell back but I do shove him out of my way. I've never seen Needles so angry but I'm pretty pissed too that he could even think shit like that.

Again he stops me saying he still has to talk before I go in to see her. I'm tempted to brush past him but his serious look stops me.

"Viper, Dora has been deeply traumatized for weeks now but instead of collapsing she's internalized the stresses. I've given it some thought, discussed it with Banger, and I surmise there are two reasons why she hasn't completely fallen apart.

One, she's in shock and the facts haven't sunk in yet.

Two, she's led such a sheltered life that she's experiencing her current reality as if it's a movie or a story in a book. Not real, not something that touches her."

"Or maybe she's a strong girl." I counter.

"Oh she's definitely resilient but... fuck, I just can't emphasize enough how fragile I think her grasp is right now. I mean, I really believe it won't take much to tip her over the edge and—"

"And I'm what? some thick asshole prick who's gonna make everything worse? Is that what you're saying?"

"No! I don't believe that at all. Look, I guess I overreacted with you when really it's Casso I'm mad at. Fuck man, the sight of those bruises... I'm still fucking pissed. But he's gone, it's over, so let's move on.

I believe you've got real feelings for this girl and I want you to acknowledge that and act accordingly. You care for her, Viper so let her know. It will help her heal."

He waves me inside before I can say anything and then closes the door again behind us. I'm immediately distracted by the sight of my girl in tears.

"Why is Dora crying? What did you do to her? What did he do to you, sweetheart?"

I can hear Needles chuckle but he's just background noise, the only person I can focus on is Dora. She's so pale and her cheeks are wet from tears. She looks so vulnerable, fragile, and needy. I need to shelter her to keep her safe and take care of her.

"Viper, Dora has authorized me to share what we've been discussing. In a nutshell it's simply that Casso abused Dora but not sexually. After hearing the details I'm certain he wanted to but his knowledge of their close blood relationship held him back. Being aroused but thwarted maddened him and he took it out on her with his fists."

Dora is certain he was simply vengeful but I don't think she realizes what a beautiful and alluring young woman she is."

She blushes when he says that and I want to punch the smile right off of his face. Instead I just scowl at him and he laughs before continuing:

"The night Casso got shot he spoke at length to Dora, even threatening her life, and I know she told you most of that conversation. But not everything. She didn't tell you about his accusations because they made her feel guilty and responsible.

Since Dora was unaware of their true relationship, believing they were simply good friends, his behavior when he was enraged was completely bewildering to her.

Casso made all kinds of accusations to justify his actions like claiming *she led him on*. Hearing that often enough made her believe everything must be her fault even though she didn't know what she had done, or was doing, wrong. That's why she kept quiet."

My own hands have balled into fists and the only thing keeping me from driving a hole through the wall is knowing how my violence will frighten her.

"It's my fault you didn't think you couldn't trust me Dora, and I'm sorry I made you feel that way."

The words come easily which is a surprise because I don't recall ever apologizing to a woman before. She was looking down at her hands while Needles spoke but now she meets my gaze and nods.

"I couldn't trust anyone, Viper. That drive-by shooting? the fire? I didn't know if that was aimed at the club, or at Casso, or at me. Who my family is – was, I guess – means I have enemies. People I don't even know. You were my enemy too but even so I did trust you, you know. I didn't tell you about Casso because... well, I guess because I felt that, um, maybe I, uh... kinda deserved it."

Her voice has run down to nothing by time she finishes that sentence but it doesn't matter, I've already folded her into my arms. "You don't have to worry any more, sweetheart. You're mine, my Poison, and I'm addicted. From now on I'll protect you against everyone and anyone."

"Even you?" she says with a hint of a smile on her trembling lips.

"Oh especially me, sweetheart. I know I won't be able to keep my hands off you but only to give pleasure." I kiss her then, gently, and when we pull apart I see that Needles has left us alone so I kiss her again a bit more forcefully this time.

"You know Dora I really did think I hated you but somehow... well, I'm sure my feelings didn't change but now I can see them for what they really are. Everyone else saw and they all told me too, but... I've never felt like this for anyone before and... and I didn't think I could. What I feel for you isn't hate and never was Dora."

In a tiny, uncertain voice she says: "The opposite of hate is..."

"Love. What I thought was hate was really love and that is so... unbelievable. For me, I mean. Growing up I never learned to love.

When we're kids it's normal to cling to our parents and never question what they do. I only had a mother while growing up and for the longest time I believed she loved me but well, when I learned otherwise I swore off those feelings for good.

Until you told me about the diamonds and put me first. No woman has ever put my well-being or my safety first. Everyone has always wanted something from me in return. Except you, Dora. Even though I was so mean to you."

By now I've pulled her off the examining table and onto my lap. We sit together like that in the armchair kissing and cuddling for a long time before Needles is back telling us he needs the room.

"Now that Fiona's not here to keep them in line the club whores are fighting with each other and involving the men which means Dog had to get right in the thick of things so now I've got a sprain, a bloody nose, and some black eyes to treat. Also Banger's looking for both of you."

I lift Dora up off my lap and watch her give Needles a hug along with a whispered *thank you*. To my surprise and his shock I shake his hand and thank him as well before we leave.

Dora

It's kind of awkward sitting with Viper, Banger, and Kim in the den of their suite. Kim's just explained that they have their own home but keep rooms at the clubhouse as well.

When I first saw Kim in the Road Lightning's clubhouse I noticed her striking good looks but now I have the leisure to really see her and she's a knock-out.

There's a family resemblance with her red-haired cousin but what's ugly in him is beautiful in her.

Midnight black chin-length hair and a porcelain white complexion perfectly frame her emerald eyes. They steal the show. Characters in books have green eyes but I've never actually met anyone with them before. Kim is stunning.

She's changed from a casual fleece-set into a denim mini-dress and her club vest. Although I can't see the back I know it will read *Property of Banger*. He's rubbed his hand over the words a few times.

I notice that the two of them are constantly touching each other. Not in an obvious way, but keeping connected. His leg leans against hers, and she rests her head against the arm he's stretched across the back of the sofa. I know from the gossip that they've been living apart for a few weeks.

As for Viper and I well Banger just sits there glaring and fuming at us.

The Prez has been waiting for us ever since he was told about the to-do in the parking lot. Naturally he expected us to come here straight to him so he's scowling when we do arrive because we're so late.

I start telling him about Needles coming outside to deal with my bleeding arm but he waves his hand like he's shooing a mosquito. He couldn't care less regarding my injury or health.

Viper takes over and explains about the diamonds and how they're too risky to pawn. Now Banger gives me a sour look while Kim is simply puzzled. When Viper hands over the jewelry to Banger her eyes grow wide before she laughs, saying: "Those can't be real."

None of us answer her as Banger pockets the stones. "Let me think about this," he says. "I trust our fence but not enough to risk anyone's life."

"Prez, I got to thank you for getting Fiona outta here. I know she's your sister but I swear to God I just want to strangle her for what she was trying to do to Dora."

"You're not wrong feeling that way, Viper. Fee was so far out of line... I mean she's my twin but today, tonight, I feel like we're a million miles apart. But you should know, and you too Dora, that Goblin would never have allowed it.

Road Lightning has an unwarranted reputation for sex trafficking but those girls at their club? they're actually rescues. They only ever did one shipment and wanted to bow out in the middle of it when they saw the conditions those women were kept in, fucking horror-show stuff. But Goblin told me if he didn't follow through his crew would be killed. He felt sorry for the girls but he wasn't sacrificing his brothers for them.

So they were guarding the transport *en route* when some rival of the cartel ambushed them and most of the women ended up getting killed in the cross-fire. It was a fiasco as a job and a terrible waste of human life.

He smuggled our house mice away but couldn't keep them at his club because they were too young and fresh to escape notice. He refused to accept the payment his club had earned though, and he figures that's why they were able to walk away from further cartel business."

"Business," Kim snorted her disapproval. "That's no business, that's despicable criminal activity and I told him he was no cousin of mine if he got his hands into that filth.

I mean, the drugs are bad and we all know it but at least you've got adults making their own poor choices, not girls grabbed off the street then terrorized and forced into prostitution. Like our two girls. The sisters came to America to work together as nanny-domestics to a family with 5 kids but instead were sold by this so-called family to the sex-trafficking cartel. It's modern-day slavery and all for sex. Men are pigs."

I can feel my eyes stretched wide in fascinated horror. Kim sees my look and grabbing my hand insists I was never in danger of being sold on. Crusher found out what was going down before the guys even left the clubhouse to come and pick you up.

"Some of their members wanted to keep working with the cartel because it's such a lucrative market I mean the money is huge, really huge. But these guys, led by one of their enforcers called Hammer, got voted down by a vast majority. Just because we're 1-percenters doesn't mean we're without our own moral standards."

Turning to Viper Banger adds, "It was Hammer who Fiona contacted to move Dora on. He involved Hornet who immediately notified Crusher."

"None of the brothers want to get on Crusher's bad side," Kim explains.

Viper raises an eyebrow asking: "Does he have a good side?" and Banger laughs.

"He does, actually. Him and I found ourselves the only two sober people late one night and ended up having one of those revealing conversations that only seem to happen if it's the wee hours or you're very drunk. He was in the mood to talk and since the subject of his conversation was my bitch of a sister-in-law naturally I wanted to listen.

First off, she's in no danger of being hurt by Crusher. He's crazy in love with her but he's the one who ended things between them."

"That's not what Fee said," puts in Banger. "I remember being really surprised because as a couple they seemed perfectly matched."

"Yeah, he's a psycho and she's an instigator who knows how to push his buttons. Although, come to think of it she did pretend to worry about him stalking her," adds Viper. I think back to the tall man with the fearsome aura and almost sympathize with Fiona's plight. I think Kim must have been really lonely for company if she was desperate enough to sit and talk with him.

"Crusher loves Fiona but they split for a good reason and she knows his terms if she wants them to get back together. He's been waiting for her to come around. He didn't want to break up with her but things had reached the point... okay, I'll just tell you what he said as closely as I can recall.

First off I asked him *what terms? what happened with you two?* and he said he caught Fiona kissing another guy and not just kissing, *her tits were in his hands and she was stroking his dick through his jeans.* I thought about how angry Crusher must have been seeing that and I shuddered wondering what he did to the guy.

Crusher told me: *I broke all his fingers and slashed my knife across his palms. He'll remember me every time it rains and his joints start to ache. And every tit he ever fondles in future will feel his scars.*

So then I asked Crusher what he did to Fiona and he said nothing. He accepted her story that she was drunk and didn't know what she was doing and the guy took advantage of that. It was *only a kiss and a grope* so he let it go.

He acknowledges now that that was a mistake. We all know how Fiona is... like Mae West said about men: *Give a man an inch and he thinks he's a ruler.* Well that's Fiona, always quick to suit herself.

She got in trouble again when he discovered a brick of cocaine was missing and Fiona was the only person who could have taken it."

"A brick?" exclaims Viper just as Banger says: "That's a fuckload of money's worth of coke!"

"Yeah and Crusher said he'd been missing money and pills here and there but you know how it is, you don't immediately suspect the people close to you, you're more likely to blame yourself for having brain fog and forgotten. I totally got what he was talking about. He said he figured that in the back of his mind he must have guessed it was all down to Fiona but it didn't seem worth pursuing.

Again, that was a mistake because stealing from him was one thing but *stealing the coke from the club? no way could he put up with that.*

Of course she denied it but as the Road Lightning's interrogator Crusher is very good at his job. It didn't take him long to get a confession. He made sure I understood that he didn't maim or torture Fiona, but he did scare her badly. Luckily she hadn't sold the cocaine so he got it back and never did have to *fess up to his brothers,* as he put it. He knew the time had come *to fix things with Fiona or kick her to the curb.*

Once he was able to look back with some perspective he figured she was pushing him into making a declaration, a claim on her. He's not a stupid man and he reasons things out before he acts. At least he does in his relationship with Fiona because he has no illusions about her. He's ready to make her his old lady and give her status because he loves her. He has since the very first time he saw her.

So what's the problem? I asked him and he said Fiona needs to accept her punishment. He said *I can't make her mine until she gives herself to me under my terms. Total submission. That means she enslaves herself to me for one week. During that time she'll live in my room naked except for a dog collar. I will fuck every orifice with my fingers, mouth, dick, and dildo. She'll be mercilessly edged and since I'm a spanko she knows how the rest of her punishments will go.*

He has to explain to me what a spanko is and then I tell him about our horrible attempt at a little *Fifty Shades* action and, just like you Banger, he thought that story was too funny, laughed his head off. I still don't understand why you men have such warped senses of humor.

Viper coughs and chokes over nothing and I give him a suspicious look. I figure he's covering up a comment or a chuckle. Banger is very pointedly not making eye contact with him and from Kim's narrowed gaze I can tell he'll be quizzed about that later.

Anyhow, Crusher not only has it all figured out in his mind but he's already got his props ready. This guy is prepared. He said each day he'll attach a leash to Fiona's dog collar and lead her to the kitchen to fix him a meal. I'm like *naked!?* and he says *no, he's bought her a bathrobe, the kind that the woman in the lingerie store called a wraparound.* I told him I would have paid good money to see him in a lingerie shop. At first he scowled then gave me a devastating grin. When he's not looking stern and mean he's really quite good-looking, you know. He's a very manly man, but in a good way.

So, he's got what he calls *a bag of goodies* from the adult sex store and he's bought this silk shortie robe that she'll have to wear with high-heeled slippers and the collar-and-leash combo. I know Fiona will be awfully humiliated being led around like that in front of the brothers but I also know she'll look hot as hell and when they're all eyeing her and giving wolf-whistles she'll revel in the attention. Well, after I heard all that I just had to connive with my husband to make it happen."

"You orchestrated this?" Viper exclaims with shock and delight.

Putting on the strong accent again Kim says: "Well, I'm a big softie matchmaker underneath it all, aren't I Banger? Plus, I get the added benefit of not having Fiona around when I'm visiting here."

He takes his wife's hand and lifts it to his lips. Never taking his eyes off her he says: "Viper? it's time for you two to fuck off now."

"Wait!" I call and feel Viper tense up beside me. "Oh! maybe this isn't the best time but the idea just came to me. What if you give those diamonds to that guy Hammer and tell him it's my payment for him to leave me alone? Will be believe that? It would sure take care of him because if he tries to sell them then he'll be the one who gets caught and when he gets tortured he'll admit he's from the Road Lightning motorcycle gang–"

"Club," the three of them say in unison making me blink in surprise. That's not the first time I've been corrected on the wording but I didn't realize how important the distinction is to them.

"Anyhow, the Vendettis will think Road Lightning took me, not Satan's Tears, but they won't care about that because they'll have their heirloom jewelry back. Do you see? that way no one will need to come after you because of me.

I don't think that drive-by shooting was my fault, I think Casso was always the target but even if was because of me well, you won't have to kill me now."

Banger and Viper laugh at that remark while Kim mutters about nobody telling her anything. Banger says he *likes the way I think* and pinches my cheek as if I'm a little girl or something and Viper pulls me close against his side while we walk out of the suite.

As we head down the hallway to his room I recall Banger's words about knowing Viper would wait until I was his and now... well, I've been given to him. Now I am his so I guess the waiting is over.

Love

Dora

Of all the crazy thoughts to have racing through my head is the story of Adam and Eve as I learned it from the nuns at Sunday School. Their version, and maybe it's the real one? like if it really was a true story... I try to be a good Catholic girl but it's hard when your family is mafioso.

The nuns focused on how Eve corrupted Adam and her punishment was the pain of childbirth for which all women do penance. I remember that even as a kid I wasn't impressed by Adam blaming the female for his weakness. I didn't think he was much of a man.

Of course as a child I didn't understand why awareness of their naked state was such a big deal. Being back in Viper's room, knowing what we're about to do, I understand now and suddenly feel shy.

This is pretty much my first time because I've decided Walter didn't count. Losing my virginity to him was like losing it to the seat of a bicycle.

I'm standing awkwardly by the bed, arms crossed in a pose that is neither sexy nor inviting. I can't look at him, but I'm very aware of his presence close behind me. I'm not just uncomfortable... I'm scared.

Viper reaches for my hair and gently pulls it all over my shoulders to fall straight down my back. As he catches the loose strands his fingers brush against my neck and when I shiver he continues stroking from ear to shoulder. I was holding my elbows but now my grip loosens and finally lets go. The chill tremors go straight to my nipples and I arch my chest as his fingernails lightly scratch under my hair and along my jawline.

My eyes are closed but when Viper turns me around to face him I slowly, hesitantly, open them to meet his gaze. Startled I gasp in a breath when I see his look of raw wonder.

His hands cup the sides of my head, fingers massaging my scalp, while his eyes explore my face like he's never really seen me before.

He stares for the longest time then tilts me into the light and studies some more. Leaning in he brushes feather-light kisses across my forehead, down my cheeks, and just before he reaches my mouth he breathes *perfect!* and when his lips land on mine it truly is a moment of pure perfection.

It's not our first kiss, but this is... this is me, Dora, as a lover. Not a liar being punished or a victim being comforted. This is the natural coming together of a man and a woman, *a wonder and an amazement.*

I'm stunned and awed by the wave of love that emanates from this man towards me. I'm bathing in his affection and my feelings overwhelm me. Time doesn't stand still – it simply no longer exists. Nothing exists except our joining. His kiss is a loving promise and I hope mine shows how much I want – and need – to fulfill that desire.

I know I've forgiven him too soon but omigod this kiss!

When we do finally draw apart Viper smiles tenderly before crushing me to his chest in the tightest embrace. He's holding me so close it's like he's absorbing me into his body. Every inch of me is pressed and pulled and held as he murmurs *my girl, my baby girl* before lifting me in his arms and gently laying me out on the bed.

He undresses me so slowly. First lifting off my – our – hoodie, being careful not to brush against the bandage on my arm. The fleece is loose enough that I didn't need to wear a bra which I couldn't have managed to put on myself anyhow.

So now I'm naked from the waist up and his look is full of admiration but I'm feeling self-conscious. I have to fight the urge to either cover up or pull his shirt off of him. My shifting around must give him a clue because he lifts my arms above my head and clasping both wrists in one hand keeps me securely pinned down. With his free hand he drags the boxer shorts off me, slides them down my legs and motions for me to kick them off.

Once again I feel the excitement of being naked while he's still fully dressed. The wanton reveling is incredibly erotic.

I can hear music with a heavy rhythmic base, some kind of old rock or metal, and know the club members are gearing up for a party. Good, that should mean no one will disturb us. It also means no one will hear me if I scream but... they probably wouldn't come to my rescue anyhow.

"Don't move your hands," he orders, getting up and stepping back to fully examine my body. I feel goosebumps forming and discover I'm pressing my thighs tightly, trying to rub my hidden spot. I'm sure he notices but he doesn't smirk or tease me. Instead, his gaze is worshiping me.

His eyes rove over every inch of my body adoring me like I'm a sacrament and I feel blessed. I feel like a gift that I hope with all my heart is enough.

He strips off and I ogle this beautiful man, this ideal specimen of maleness. Tall and muscular, graceful as a panther, tattooed and tough. His masculinity makes me feel so feminine, so womanly. The power of my sexuality surges through me.

"Sweetheart I'm just going to hold you tonight. The last 24 hours has been insane and all I want to do is keep you thoroughly kissed and cuddled and safe with me."

A pang of disappointment lodges in my chest making me look deeply into his eyes to penetrate his thoughts. I didn't realize how anxious I was until seeing his calm certainty made all tension leave my body. Closing my eyes I snuggle into his arms and am enfolded in his warm, loving embrace. I was so worried about having to have sex and now... now I don't have to think about it at all.

Last night and today has been a horrendous ordeal but here in our bed I can safely relax feeling the strength of Viper's arms, the steady beat of his heart, and savoring our closeness.

Viper

I surprised myself when I didn't push Dora for sex because I fully intended to. Now my raging hard-on has woken me up early. It's just turning light with the dawn. My cock has grown impatient after pressing into Dora's soft naked body all night.

Bending down to play with her pretty pussy I'm ready to first drink her up and then bury my cock deep.

Yesterday I reveled in Dora's explosive reaction to an orgasm from oral. I have a new mission in life. Driving my girl crazy with lust and pleasure is gonna be my new go-to thing. I can't think of a better goal than to drown in the savory, salty taste of her cream while she begs for more.

It felt like *deja vu* last night when Dora lay motionless on the bed while I undressed her. Partway through it became a repeat of me surveying the damage Casso had inflicted. Back then her frailty frightened me and I was barely able to touch her. She was like a damaged doll, dainty and breakable.

But then the scent of her arousal led me to inspect her precious pink nub and once seen I had to kiss and lick and suck. When my girl freaked with trembling legs and bucking hips I realized she wasn't something fragile but a highly sexual and sensual young woman.

I was prepared to make love to her sweetly the first time - but with plenty of savage fucking to follow - when something held me back. It wasn't right yet.

Now I can't wait so I part her thighs and kneel between her legs deeply inhaling her delicious scent. I won't last long until the need to be sheathed inside her wet warmth is overpowering but there's still time to fuck her with my tongue first.

Dora squirms and squeals while begging for more. Her breathless cries are sweet and pretty, and they go straight from my ear to my cock. When Dora shouts my name, my real name, I can't hold back a second longer.

I need to RSVP that invitation to her pleading pussy.

Even though I threatened to go bareback with her I know I have to wrap it up because who knows where Walter was dipping his wick? Quickly rolling on a condom I slip between her widely spread thighs and push my way in. Dora winces slightly as my cock stretches her open but her eyes hold my gaze while her sweet pussy welcomes me in and holds on tight.

I'm aware that I need to take it slow. Although technically I'm not her first the truth is I pretty much am. I mean, there's no barrier to break through but her entire passage is super tight. It feels fantastic: hot and pulsing and frazzling every nerve ending.

I'm trying to keep still to give her a chance to get used to me but fuck it's hard to hold back. I'm not used to being gentle. Fuck, I'm not used to giving a shit how the bitch feels. Dora's not a bitch but I still have to adjust my thinking. Giving as much or even more than I'm taking feels righteous with my girl.

"Sweetheart, are you doing okay?"

Dora's eyes are still glazed from her orgasm and she gives me a lazy smile accompanied by a happy sigh.

"I am so okay... are you?"

"Uh yeah, but going slow is really hard and I need to start moving like now, okay?" In my head I'm screaming *say yes, say yes, say yes.*

"Of course it's okay, you know I've done this before."

"Well no, you really haven't. You had a cock slip in and out... I hate the thought of some other guy even having that much of you," I add, feeling my hands clench.

"But he's dead so you can't really hate him."

"I can fucking hate anyone I want to but, okay forget I said that, this is gonna be totally different."

"Well yeah, I guess I am expecting you to be better than the dead guy."

I close my eyes to distract myself because if I start laughing I'm totally gonna blow my load. I know what she really meant but the way it came out... fuck me!

I'm biting down hard on my tongue when she asks: "Should I be doing something like moving around like this?" and she starts to wiggle her hips making my balls tighten way too soon..

I feel her hot walls throbbing around me so I inch in until I'm fully seated and so deep. My girl is chewing hard on her bottom lip but stroking my shoulders, urging me on.

"Jeez Dora you are so fucking tight," I groan.

"Is that a complaint?"

"Christ, no!"

"Because it's your fault... I mean with a dick that big all the girls must feel tight to you."

I snort a laugh then tell her: "Stop joking! I can't laugh while I'm fucking and I need to do a good job for your first time."

I see the happiness shining in her sparkling eyes and shake my hair back so I can keep sight of her face as I withdraw then push back in again and again. We soon establish a rhythm and I move her hands to her tits so I can watch her knead and caress them. I need to keep my hands free to hold my weight off her body.

Swiveling my hips I concentrate on finding her g-spot. Her eyes go wide before she squeezes them shut. Lifting up on my knees I hold her by the shoulder and start driving hard while my other hand snakes between us to rub her swollen, wet clit. Dora's body goes spastic underneath me and I can't keep my orgasm back. I cum so hard it almost hurts and feels never-ending. The best I've ever had.

I know for certain that this is the first time I've ever made love instead of simply fucking and when she breathes out *Oh Gray* my cum shoots from my balls via my heart.

I flop down beside her breathing heavily. Dora's face is glowing and her smile is so sweet. She reaches across my chest and her hand looks so little as it strokes one of my Celtic tattoos.

"I don't ever want to move again but I've got to get rid of this then I'll be right back." Walking to the toilet I can't even remember the last time I got laid and for some reason I say that out loud.

"I don't know what to say to that," she calls out after me and I chuckle.

"Sweetheart you've got to get up as well because you need to pee, girls should always pee after sex."

"Is that so I don't get pregnant?" she asks coming up behind me. I love that she hasn't tried to cover up to hide her beautiful body.

"Um, no my little innocent, it's something to do with your plumbing. The condom is what keeps you from getting pregnant–"

"Oh so if I go on birth control you won't need to put one of those on anymore, right?"

"Now you've really got me thinking back and... hmm, nope I've never had sex without wearing one." Wrapping my arms around her we kiss and I tell her I will love fucking her bare. "We'll both get tested and you can get protection. I don't want you to get those shots because I don't think that can be good for you but one of those wire things will be okay and then no more condoms."

"And we'll have sex even if I'm on my period? You won't be disgusted?"

"Never disgusted by you or your body Dora but I probably won't go down on you... although I might, just you know, just to taste." Now she's the one wrinkling her nose.

"And will you show me how to do that to you? I mean, I know it won't all fit in my mouth but I'll do my best."

Just the conversation is getting me hard again.

Although she waves me away I wait for her until she's finished on the toilet. When I grab her as she's washing her hands she cups water from tap and throws it at me.

She gives a little yelp when I smack her ass stating: "Oh you can't cool me off like that baby girl."

"Dora is your pussy too sore for my cock again? I mean, I can fuck your mouth..."

Her reflection in the mirror shows the little devil licking her lips as she meets my eyes and says: "Why not do both?"

Grabbing hold I swing her across the room onto the bed. Her squeal turns into peals of laughter when I leap beside her, reaching for another condom.

Dora

I never want to get out of bed again. Lying here wrapped around Viper's lovely body is the best feeling ever. I never would have believed that a couple of weeks ago. Not even a couple of days ago!

The experience of being kidnapped by Fiona and her men was terrifying. If I'd known the plan was to hand me over to sex traffickers I'm sure I'd have been even more frightened but I knew Viper would rescue me. Really weird that the man who was my first abductor would later be my savior, rescuing me from the second attempt.

Realizing I was 100 percent certain that Viper would come for me proved he was my man, no matter what. I knew that even before this marvelous experience that he's given me. That we've shared.

Every time Viper touches me he can't resist mentioning how incredibly soft my skin is. His skin isn't soft at all, it's hard. Not rough-hard, but muscle-hard. Muscles all over and a hard... cock. A giggle is rising to my lips just for thinking the word. I'm such a loser and yet, I can't be if I'm in bed with a man like Viper.

I'd rather call him Gray but Viper is his chosen name. Or maybe it was bestowed on him by a club president, I'm not sure how that works. But I prefer Dora to Loretta so I should go with his preference. He actually growled, in a very sexy way, when I called out Gray in our most intimate moment so I know he liked me saying it then.

I want to do everything exactly the way he wants. I want to be everything he expects, needs, desires... Waking up to his fingers prying into my vagina, parting my folds so his lips could suckle and lick, gave me unimaginable pleasure.

I'm not very good at stimulating myself and even though one of my cousins gave me a dildo to practice with I never had the nerve to put it in. Another cousin talked about her vibrator and everyone joined in on that conversation except me. I wish I'd been given one of those instead but I guess they just took it for granted that I already had my own *magic wand*.

So everything that's happening in bed with Viper is totally new and very exciting.

Playing with my pubic hair her comments: "You're a furry little thing, aren't you?"

"I'm just normal... right?"

"Well.... most women wax so they're hairless or just about."

"Aren't all the women you know strippers or club whores?"

"Fair enough," he laughs then continues: "But I do know that while men have hair on their asses women shouldn't."

"I don't!" That was uncalled-for and I'm indignant.

He laughs again and answers: "True, not *on* your ass but around your asshole. I saw it when I was doing your body art—"

"You mean scarification - ugh! that's an ugly word, isn't it?" I interject.

"Oh Dora. I am a brutal man full of ugly words and cruel thoughts and I have been for a very long time. I'm not going to change – I don't think I can. But—" He flips me onto my stomach which immediately makes me struggle and squirm but he holds me down and plants kisses all down the crack of my behind. "I'm sorry Dora's ass– what's the word for that in Italian?"

327

"*Culo* for bum."

"Oh that sounds nice. Okay, I'm sorry Dora's *culo* for the pain from the carving and healing. And Dora, I promise that the only brutality you'll ever encounter from me is witnessing how viciously I'll take out anyone who tries to harm you."

"Umm, that's sweet? I guess? Anyhow *if* I do actually have hair there it doesn't matter–"

"Sweetheart you could be as hairy as Sasquatch and I wouldn't care," he declares laughing loudly. "Fuck, there's so much you don't understand about men. Besides, this hair of yours is soft and silky. I like playing with your curls."

Although I love to see him really laughing and happy my cheeks feel like they're on fire. I remember my cousins explaining a joke from a TV show about *the drapes matching the carpet* but I've never given any thought to shaving away that hair. Now I'm wondering *would he like it better if I did?*

I give him a halfhearted smack saying: "Can we change the subject now? This conversation is too embarrassing."

"Sure but one last thing on that subject for now: believe me when I say that anal sex can be very pleasurable for the man and the woman."

"Oh ewww! it'll be a cold day in hell before anything like that ever happens," I remark.

"We'll see," is his reply. I'm about to argue the point but the look on his face is so confident that even I start considering *well, maybe*. I do trust him to know best when it comes to doing sex stuff.

Holding my chin he leans in to give me a gentle kiss but stops just short of my mouth and wetly licks my lips staring into my eyes the whole time. After a few moments of this he tells me: "I saw you spit in my coffee at the tattoo shop so this is me paying you back."

Then he crushes my lips against his as he swirls his tongue all around mine, transferring his saliva. It's gross and sexy and erotic and for some crazy reason it makes me chuckle. I just love this playful side of him.

I can't believe he saw me do that to his coffee but never complained about—oh, he did say something about how great the coffee tasted. At the time I thought he was just making fun of me. Hmmph, turns out I was right.

When he's done he asks: "Are you hungry, sweetheart?"

"Well I *was* but after that I have no appetite..."

He flips me over and gives me a few sharp swats on my bum. It stings and at my indignant cry of *Hey!* he tells me *cheeky girls get their cheeks spanked.* I roll my eyes then quickly roll my body out of his reach. Kneeling I pout at him while rubbing my sore bottom with both hands. Since he moved away instead of coming after me I don't react until his phone appears in his hands and he quickly snaps a photo.

"Viper! No! Delete that right now!"

He's grinning at the picture he's just taken and shaking his head slowly tells me: "No way, this is really hot. You're so pretty showing off your tits and pussy. I can get a hard-on just from this look on your face."

One time my cousins were fooling around taking selfies with the cameras on their phones and forgot to delete the pictures. One of the aunties discovered the photos and we all got grounded for a month. Since I almost never went out a grounding for me meant no TV.

Viper turns the screen around to face me and I'm speechless. Other than glimpses in the mirror as I get dressed or step into the shower I never see my naked body.

This candid photo of me wearing a petulant expression while my breasts are thrust forward from my hands being behind my back really is... slutty and sexy. My waist dips in with a nice curve and my hips flare down to round thighs. And despite the coverage of my pubic curls the pink flesh of my labia shows through. I look like a girl in a dirty magazine.

"I'd make this my screensaver except I can't hack the thought of anyone else seeing it. I guess I'll edit it to save just your face. Every time I see it I'll remember what the rest of the picture looks like."

"No Viper it's not allowed!"

He cocks one eyebrow asking: "Do you want to rephrase that, little girl?"

"Oh stop with the macho bullshit. I'm serious. Spagnolos aren't allowed to have their picture taken. I'll bet your tech guy didn't find any, right?"

He thinks for moment before giving a single nod. Looking at his phone again he studies it then tells me: "Tough. Nobody's messin' with my phone so don't worry about it. I like this photo and I'm keeping it, I mean look at yourself you're really hot."

Viper turns the screen back towards me and again I'm struck by the image, especially with his words ringing in my head: *I'm hot!*

I drop down to all fours so I can move faster as I crawl onto him in a hurry to fasten my mouth to his in a hungry kiss. I can't believe how forward I'm being and how much I love it.

Seeing the admiration in Viper's eyes as he stares at my boobs makes me want to flaunt myself even more. I don't feel the slightest need to hide myself under covers or clothes. I'm... relishing my unexpected exhibitionism and his obvious enjoyment of my nude body.

Just as much as I adore studying him. His tattooed skin bulging with muscles and veins, decorated with intricate Celtic designs I can trace around with my fingers, followed by my lips. I want to explore every inch of him and he'll indulge me. This playful intimacy is something I would never in a million years imagine I could someday experience.

"Oh baby," he laughs lightly, "Dirty photos turn you on, huh? We'll definitely have to make a video."

I squeal *no way* but quickly forget those concerns as I lower myself to rub against his hard cock. Another condom and then I drop down, absorbing him deep inside me. Yeah, I guess he's right because despite the soreness from all this new sex I am really, really horny for my man.

He has access to all of me when I'm on top of him like this. His hands move from holding my hips to cupping my tender ass and riding him hard makes my tits bounce in his face. He leans forward to lick first one hard nipple then the other. The sticky slapping sound of our flesh and the sight of our joining where I slide up and down his dick adds so much to our pleasure. My every sense is engaged with him.

I drop my head back as the wave of bliss takes me under and I scream in ecstasy. I feel his hot mouth sucking the skin of my throat. Being marked makes me shudder with chills of orgasm and then he explodes hotly inside me.

We're both panting as we fall back down on the bed. Flickering through my mind is the thought that the house mice will be impressed and I huff a laugh.

Viper says *hmm?* and I tell him my appetite *for food* is back.

"I'll take you out for a meal. Get dressed for riding on the bike."

I clap my hands with delight and hustle to get into the leathers Kim passed on to me. Viper whistles appreciatively at the result then takes the hairbrush from me and fixes my hair. I lean into the pleasure of his hands combing out my tangles.

When he's finished he again lays kisses on the side of my neck that make me shiver – he remembers everything that turns me on! I just can't get enough of him.

Viper

I lead Dora towards the kitchen and wave Bebe in to join us. She arrives with Bunny in tow, both of them complimenting my girl on her cool biker chick look.

"Bebe help us out here," I say. "Dora's covered in hair. Legs, armpits, snatch. I don't care but she does so what's the best solution?"

"Wax that pussy–"

Bunny interrupts to specify: "A *Brazilian*, to get everything."

Bebe gives Bunny a considering look. "Do you think so? I thought maybe just leave a landing strip, to get her used to it."

"Nope, go the whole hog first time and then she can decide if she wants anything different afterwards."

"Yeah okay, that makes sense. So, a first-time Brazilian will cost about fifty bucks and last you a couple of weeks but you'll have to wait longer until the hair grows enough to do it again. Honestly? I can't remember how long that takes because the first time I got it done was ages ago. But I do know the more you have it done the longer the time in between. Come to our spa, the club owns it, and–"

"We do?" Now I'm interrupting because I had no idea about this.

"Viper! you know about the nail salon. It's expanded and now we do everything from hair removal to hair extensions."

"Yeah we do work you know." huffs Bebe. "In fact, I'll be the one doing your laser." At Dora's puzzled look she adds: "Pits and legs, laser is the only way to go and it lasts forever."

"So Dora can go to the salon and you girls will see that everything gets done?"

"Sure, it'll be fun!"

"Yeah, now that Fiona's not around we can have a good time with Poi...Dora."

Dora ducks her head smiling shyly and I can see she likes the idea but then her mouth droops down and she whispers to me: "I don't have any money!"

Bebe hears her and says: "Don't worry about the cost sweetie, Viper will pay. After all," she pauses to smirk at me, "he'll get all the benefit."

"Yeah, yeah how much do you want?"

"Give me $500 and we'll open an account. We do that for the strip club staff and send them a monthly accounting of how much per girl. We'll do the same for Dora and then let you know when you need to top it up, okay?"

Viper pulls a wad of bills from the front pocket of his jeans. He separates a stack and hands it over to Bebe who quickly counts it.

"This is $1,200," she says.

"That's good, she can do her nails too, if she wants, and give yourselves the usual tip." That makes the women happy.

"Oooh we'll do her make-up too, Dora you're gonna love it. And maybe a sexy slip or something from the boutique..."

"Omigod that new lavender baby-doll nightie would look perfect on her!"

I look at Dora who has perked right up with her eyes moving back and forth like she's at a tennis match. "It's up to you to let them know what you want or don't want, right?" She nods vigorously.

"Oh and Viper no sex right after the waxing. Not her first time. She'll a bit sore and red and will need to smooth on *aloe* lotion... I'm sure you can help with that." Bebe says with a wink.

"No hot bath or shower, either. Just lukewarm so the skin doesn't get more irritated."

"But you'll be fine Dora, you're not super-pale like Kim... shit do you remember how she reacted to the treatment?"

"Oh yeah, she was hurting but only 'cause her Irish skin is so fair. You're right about Dora, it'll all be good."

"Okay so no fucking because her pussy will be sore but she can still blow me, right?"

Dora rolls her eyes at me but the club whores nod in agreement understanding that it's a perfectly valid question. Huh, I thought it was. Just for that I'm not telling her how obvious that hickey is on her neck, Not until we finish eating and I'm paying the bill. It'll be fun watching the waitress staring, and once Dora realizes why she'll be blushing and trying to cover it with her hand or by ducking her chin down. She'll look so cute!

We have a great twilight ride and then stop at a Mom and Pop diner out in the countryside. Plenty of good food and a friendly – nosy even – atmosphere. Dora's neck is stared at and we're both given knowing smiles but it's all done in good humor. There's no censorship in the older couple's eyes, just a happy salute to young love.

When I reveal why she's getting such close scrutiny Dora's reaction is everything I hoped for. She gasps, blushes, and hunches up her shoulder whispering *can you still see it?* She's a fuckin' cutie.

Back in my room I let her make me grovel over her public embarrassment before she's willing to even consider sex. It's fun. We both enjoy the dramatic retelling of her shame as she carelessly unzips her leathers. Wearing just her underwear and high-heels she flops down on the bed. Apparently she thought she *was going to die!!*

"Will it make you feel better if I kiss your foot?" I ask, kneeling to pull off her high-heel. "Or if I kiss you here?" as I lift her leg to reach the back of her knee. "Or here?" now I've moved up to the inside of her thigh.

She's gone from giggling to gasping. Kicking off the other shoe Dora brings both feet up on the edge of the bed, spreading her legs replying: "Maybe."

"Maybe? let's see." I yank her thong down but instead of sliding if off over her feet I twist it into a knot tying her ankles together. Grabbing hold of them I lift her legs straight up and attack her exposed pussy with my fingers.

"Maybe, hmm?" I smirk as we both hear the sucking sound when I tap my fingers in her wet slit. She squirms from a mixture of lust and embarrassment that spreads a blush from her cheeks right down across her chest.

Threatening: "Little liar! I should spank you..." I give her ass a pinch adding, "but I promised your cunt a kiss."

"Ugh, do you have to use that word, Viper?"

I'm honestly puzzled so she elaborates saying: "You know, the c-word."

"Cocksucker? oh, you mean cunt. Uh, yeah Dora, it's a great word. It's got that nice sharp bite when you emphasize the T."

Again she rolls her eyes at me. "OK brat, your cunt-t-t-t is about to be punished."

I torment her to the edge, back off, then tease her again. It's such a turn-on to watch her squirm and hear her moans as she begs for my cock. She's so responsive! I'm gonna be edging her for all our foreplay in the future.

I finally remove her panties but I don't free her ankles. Instead, I take one in each hand and spread her legs wide pushing them down by her shoulders. When I plunge into her welcoming warmth we can both see how eagerly she pulls my cock in.

"What a greedy little cunt you have, Poison," I taunt her.

"It's hungry, not greedy. And it's my pussy—"

I interrupt asking: "How about snatch? twat? bird?—"

"Bird?"

"Yeah that one's not so common."

"Well whatever. But I decided it's okay if you want to call me Poison sometimes. It's kind of a bad-ass nickname."

I laugh at the very thought of Dora being bad-ass but I play along asking: "Oh? are you some bad-ass bitch, Poison?"

"The baddest!" she happily exclaims.

I pull her into my arms and kissing the top of her head tell her she can give me a hickey any time she likes. That catches her attention and she props up on one elbow to ask *how?* After I explain she practices in the spot where my neck meets my shoulder and I'm sure she's left several bruising marks.

Her sucking kisses are enough to make my cock stir with interest but we need to wait a bit. *Fuck!* I think, *I didn't use a condom just now. No wonder it felt so good.* I decide not to say anything but tomorrow I'll see about getting her one of those morning-after pills.

Once she settles back in my arms again I comment: "So... you'd be a married lady right now if everything hadn't gone tits-up."

Dora wriggles in a little closer against my chest. I tighten my hold and she's delighted when I flex a pec several times, making her face pop up off my chest. The club has its own gym including a boxing ring so we work out all the time. I show off to her a little.

"The club arranges fights and we all bet on the outcome. I win most of mine."

"You mean punching fights?"

"Yeah, boxing. It's a great way to relieve pressure although some guys prefer grabbing a club whore for a blow-job to ease their stress."

That gets me a squinty-eyed look and a raised eyebrow.

"Not me, though," I add. "I like fighting. Dog and I are pretty evenly matched so the stakes mount up when we square off. Same with Hardware and Tiny. Tiny is bigger but Hardware is more agile.

Banger never fights now that he's the Prez and I'm sure he misses it. I'm equally sure Kim doesn't, her husband's nose has already been broken enough times to detract from his good looks."

"What about your good looks?"

"You think I'm good-looking, Dora?"

She huffs her reply: "You know you are. The club whores all fuss over you."

Squeezing tight I chuckle when my girl makes an *oomph* sound. It feels so good to have her settled securely in my arms. "They won't any more, not now that we're together."

"Some might 'cause they'll be jealous."

"Yeah probably." I'm matter-of-fact about it, it is what it is. "But you let me know if anyone's causin' you grief, okay?"

"No worries, bad-ass Poison can take care of herself," she declares.

"Oh, baby." We kiss for a while then I remind her where we left off in our conversation. She agrees saying:

"I guess if the engagement party, or at least the shoot-out, hadn't happened then yeah, Walter would have officially consummated our marriage and, no doubt, performed his duty nightly until I fell pregnant. We'd be parents to our child but strangers to each other."

"Nah, he'd have fallen in love with you in no time."

She gives a dry humorless laugh. "There's no room for romance in mafia marriages, Viper. My cousins told me Walter had already set up his mistress in an apartment. She's the one who could indulge in romantic notions and fun. Walter would escort me to a family dinner then drop me off back home so he could hit a nightclub with her."

That doesn't make sense to me. "You mean you'd be okay with that? knowing you were sharing your husband?"

She's blows out a heavy breath and the breeze makes my nipple tingle. "No you don't get it. You see *officially* I wouldn't know I was sharing him. I'd be expected to turn a blind eye to anything Walter did and, in return, I'd get a platinum credit card, jewels in every color, and a convertible to run around in. Plus a mink coat on the birth of my first child. From the outside my life would look perfect and, funny enough, the mistress would be deeply jealous of me."

"Why? she's the one having a good time while you're stuck sitting at home."

"But she has no status, and that means everything to the *famiglia*. He could cut her loose at any time or even gift her to one of his men if he felt like it. Hmm, like Banger did to you with me. I guess the macho man mindset is the same everywhere.

Anyhow, her luxurious home is built on quicksand knowing the day will come when some younger, prettier *putana* will catch his eye. Ugh! why are we even talking about this?'

"My fault, I wanted to know what kind of life I stole from you. Now that you've told me all this well... I don't feel guilty about it at all."

"Oh I wasn't planning on living that life. I wasn't sure how I'd accomplish it but I was determined to escape. That's why I gave all that money to Auntie Angie to hold for me.

She was happily widowed after a short marriage to a violent man and that's why she was willing to help. She knew what was in store for me if I stayed. The only thing I've ever wanted is the freedom to live my life in the way I choose."

I push her back from me in order to see her face when I ask: "Do you feel like you've exchanged one prison for another?" Dora doesn't reply right away and I experience a shortness of breath while suddenly feeling her answer is the most important thing ever.

"To be honest I did, at first, and I had figured out a plan on how to get away from Casso – it meant robbing him which I didn't mind at all! – but now? with you? No. I'm exactly where I want to be, Gray."

I know from the love I see in her eyes that she means what she says. Something inside me eases at her words and when she uses my real name everything feels utterly right.

Dora

Viper looks so earnest when he apologizes. "I really am sorry about the, you know, punishment. It might have seemed like ... and yeah, maybe it was an assault since you didn't consent to the carving so as I say, I'm sorry I hurt you."

"It really hurt a lot!" I whine at him adding: "There really wasn't much physical pain it was the thought of having that nasty phrase on my butt forever!"

He looks suitably ashamed about teasing me over what the carving said. "Aw baby girl what can I do to make it up to you? please? I need you to forgive me so we can move on."

With a big sigh I explain: "Actually... I already forgave you. Being beaten by Casso showed me the difference between your punishment for the threat to the club and violence for its own sake."

"Dora honey, you're the best!"

"Well I have to forgive you 'cause if I don't I'll never get to enjoy your dink again."

He pulls back with an expression of horror mixed with hilarity: "Did you just say *dink?*"

I nod and he laughs loud and long. "Fuck me, Dog's gonna love that! It's a cock, sweetheart, it stops being called a dink once a boy is potty-trained."

I roll my eyes at him asking instead: "Umm, how about dick?"

"No, cock. C-O-C-K, say it."

After pausing long enough to feel the color flame in my cheeks I mutter *cock*. It's hard for me to say that word even silently in my own head.

"Oh baby your pouty lips and blushing face are making my balls tight with the need to fuck you. C'mon, say it again. It sounds so pretty and dirty coming from you."

I twist my lips to hide a smile and pretending exasperation say: "Cock, okay? now stop it."

"No, again! Louder this time and stress that K at the end."

My sarcasm can't disguise the laughter in my voice. "Oh do you need me to use it in a sentence? Is that what you want?"

"Yes! Yes, that's perfect. What have you got for me?"

In what I hope is a seductive voice I whisper "Oh Viper, I just loooove your big *cocK-cocK-cocK* and I need it in my pussy ALL the time."

I guess my attempt at sexy worked because suddenly his hands are caressing me everywhere and I've hyped myself up too. I really do want his cock in my mouth and down my throat. Squirming free from his arms I slide down his body with my hands busy caressing. He smells musky and manly.

His pubic hair is dark and thick and short. I'm curious and ask: "Do you cut this?"

"Yeah, every now and then I hack it down to keep if from getting caught in my fly because I go commando a lot."

"Mmm, I noticed that, but not when you sleep at night."

"Mmm-hmm, and I noticed you noticing."

I tell him to *shut up* and when I take hold of his cock and put the head in my mouth he does. For a little while, then he groans and tells me I can grasp him harder because *it won't break, and I can give him more than just the tip of my tongue.*

The first time I saw his cock I thought it was ugly with its red color and thick veins, the whole thing frighteningly big. I've come to realize those same veins rub along the inside of my passage in the most delightful way and surprisingly his cock fits.

After screwing for the third time it leaves me sore at the end of my hole, I'm not sure what he's hitting: womb? cervix? some part of my internal plumbing. So it's easier to take him down my throat this time and once I start lapping him all over like he's a melting ice-cream cone he really seems to like it.

He gives me instructions on what to do and I like giving him pleasure. When he cums I swallow and I'm surprised at how hot his jizz is, and how much there is, and how quickly it shoots out of him... but it doesn't taste bad.

"Fuck Dora that was... fuck!" Viper collapses in sweaty exhaustion with a huge grin on his handsome face. His heart still pounds making his chest rise and fall with his rapid breathing.

Giving him a mischievous smile I draw circles around his nipples and stretching out the words drawl: "That was fuuuuun..." deliberately leaving the sentence open.

"Fun? I'll give you fucking fun you naughty little girl," laughs Viper swinging my body on top of his and using both hands to lightly smack my butt. I wriggle and giggle and nibble my bottom lip which catches his gaze making him growl playfully. Looking into each other's eyes the world goes on pause for a long moment while we smile and stare, seeing something more than lust.

"Fuck! I'll fucking teach you everything about fucking sex, and everything else you need to know, Dora," he promises.

"Oh I know you will, Viper. You've already taught me how to say *fuck* as an adjective, a verb, and a noun."

Respect

Crusher

Taking Fiona by the arm I reach to hold the back of her neck and steer her away from my bedroom. *It's been quite a while, too long,* I think, *since she was in there but, happily, we'll have plenty of room upstairs.* I lead her up to the second floor, our home for the next few days.

"Why are we up here? Why aren't we going to your room? I don't think I've ever been up here before." Fiona keeps asking questions, trying to hide her nervousness.

"Probably not. We only use these rooms for out-of-towners who need a place when they come in for a meet-up."

"So why are we here?"

"We need the privacy. You're going to make a lot of noise."

"Look Crusher, I know you're pissed at me but–"

I interrupt her, my gravelly voice insisting: "Fiona, you know you deserve this. It's warranted, and you won't be content until you've been thoroughly punished."

She yanks her arm trying to free it from my grip but my fingers are like iron. This reminder of my superior strength leaves her apprehensive but also aroused. She hates to admit how my dominance thrills even as it irritates and frightens her. She's an impatient woman who doesn't know what she wants. Not a good combination.

I carefully choose words I know will excite her even more: "Behave, little girl. You've been very, very naughty and you're due for correction. To be mastered. By me. Soundly spanked and thoroughly disciplined. You were unfaithful, you lied, you stole—"

"I didn't!"

"You didn't get away with it but you tried which is just as bad. And you're a shit-disturber. Kim and I have talked quite a bit in the short time she's been here and Fee you've been getting in everybody's business trying to break up couples and start fights between the club brothers.

But what you were planning to do with that young girl was the worst, Fiona. You must know what happens when they're trafficked so how could you do something like that to another woman? and don't give me any bullshit about being jealous over Viper. I fucking know that you panting after him is all for show, just a way to tell every other guy to back off."

"We're friends, we have history together."

"Exactly, you two *are* history. And you don't get to be friends with another man, trust me men aren't built that way. Jesus Fee, you need to learn how to be respectful—"

Again, she tries to interrupt saying: "People have to earn—"

But I just talk over her continuing: "And I'm going to have all your respect and loyalty by time I finish disciplining you."

She tosses her head and sticks her chin in the air exclaiming: "Oh you and your *punishing* crap. I know you're gonna be spanking me 'cause you get off on it. Go ahead and call it discipline if that makes you feel better but we both know the score. It's no big deal if I get a sore butt, I can handle that."

"Yes, I know you can which is why I have so much more planned for you. You're gonna be my very well-trained and respectful pet."

Good, now she looks scared, I note with satisfaction. No need to explain myself when a cruel smile will get her imagination do all the work.

Finally I tell her: "Here's a hint," and it's very satisfying to see her hanging off every word. "Your body will very much enjoy the torment which is going to be much, much more than merely *a sore butt.* True, you will spend most of each day tied down on my spanking bench so I can keep your ass red-hot at all times and your body flooded with pleasure chemicals. Then I'll... do you know what figging is, Fiona?"

Her eyes widen in horror: "Is that the thing with the chili peppers?"

"No, that's Capsaicin but I don't have... oh! that would work really well. I'll place an order, I'm sure you're going to need some refreshers in the future.

No figging is done with ginger. Same principle but it's not as hot as chili. Still, it's hot enough to make you squirm and beg for relief. Anyhow, I'll plug your butt with the burning root while grinding your clit with the magic wand. Simultaneous pain and pleasure will have you screaming *stop!* and *don't stop* at the same time.

That's just one example of the many fun games you and me are gonna play over the next few days."

"Why do you keep saying I'm your pet?"

"Because you're going to wear a dog collar and nothing else while I leash you up for daily exercise running up and down the hall. Well not really running... I'll be jogging and you'll be scrambling on your hands and knees struggling to keep up. Don't worry, I got you knee-pads to wear and I'll use my riding crop to help you with your speed. That's why we need the second floor to ourselves."

"I'm not doing any of that."

"You will," I assert, my smile smug and confident.

"No, you don't understand you can't... we can't... oh fuck Crusher there's no time. I can't believe I'm telling you this but I have to. Fuck!"

"What?" Seeing her chew her bottom lip while refusing to meet my gaze set off alarms in my head. Grabbing her by the upper arms I hold her in a firm grip and demand: "Tell me what you've done, Fiona!"

She blurts out: ""I called the FBI and they're going to raid this clubhouse tonight."

I feel the color drain from my face as the dire consequences of her actions rush through my brain. Our very lives are at stake.

Fiona rushes to fill the silence saying: "I was never going to let them actually sell Poison, I'm not that much of a bitch, getting her here was just to have some evidence..."

"That's entrapment!"

"But the club does traffic women and—"

"No, we don't. Jesus Christ, okay give me a second here." When Fiona tries to explain herself some more I cover her mouth and the look on my face is enough to shut her up.

After thinking through a few scenarios I tell her to call her brother. Banger answers by saying: "Forget it Fiona, I'm not—" but I take over the call.

"Banger you're on speaker at our end but make sure we're not on yours, okay? Something seriously fucked-up is going on so just... Christ, just listen. I can't fucking believe what I'm saying but okay... Fiona called the FBI to raid our clubhouse... tonight, Fiona?"

"Tonight or really early in the morning."

I have to interrupt a loud shout of "Fiona why the fuck would you—"

"Banger, stop! There's no time. I want you to call Goblin and say a law enforcement contact just gave you a heads-up that your club and ours and the Wolverines are all being raided simultaneously by the FBI. None of us want any heat or attention so you're passing the tip on.

Call him right now and Banger make it convincing because if the truth gets out Fiona is dead and our clubs are at war."

"Pat! You've gotta believe me, I did it for our club, I thought—"

Cutting right over his sister's explanation Banger tells Crusher he'll call Goblin now adding: "You're banished Fiona, don't call me again," before disconnecting.

"Banished?" Fiona wails before bursting into tears sobbing: "Oh Crusher, I'm sorry, I didn't realize—"

"Stop. You and I are going to face this together and we'll figure it out. Meanwhile we act surprised when Goblin sends out the alert and yes, your punishment is put on hold until the FBI have been and gone—"

"I can't be here!"

"You have to be. It will look too suspicious if you aren't. Fiona, I wasn't kidding when I told Banger my Prez will kill you for this and if he doesn't any other club member will."

"Including you?"

I force my face to be impassive and don't reply. She needs to understand how deadly serious I am.

With our eyes locked on one another the air acts like a force field holding us in its beam. It's totally fucked up but the danger only adds spice to our mutual attraction.

Fiona's chest moves rapidly as her breathing quickens and her pupils are so dilated with lust that the blue of her irises barely shows. I know my arousal is evident but maintaining control is a huge part of my pleasure so I'm showing a cool exterior.

Pulling her close I cover her mouth with a firm, demanding kiss.

As I feel Fiona melt into me I roughly pull her clothing off and use her panties to bind her wrists together. Easily tossing her over my shoulder I stride down the hall to a bedroom at the end, lightly caressing and pinching her ass.

Entering the room I tell her: "Your delayed punishment is gonna be doubled... at least. Meanwhile, I'm gonna fuck you silly and Goblin or whoever will be suitably impressed at what a good girl you are when they come interrupt us."

I drop her on the bed and Fiona looks so enticing lying splayed out with her flushed face and bound wrists.

"Change of plans. I don't want to be naked when somebody comes knocking."

Quickly unzipping my jeans and push them down over my hips to free my cock. I give myself a few strokes before pulling Fiona onto her knees. "Take me deep, baby. You need to earn lots and lots of brownie points."

Fiona struggles to balance on the bed but I hold her head in both hands to control her movements. She manages to cup my balls while opening her mouth wide so I can push in and out.

We hear my phone buzz with an incoming text but but I deliberately ignore the summons and keep driving hard down her throat. Two minutes later two bikers are pounding down the hall only to collide with each other in the open doorway when they see us in action.

"Oh fuck. Crusher, man, sorry but this can't wait," says Slick, admiring the sight of Fiona kneeling on the bed with her face pressed up against my pelvis while my cock fills and chokes her.

Hornet, a closer friend who knows all about my feelings for her, smirks while casting an appreciative eye over Fiona's naked assets. Everyone in the clubhouse is used to public nudity and fucking although I'm pretty sure Fiona has only ever been a spectator. Well I guess being caught servicing her man can be her first lesson in humility.

"You've got thirty seconds to finish and get downstairs, both of you, Goblin's orders."

I reply by letting my head drop back as I give several more hard thrusts and groan as I release down Fiona's throat. Seeing that the two men are still standing there, unabashedly enjoying the show, she does her best to cover herself. She has no idea how sexy her submission looks with cum dribbling from the corner of her mouth and her tied hands cupped between her legs.

I chuckle hearing my brothers comments as they head back down the hall. Fiona's mortified look pleases me, too. Reaching down I slip a finger inside her folds and smile at the hot wetness. Giving her swollen nub a few strokes I leave her itchy and unfulfilled while ordering her to hurry and get up.

"C'mon, your clothes are in the hall."

Fiona

The Road Lightning members don't like me. They aren't hiding the fact that they don't want me here in their clubhouse. Nobody says anything, not in front of Crusher, but the looks I'm getting tell me plenty.

I suddenly realize he's right, if the truth comes out they won't hesitate to rip me apart. Being Crusher's bitch won't save me. Not even if I was his Old Lady. That's an odd thought. Is that what I actually want? I can't deny the chemistry between us although I always seem to be challenging him. I think he likes that, though.

Goblin's voice rings out, catching everyone's attention.

"We've gotten word the Feebs are gonna raid our clubhouse and it's vital they leave empty-handed. That means anyone with outstanding warrants get the fuck outta here now, and the rest of you pack up all the drugs and weapons – everything! - and we'll move them away.

Prospects, I need you to haul all our shit over to our safe house. I don't want any of you here. All the unattached pussy leaves as well. Go to your homes or if you don't have a home go with the prospects.

I only want members to be here and only a few, but we gotta look surprised so let's keep all the executive and we'll stage it like we're holding a private top-level meeting."

Some bikers have to go and they fist-bump and man-hug their brothers. All the women start scurrying around packing up their things in preparation for leaving. A few have their own cars and they drive off together.

A couple of wives announce they're staying with their men and Goblin agrees, realizing that's a good idea. It makes sense that no club whores are present when the old ladies are around.

I do my best to stay out of the way. I don't know where they keep their stashes and caches so I can't help pack up. Crusher is boxing files, members are dropping their guns into open duffel bags, and cases of untaxed booze and smokes, plus a lot of drugs are being passed to the prospects. Those guys are rushing back and forth to and from the parking lot when they've pulled up several pick-ups.

One of the men writes out a sign stating the club is *Closed until further notice for official business, Executive Members only*. He sticks it on the front door. That won't stop the FBI but it might help explain why so few bikers are on the premises.

I wonder who is taking charge of the clean-up at our clubhouse when I realize that one, Satan's Tears isn't actually being raided; and two, it's not my clubhouse any more.

That shakes me up and I feel lonely and alone until I sense I'm being watched and looking up catch Crusher's eye on me. He's busy, but he's still keeping me in his sights. That's reassuring. It means he'll take care of me publicly as well as when we're alone. Of course the thought of what he has planned for me when we are by ourselves isn't reassuring at all...

It takes almost two hours to get the clubhouse sorted to Goblin's satisfaction. The old ladies head into the kitchen to cook a meal and I follow them.

I'm not exactly welcomed with open arms but the men need privacy so my presence is tolerated. My offer to peel potatoes makes everyone happy.

Potatoes, onions, and carrots and loaded up on the counter and I get to work. The conversation flows around me and I feel myself relaxing in the women's company, easily managing my mindless occupation. Once the prep work is done I pour myself a cup of coffee and sit down at the big table, so reminiscent of home. Except that this is my home now, I guess.

Since my hands aren't occupied my thoughts again circle back to my recent interaction with Crusher. Our conversation, not the blow-job although that was epic despite the audience.

I'd forgotten how pleasurable it is to use my skills to make him moan and groan. The two of us have had plenty of practice and I know exactly what he likes. He knows his way around my body too and I'm looking forward to enjoying his expertise.

Except... he wants to do some kinky shit to me first and I know it's not going to be playtime, it's going to be punishment. A shiver runs through me and one of the women, Brandy I think her name is, asks *is somebody stepping on your grave, Fiona?*

That's a little too close for comfort! But I answer her honestly and say Crusher has some conditions for us getting back together and I'm a feeling a little apprehensive about the stuff he's got in mind.

A few chuckle and I realize they'll have heard about his predilections and maybe even witnessed him spanking some of the club whores. He's a disciplinarian by nature and I find myself hoping, unfairly I'm sure, that he hasn't been fucking anybody. I'm sure he could find himself a submissive or two amongst the club whores and I really hate the thought of that.

When the food is ready and laid out the men come in and get plates fixed up for them. Some sit at the table with their wives while the rest head back out to the bar area.

Crusher lets me know what he wants and then tells me to serve Goblin too so they can sit together and talk. Almost as an afterthought he says I can grab something as well and follow them.

I'm not sure how I feel at being ordered around like I'm his subordinate or something but I have no friends here so I have no choice but to obey.

The three of us sit down and after eating in silence for a bit Crusher blows me away by dropping one bombshell after another.

"Goblin, I want to make Fiona my Old Lady but I know that will be awkward because of who she is and the way she is. I know she's a bitch and nobody likes her, but I guarantee to make her act friendly and get along while she's here.

I realize nothing can happen until after this raid is successfully concluded in our favor but I'd like to give you a heads-up now that I'm officially claiming her and applying for Nomad status. I think that's the most satisfactory outcome for our club and for Satan's Tears, for me and her, and... I'm drawn to traveling."

"With your *second time around* backpack," states Goblin with a nod in my direction.

I'm not even trying to eat, I'm just sitting there with my mouth open in surprise at this news of Crushers. He wants to go Nomad? I had no idea. Or is this simply a way to protect me? Would he really go that far?

Going nomad is something we all hear about and we've offered hospitality to Nomads from time to time, but I've never envisioned that life for me. I never expected to leave my clubhouse. Of course I sure as hell never expected to hear Crusher ask for permission to make me his Old Lady, either.

I'll be completely under his thumb if we're far away from everyone and everything familiar but... I'm actually not opposed to that idea. Maybe it's because I'm in a difficult situation here in this clubhouse, just as I will be at home. My old home.

I'm 32 years old and my future is looking an awful lot like my past so a change - an adventure - might be exactly what I need.

Plus it's awfully uncomfortable being this horny. I can't stop inhaling Crusher's sweaty smell, it's such a turn-on, and his scarred, ugly face has always been the manliest look I've ever seen. The heels on my motorcycle boots add to my already impressive height so not many men are taller than me but Crusher towers.

Another thing about Crusher is that underneath the threats and the tough exterior is a man who cares deeply for me. He'll keep me safe well... safe from everyone else, I'll still be subject to his discipline. And yet I know he will be fair.

His motivation comes from a good place even if his methods are questionable. At the end of each punishment I know I'll be thoroughly aroused but I bet I'll have to beg for every orgasm.

The two men have been discussing logistics while I've been thinking my thoughts and they've come to an agreement because they're shaking hands.

Goblin turns to me and says: "Welcome Fiona. I'll make the announcement now." I can see that his smile does reach his eyes, but I'm glad I won't be under his watchful gaze on a daily basis.

Standing he calls out to the members: "Under the circumstances I've made this decision outside of church: everyone welcome Fiona, Property of Crusher, who has chosen to become a Road Lightning Nomad."

The pleasant lilt to his voice can't stop the rest from all talking at once, questioning and wondering what's going on. None of them sound happy but then Hornet speaks up and the mood changes.

"Congratulations Crusher. I know you've had your eye on Fiona for a long time. And welcome Fiona, I happen to have personal knowledge of the fact that you make Crusher very happy."

From the sniggers I know he's shared details of the scene he witnessed in the bedroom and I press my lips tight together to keep from speaking out. These are Crusher's people and I can't shame him. Besides, I need them to accept me as his Old Lady.

Hornet continues stating: "None of us want to see you leave man, but I think each of us has a secret desire to go Nomad for a time and well, go with our blessings, but don't go forever."

As Hornet concludes his statement the group raise a cheer and stomp their boots – a loud sound even without the full membership present – yelling *Crusher! Crusher! Crusher!*

When they finish Crusher hoists me up onto his hip and calls out: "It's time to fuck my Old Lady for the first time as my Old Lady." The happy, wide grin on his face when he looks at me makes him the handsomest man I've ever seen.

We leave the room to a chorus of wolf-whistles and cat-calls. I hear Goblin telling everyone to crash for a few hours' sleep before our unwanted guests arrive.

Crusher takes me up the stairs with my legs wrapped around his waist and my arms around his neck. I rest my head on his shoulder and don't speak until we're in our bedroom.

"Old Lady? Nomad?"

"Say yes, Fee. I think this is the best solution for us and our respective clubs."

"I don't have a club anymore," I retort and am ashamed at my trembling lip heralding tears.

Crusher captures them in a tender kiss that makes me even more emotional. As my tears fall he leans in to lick them off my cheek.

"You and me are our own club Fee. That's all we need for now. I told Banger I'd let him know how things go here so I'm going to give him a call. I better use my phone in case he won't answer your call so here put his number in it for me."

He doesn't realize how my twin's rejection stabs at me but I do as Crusher asks and lean in so I can listen to their conversation. Unfortunately what I hear is painful. Crusher explains that he's got Goblin's permission to go Nomad with me as his Old Lady.

"Nomad? Cool and... yeah, that's smart Crusher. That solves a few problems."

"We're planning to head out right after the raid is done and dusted so do you want us to stop in to say our goodbyes before we go?"

"No, I warned Fiona years ago that the next time she interfered in club business her punishment would be public. That can't happen if she's not here so don't bring her over. Nomad, eh?"

"Yeah, I think it will be good for us. Something new, strangers to everyone we meet but sharing the fellowship of the road."

"Where will you go?"

"Wherever we feel like!" Crusher laughs before adding that with winter only a few months ahead we'll be aiming for California where we can bike year-round.

"Of course I'll be available if Goblin urgently needs me back but well, Fiona really doesn't fit in with our club and I figure time away from everyone will be best for us. When we come back it'll be without all the baggage and rivalries.

I've got plenty of money just sitting in the bank so we can travel for at least a year. Maybe we'll find some place where we want to settle down, who knows?"

"You're taking on quite a responsibility, Crusher."

"Oh I'm confident I can keep my girl in line." The look he sends my way makes me quiver inside.

"I'm so fucking angry at her right now but... I love my sister and I hope for good things for my twin. We'll meet again."

I've forced myself to keep quiet but at Banger's words a sob escapes me and I'm overcome by the strongest wave of regret for my past and present behavior.

"I love you too, Pat and I'm sorry and I'll miss you."

"Take care, Fee," he says and ends the call.

I'm crying and my thoughts are racing round and round. Have I lost Pat? Do I want to be Crusher's Old Lady? What will going Nomad mean for me? What about all my stuff at our clubhouse? Some of my things there are private... but Crusher knows how to deal with my anxiety.

He pulls my clothes off again telling me: "We've probably got a few hours to kill before the raid so you're going across my knee to be spanked until you're sobbing from a stinging bum instead of a broken heart. Then I'm gonna fuck you and you're gonna fuck me back and after that we'll make love."

He keeps talking as he fondles my butt saying: "I'm sorry I'll have to pack up my bag of nasty goodies unused but we'll get a chance for our pet play someday."

"Mmm, gotta be honest and say I'm not looking forward to that."

"Aww, sweetheart. Everything I ever do to you will come from a place of love because I love you with all my heart and soul, Fiona. I know that's a cliche but we understand cliches, they make sense to us.

What I bring might not be the kind of love you expect but it's the kind you need and it's the kind I understand and can give.

In return I want all of your love and devotion, and I demand your respect, it won't work otherwise and we're in this for the long haul, Fee."

I'm resigned to acknowledging just how aroused I am by his words. I know I'm in for a rough time riding on the back of a bike for hours with a well-spanked ass but exhaling on a sigh I quietly agree:

"Okay Crusher, you win."

Laying down a stinging smack he coolly commands me to *try again* and I quickly reply:

"Yes, Sir!"

Epilogue

Viper's eyes light up when he spots Dora walking from the clubhouse towards him. The sun has brightened her tawny hair to the color of honey and added a dusting of freckles across her nose.

She has a curvy, short-waisted figure and her 5-foot-2 of height is all legs. Seeing him standing beside his bike with her helmet in hand she picks up the pace and practically skips across the parking lot.

Planting a kiss on her nose he asks: "Did you bring a jacket?"

"It's like a 100 degrees out here, I don't need a jacket!" she argues as he buckles on her lid.

With a sigh Viper explains she'll be cold once the sun goes down, especially riding on the bike. She gives him a pretty pout and he knows he'll be wrapping her up in his hoodie when they're ready to come home.

"We're really lucky to have such a hot day this late in the year for our ride."

"And our picnic," Dora adds patting the saddlebag she's filled with their favorite snacks and drinks.

Stepping back Viper looks her up and down. He admires the way her tanned limbs contrast with the gleaming black of her vest, skort, and ankle boots.

Then he asks: "Did you do what I told you?"

Still smiling but avoiding his eye Dora nods.

"So once I strip this leather off you'll be bare-ass naked, right?"

Looking down to hide her blush she nods again then says: "I was thinking maybe you could add another word to my design?"

Viper took a photo of the POISON scarification he'd carved on Dora's right bum cheek and she studies the picture all the time. Now he quirks an eyebrow, waiting for her to continue.

"Yeah well I just wondered if you could write on top the word *VIPER'S* so it will read *VIPER'S POISON*. What do you think?"

His happiness is reflected in the loving kiss he gives her. "I think that's a brilliant idea sweetheart, and I'll curve my name in an arc so that it embraces your name, just like I will always hold you."

Dora bites her lip and coos: "Ahhh, that's so sweet Viper."

"Yeah and you know what's really sweet?"

When she shakes her head he leans in to whisper in a wicked tone of voice: "Thinking about how the vibration of the bike is going to stimulate your hairless pussy so much you'll be squirming the whole way there."

Meeting his gaze with a grin she replies: "I also know that feeling my braless breasts moving around freely as they rub against your back is going to make you crazy, too!"

Viper gives her a wicked grin saying: "I can't wait to snap some photos of you posed naked on my bike."

"Good idea! You know how much dirty pictures turn me on. And I'll get some of you too now that I have a phone to keep them in."

Groaning he complains: "Baby girl you're gonna get me so distracted I'll probably wipe out and end up killing us both."

"Oh Viper, don't even joke about stuff like that!" she exclaims with a worried look that he kisses away with an apology.

"I'm sorry sweetheart, but I promise you this – no joking at all – that I'm going to make sure I hit every bump in the road. Every. Single. One. Your pretty ass will be bouncing all over the place and you'll be squealing with excitement."

Her delighted laugh rings out over the roar of the Harley's engine as she hugs him tight. The prospects open the gate and they peel out enjoying the late September sunshine.

The name on Dora's vest is *Poison* and the patch across the back proudly proclaims for everyone to see: *Property of Viper*.

Also by Lori Laidlaw

Lockdown + 3 Alphas = Heat: An Omega's Thrilling Dark Romantic Adventure
Girlie: Undeniable Attraction Enemies to Lovers Steamy Standalone
Cruel Obligation
Jane's Special Adventure
Captive's Deception
Finn and Marbeth

Watch for more at https://lori-laidlaw-novelist-bvwonn.mailerpage.io/.

About the Author

Lori says:

I'm a bit shy... but I love reading and writing in the Adult Romance genre with all its sub-categories.

I fall in love with my characters whose moods range from playful to dangerous and everything in between!

My stories are multiple POV expressing mature themes and passionate encounters with enough steam to stimulate your imagination.

It's all about the love.

Email: AuthorLoriLaidlaw@gmail.com

Website: https://lori-laidlaw-novelist-bvwonn.mailerpage.io/

Facebook: https://www.facebook.com/people/Author-Lori-Laidlaw/61555470454210/

Goodreads: https://www.goodreads.com/author/show/29566696.Lori_Laidlaw

Read more at https://lori-laidlaw-novelist-bvwonn.mailerpage.io/.